Sold Out

BY STAN R. MITCHELL

Edited by Desiree Kamerman

Cover by Danah Mitchell

ISBN: 1479140945
ISBN-13: 978-1479140947

FOREWORD

To Danah, my perfect wife. Thanks for believing in me.

To my Mom and Dad. Thanks for all the love.

To Mike Rose, Henry Greer, and Bobby Fisher (GySgt, USMC). Three men who taught a boy what he should aspire to become.

To Capt. Eaton, United States Marine Corps, and Sgt. Major Hill, United States Marine Corps; two men who epitomized leadership and strength, and who made an unforgettable impression on me.

To my fellow Marines, SSgt. Frank Kovach and SSgt. Jon Rumbolt, who helped me on a couple technical and tactical points with this book.

And I would also like to thank Dave Conrad and Rodney Reed for their editing suggestions. All mistakes, of course, are mine.

Learn more about Stan R. Mitchell and his other works at www.stanrmitchell.com.

CHAPTER 1

Allen Green, a seasoned reporter of thirty years, walked into the bar that night believing that locating the man he had tracked for months would solve all of his problems, and it was hard to disagree. Finding the man would provide Allen the final link in breaking the biggest story in journalism since Watergate in the '70s.

Allen could almost taste the acclaim and cash that would follow. He would win the Pulitzer Prize, without question. *(It was, after all, one of the biggest news scoops ever.)* He would finally have the opportunity to be rich. Book deals would follow, prepped by juicy, prime-time TV interviews. Then, perhaps a multi-million-dollar screenplay.

He knew when he walked into the bar that he was oh so close to his goal.

If asked, Allen might deny he was seeking the Pulitzer Prize and say he was just doing his job. But that was a lie. A big one. Allen wanted to break the big story, not because it needed to be broken -- he was past that naivety -- but because he was tired of shitty stories and shitty pay. His attitude was well earned: thirty long hard years of breaking decent stories, but never gaining the deserved recognition.

The bar was in the testosterone-filled, Marine town of Jacksonville, North Carolina. Named Leatherneck, the bar had a neon sign on the front window that claimed it had the coldest beer in town. Allen didn't know if it had the coldest beer or not, but it for damn sure might have the loudest music.

Rock music blared loud enough to make its occupants temporarily forget the misery synonymous with the desolate, pathetic city of Jacksonville, North Carolina. Well, almost loud enough, he thought with a smile, trying to come up with at least one positive thing about the place.

Allen walked through the darkness and headed toward the back of the room, his eyes trying to adjust to the darkness and flashing lights. The place didn't seem like the kind of bar his target would hit, but after finally locating the mysterious man's house, he had followed him here one week ago.

Well, it wasn't that easy. He had trailed him about halfway here and lost him, worried he might blow his cover by following too close. Then, he had spent nearly two hours checking every parking lot in town looking for the man's black F-150, license plate CBH-194. This wasn't an easy task in a town disproportionately crammed with men, who all seemed to drive big trucks.

For tonight's stake out, Allen wore a flannel shirt, blue jeans, and military-issue jungle boots. His dress was a fashion no-no, he knew, but that's what most people seemed to wear down here, except for the officers, who favored collared shirts and khakis.

Allen met the stare of many young, defiant Marines as he made his way to a rear table. He hoped he looked like a salty Gunnery Sergeant, or Gunny, as they were known in the Marine Corps, because the only thing he planned to use if things got violent with these brutes was his cell phone. Well, maybe he would bluff about his "rank" first.

One thing was certain though; he didn't intend to fight any of these mean bastards.

At the back of the place, he took a seat at a table for four. He kept his back to the wall and prepared for a long night. The bar had about twelve or fifteen round tables and probably could hold a hundred thirsty Marines, if a hundred ever succumbed to the "lure" of the "coldest beer in town."

It sure wasn't much. Just a dingy, dark dump, with three pool tables and two pinball machines for entertainment. It could hardly compete with the titty bars and dance joints sprinkled throughout Jacksonville. No, this was where you went when all you wanted to do was drink and forget, or drink and fight.

Allen pulled out a pack of Marlboros and a chrome Zippo that bore a Marine logo with the words "Death Before Dishonor" in capital letters. The words were written in a curved, half-moon shape above a hollowed-out skull, which was ghostly white. Behind the skull lay crossed M-16s. He'd bought the lighter at a local surplus store two days ago along with the jungle boots he wore and as he lit the cigarette, he wondered if anyone actually believed in "Death Before Dishonor." He thought on that for a moment. Perhaps some did. These military types were nuts.

A Marine walked past him to the restroom, a black tee shirt proclaiming "Kill 'em all and let God sort 'em out" stretched tight across his tank-like upper body. Allen dropped his chin a couple of inches in a nod, imitating the dignified, Southern nod he'd picked up while down here. He placed the lit cigarette in his mouth, letting it dangle down from his lips, tough-like. Christ, he was beginning to talk like them. He'd definitely been in the South too long.

As took a draw, he felt that familiar feeling of "everything's going to be alright" sweep over him. He couldn't imagine life without cigarettes. The breaks from the office, out in the cold New York air. Fellow smokers talking about sex or the Yankees or the editor, a real ass. He inhaled and for the umpteenth time of the day, realized he'd never be able to quit smoking. Truth be told, half the time he wasn't sure he even wanted to.

He laid the Zippo on the table, description side up, and

tried to relax. A bargirl came up, her big tits bouncing braless under a thin, white halter-top. She stopped those tits about a half-foot from his face and met his eyes with an inviting smile.

"What can I do for you, Marine," she yelled over the music, placing her hand on his neck and leaning over, revealing more of her tits than Allen ever wanted to see. Her breath reeked of cigarettes and God knew what else and she stroked his neck like a woman who knew what she was doing. Allen shuddered at the thought. He remembered venereal diseases were not passed by hand, stayed in character, and leaned closer. He met her eyes, glanced down at her tits "lustfully" and smiled. "Honey, there's lots you can do for me, but let's start with a beer." He winked and knocked the ash from his cigarette in the ashtray.

She looked tantalizingly down at his crotch and smiled. "Okay, sugar," she said.

Whore, he thought as she strutted off, moving her hips from side to side as masterfully as a New York model walking the runway in a $12,000 gown. He guessed some of the Marines down here were actually attracted to her, as gross as that seemed. Shit, he'd had about as much of this "city" as he could take.

It was no wonder the country was in such bad shape. Too many uneducated idiots in the South, he thought. Well, he had wasted too much time down here to give up now. Just a little longer, he reminded himself. Just a little longer. And then money and fame, but most importantly, money. Tons of it.

The song ended and another one, just as bad and just as loud, began. He needed another cigarette already. Careful to avoid antagonizing others who needed far too little antagonizing, he kept his eyes on the bottles of whiskey behind the bar. He hoped he looked lost in thought. The front door opened and he glanced over, hoping it was the man he was looking for. It wasn't.

Three more young Marines strolled in, shoulders rolled back and cruel eyes scanning the crowd. Their blown up strut reminded Allen of roosters. Or maybe pitbulls. These three looked young. About sixteen, if he had to guess, but he knew they were at least 18 or 19. Old enough to cut you from head-to-toe without thinking twice or questioning orders, Allen thought. They were just what the government needed these days. Mean boys who hated Muslims and worshiped George Bush.

The server -- no, the whore -- returned with his beer, some kind of draft in a plastic cup with an especially thick head. Well, they had to make their money somehow, Allen thought. Allen pulled out his wallet and handed the woman a five-dollar bill. She took it and he half expected her to put it down her shirt. For a second, his hand lingered, waiting for some change, but she pretended not to see it. He couldn't stand the thought of her being near him anymore, so he let her take his change and watched her walk off.

CHAPTER 2

More than five hundred miles away, Bobby Ferguson sat relaxing on the couch in his living room. He was reading the latest issue of the magazine Guns and Ammo. His wife Anne sat next to him watching American Idol on their 36-inch TV. He couldn't stand the show, but enjoyed sitting next to her.

He stopped reading an article that compared knockdown power of various pistol calibers and looked at her. Her age was beginning to show, but God she was still beautiful. With shoulder-length blonde hair and captivating green eyes, she was quite a find. She sat there, completely engrossed by some goofy looking white guy, hair gelled in every which direction, singing some kind of something that passed for music these days. Bobby thought he looked gay.

He wanted to reach over and caress her. Maybe hold her for a few minutes. Try to remember that all of this, their life together, was real. He had actually once thought he'd spend his entire life in the Marines, that fraternity that thrived on manhood and toughness.

In the land of boots and badasses, all forms of weakness were not tolerated. It was an environment that became addictive. Once you weren't the one being screwed with, it was fun. But, it was for their own good.

It was necessary for war.

Bobby Ferguson had prospered in that pit. In that lifestyle that no civilian can comprehend. He had breathed aggression and adrenaline twenty-four hours a day, four years straight. And it never left him, not totally anyway.

He knew now that he truly had been young, dumb, and full of cum, as they so often said in the Corps. Yet now, he pitied anyone who didn't know what he knew now -- the joy of marriage, a normal job, and deep sleep at night, without fear of deployments, air alerts, or missions in foreign lands.

He loved his life now, with its routine. Of knowing Anne so well that he could tell by the look on her face when she got home whether she'd be doing the dishes that night or him. Ten years of being married to her and he still loved her nearly as much as when he had fallen for her.

There really was a life after the Corps, he thought. He had his guns. He had his woods. He had his Anne.

He returned his attention to the article, reading for several minutes before he heard a sound outside. He looked up, his eyes snapping to the door before he could stop them. The door was locked, and the deadbolt turned. The curtains, though, were pulled back leaving the window wide open and he nearly rose to close them.

He didn't, knowing doing so would worry Anne. She might start keeping a closer eye on him, or even start pestering him again to go see the doctor for some medication. Laying the magazine down on the coffee table, he shook the thought of paranoia, relaxed, and looked back at Anne.

"I love you honey."

"I love you too," she said, momentarily breaking her eyes from the show.

He leaned over and kissed her cheek and ran his hands through her hair.

"You going to bed?" she asked.

"Yeah," he said, hoping she'd follow, but not bothered if she didn't. He was about done with Stephen Hunter's latest novel, "Pale Horse Coming," and had stopped last night right before the main character Swagger and some gun fighters attacked the town.

He got up and walked in the bathroom and flipped on the light, taking in himself in the mirror. He hadn't lost much. He was tall and lean, and though his abs weren't as firm as they'd once been, they were still noticeable even unflexed. His eyes glanced to the nearly unseen mark on the left side of his chest. It was barely visible, veiled by his thin brown chest hair and healed after all these years. But, it was there and it rarely left his mind. Just two letters. Burned into his skin so long ago by a coat hanger, no differently than branding a steer. ***SS***, in the straight recognizable lines worn by Nazi Gestapo in World War II.

He peeked out the door and made sure Anne was still watching TV. She was. He bent down and quietly pulled open the right door under the sink. Looking up under the sink, he confirmed a .380 automatic pistol was taped to the bottom of the sink. Relieved, he silently closed the door. He reached for his toothbrush and toothpaste. "I hope it doesn't rain tomorrow," he thought. Construction just wasn't as much fun in shitty weather.

CHAPTER 3

The bar Leatherneck was filling up and about an hour after Allen Green arrived, his man, Colonel Russ Jernigan entered the bar. Allen knew it was him the minute he entered, but opened his wallet to confirm it with a small picture he had copied from an old Marine unit annual. He pulled another five dollar bill out, just to play off the peek into his wallet, and waved for the bar girl to bring him another thick-headed, bad-tasting beer.

Now came the tricky part. He lit another cigarette. He was getting nervous, like a boy who has walked his date to the front door and can't make the move to kiss her. It had been years since Allen could remember being nervous as a reporter. Actually, he remembered. It was 1979. An exclusive interview with President Jimmy Carter, about the hostage situation in Iran.

Part of the nervousness came from the months and months of work that were on the line. This man, Colonel Russ Jernigan, was his only hope of nailing down the story -- not to mention that ever-elusive Pulitzer Prize. And the money.

He knew that at the age of 53, this story was likely his last shot at the Pulitzer. Too many good reporters under him, full of energy and drive. They would get the great assignments. He would get shit. Maybe even get transferred to the business beat -- one of the worst.

He blew a large cloud of smoke into the dark room. He needed this. With the award and the acclaim following winning a Pulitzer, he could shove off from the full-time work of reporting and begin writing non-fiction books. No more ridiculous deadlines. No more getting yelled at by fat-ass editors or liberal, lesbian bitches.

Get your head in the game, he thought, as the bargirl returned, her tits still bouncing. He paid for the beer and watched Colonel Russ Jernigan take a seat at the bar. This was going to be delicate at best.

What the hell, he thought. If I blow it, I get to leave this shit-hole of a town and get back to New York.

He crushed his cigarette in the ashtray and walked up next to Jernigan. He motioned for the bar tender, a young man with a hoop nose ring and purple hair, and asked for matches. Not even glancing at Jernigan, he struck a match, lit a Marlboro, and flipped his wrist three times, extinguishing it. He laid the smoking match on the counter and inhaled deep. He blew the smoke through his nose and did his best to look at ease.

Nonchalantly, he turned and said, "Hell of a night, huh?"

"Yeah," Jernigan said without looking over. Jernigan was dressed like an officer: khakis and golf shirt. He looked out of place in the decrepit bar.

Allen waited a moment, looked over at him, and said, "Hey, I think I know you."

Jernigan turned and took him in, his eyes focusing and concentrating on Allen like he was taking one of the old eye exams. The type where you stood about six feet back and squinted for all you were worth, while trying to read some damn letters you had forgotten to memorize. After perhaps five seconds or so, Jernigan said, "No, I don't think so."

"Yeah, you're uh, Jared. No, that's not it. It's uh, uh, ah, don't tell me. It's, uh, Jenkins. No, it's Jernigan. Yeah, that's it. Captain Jernigan."

Jernigan paled, as if a knife had just been driven into him. He tried to play it off, but Allen knew he was nervous as hell.

"You may not remember me," Allen Green said. "I was a nobody in Pakistan back in '88."

Jernigan took in Allen's face again, searching the deepest depths of his memory for Allen's face, while trying not to show anything, which he was failing badly at.

Allen took the reaction, and the fact Jernigan did not deny ever being in Pakistan, as confirmation of at least part of what one of his sources had said: that the U.S. military had actually sent troops to Pakistan to do work against the Soviets in the latter stages of the Soviet Union's invasion of Afghanistan during the '80s. That had always been suspected, but never confirmed. That was huge news: Americans directly engaging and killing Russians during the height of the Cold War.

"Hey, nothing to worry about," Allen said, leaning toward him. "We're both pro's. Let me buy you a drink. This deserves celebrating."

Jernigan looked unsure. He was like a deer that knew something was wrong. Not really a smell or a sound. Just a feeling that something wasn't right. Jernigan had done some shady covert work in his day and it wasn't for the world to see.

Jernigan knew he should pay for his drink and leave. But, if this guy was CIA, which he understood, "We're both pro's to mean," then maybe he could be Jernigan's ticket into the CIA and out of the dead-end career he was now experiencing in the Marines. Jernigan had always worked strictly from the military side, assisting the CIA, but never in the shadows with the CIA.

"So, what's your name, sir?" he asked.

"Rick Knight," Allen said without hesitation. Noticing Jernigan checking out his clothing, he added, "Forget my clothes. I'm in town doing some recruiting. Looking like a salty gunny usually opens the door easier for these young Marines."

"Oh," Jernigan said lamely. The explanation made sense.

Looking around, Allen leaned toward Jernigan and said in the lowest of voices, "We're putting together a team to insert into North Korea. Our overhead surveillance isn't revealing enough about their reactors."

Jernigan nodded, taking in the lie as if it didn't surprise him. As if he had known that, or at least figured that to be the case. Shit, he was a player, too. A real James Bond.

Allen leaned closer. "The truth is, they'll probably get knocked off. But, the president is looking for an excuse for military action. I tell you, we got to knock out those damn reactors." Taking a swig from his cup, he went on. "You and I know diplomacy just doesn't work all the time, but the bean counters. Those damn puss-ass pogues in Washington."

"You're right," Jernigan said, taking a deep swig of his beer. He liked the guy already.

"Say," Allen said. "I heard that you were in Pakistan to assist an American sniper team. One that was going to ambush some Soviet special forces in Afghanistan. I heard those Soviet special forces had been wrecking the Mujahideen resistance fighters in Afghanistan and Washington finally said enough. Let's send in some Americans and take care of these bastards."

Allen shook his head in disbelief, then continued. "Even though I believe the guy that told me, he's a long-time friend and all, I always found that one hard to believe."

Jernigan smiled.

"We did," he said boastfully, glad to confirm his credentials as a bad-ass Alpha male who had also worked on some cloak and dagger stuff. This cat was okay, Jernigan thought. He lifted his beer and drank greedily again. He wasn't much of a drinker, but he needed to appear tough. This guy could probably get him in the Agency.

Allen saw that Jernigan wasn't quite ready to spill the beans. Prepared for this, he began a story about a team he'd trained recently and sent into Palestine to take out a Hamas terrorist leader for the Israelis. He explained how the Americans, dressed as Israelis, raided the man's home and had to use C4 plastic explosive to blow down the door, which was bolted shut somehow from the inside. After they captured the terrorist, they had to fight their way street-by-street back into Israel.

The story was spectacular and Allen watched as Jernigan took it all in, his eyes glazed over imagining it. If there was one thing Allen could do, it was tell a story. Hell, he was a writer. But tonight, Allen outdid himself. The pressure of months and months to find Jernigan had been shed and Allen remained smooth, like a pro. Shit, he was a pro.

Allen followed that story with some ranting about terrorists and Muslims. By this time, at least an hour had passed and Jernigan had drunk three beers. He was beginning to loosen up. Allen then began a story about a CIA team trying to track down Osama bin Laden in the mountains of Afghanistan. Finishing it twenty minutes later, he took the plunge, though by then it didn't feel like a plunge. It was easier than cheating on a school test for the first time.

"So tell me about your Afghanistan in '88," Allen said. At best, he hoped Jernigan could confirm that American forces had engaged Soviet forces directly. That would be huge. "U.S. troops kill Soviets in battle," the headline would say. It would make a hell of a story.

But, what Jernigan said shook him. It was far worse.

CHAPTER 4

The day Bobby Ferguson's normal life ended was nearly perfect with great weather for construction. The temperature was in the 70s, with high cirrus clouds allowing the sun to warm what should have been a chilly fall day.

Bobby led a small crew and they were in the middle of an expansion job on Interstate 40, which cut Knoxville nearly in half. The job was expected to last another three and a half more years. Ask anyone at the site though, and they'd tell you it would take at least five years, that is unless you were a member of the media.

On this day, they were putting the final additions on many weeks of work. After tearing up a three-mile stretch of old concrete and replacing it with new, they had spent the day painting the lines, sweeping up the trash on the side of the road, and finally taking up all the orange barrels that lined the side of the interstate.

The men were in a good mood, Bobby knew. It was the weather and the feeling of accomplishment, and the chicks driving by with the tops down on their convertibles for perhaps the last time this year. Bobby let his boys -- and one woman, though she was just one of the boys -- add a few minutes to their breaks and he enjoyed the day for himself, too. They took two hours longer than expected to complete their routine tasks for the day, but Bobby knew his foreman would keep his mouth shut; he was in a good mood, too.

He was lost in thought all day, thinking about doing a little shooting when he got home. It was so beautiful that he thought he'd pull down one of his bolt guns, maybe his Remington .270, and do some long range shooting in the prone on the warm ground. He'd shot mostly just his pistols since summer struck months earlier.

Daydreaming, imagining the kick of the gun and the smell of gunpowder, he noticed a red Chevy Lumina pass by. It looked like Anne's and for a second he thought it was her. It wasn't, but he got to thinking about her. He decided that instead of shooting the .270, he would pick up some roses and a bottle of wine on the way home. Some things beat shooting a rifle, even for a former sniper who lived to be behind a scope.

CHAPTER 5

Allen Green's story appeared in "The New Yorker" magazine three weeks after his "interview" with Colonel Russ Jernigan. It read:

Americans hunt down, kill Soviet Special Forces

JACKSONVILLE, N.C. -- During the Soviet invasion of Afghanistan, America has long admitted to supplying weapons to the Afghan resistance fighters, or Mujahideen, including cutting-edge technology such as Stinger anti-air missiles. But, an in-depth investigation has revealed that American intervention was actually far more direct.

Several sources have confirmed that American snipers were sent into the northeastern parts of Afghanistan to engage Soviet Special Forces, or Spetsnaz, after Afghan resistance was nearly extinguished in that province in late 1987. Incredibly, after the operation, American military leaders purposefully leaked information of the two snipers to serve two goals. First, to tie up loose ends by having the men who were involved in the operation killed. Second, the leaked information was used to ferret out a Soviet mole buried within the U.S. intelligence community, who had been leaking and hindering Mujahideen operations for years. Both snipers were killed because of these leaks and the mole, once identified, was used by counterintelligence to leak false information that resulted in two brilliant Afghan victories, the Battle of Al Mosud and Taranka, against the Soviets. This mole was later arrested and remains in U.S. custody.

The victories of Al Mosud and Taranka helped stabilize the final years of the war in Afghanistan. . .

Allen's story went on, but the details were nothing compared to the bomb-shell revelation in the top of the article. It made nearly every respectable news outlet within minutes of the issue hitting newsstands. CNN, MSNBC, Fox News, ABC, CBS, and NBC, as well as every national paper the following day.

The government denied the story, which Allen admitted wasn't bulletproof. Nonetheless, Allen did have military records showing a Nick Woods, whose name had been used by Colonel Russ Jernigan, had gone to sniper school in 1985 and had left his Marine unit in 1987 for reasons no one from that unit seemed to know. That was odd. Furthermore, there was no record of him anywhere in the country now; twenty of the nation's top reporters couldn't find him. Lastly, two Pakistani embassy employees, one former and one current, stated off the record that eight American soldiers had been at the embassy and had brought military gear with them during 1987 -- not your normal embassy champagne party staff with dress uniforms and perfect teeth, they'd said. Those American troops had eventually left after a short time, but with two less men, according to the two embassy employees.

Allen hadn't mentioned the sniper's name, Nick Woods, because he knew that it would likely affect the insurance money Woods' family received after Nick died in a "training accident" in 1987. He also didn't want to put Woods' family through any more grief. Of course, Allen couldn't confirm the insurance money because the military had "misplaced" his records. ("It happens all the time," he had been told by a bored clerk named Sergeant Janet Lonnely, who had no clue why some reporter from The New Yorker was even asking.) Worse, Woods' family down in Georgia had practically thrown him off the porch when Allen showed up for "just a few questions" about the subject of the training accident.

What Allen didn't know, nor had Colonel Jernigan, was that both snipers were not killed. It was one of two facts in the article that was wrong.

CHAPTER 6

They came fast. And they were bold. Allen Green sat at his desk, checking his e-mail the day after the story had broke. There were messages on his voice mail for television bookings and interviews for print media. It was a media firestorm and he basked in the attention, thinking of whom he'd call first. And of the money. Oh, the money.

It was 8:11 a.m. when his phone gave the in-house ring. He picked it up.

"Yeah."

"Allen, there is a guy here to see you. He says he has an appointment," said the front-desk secretary.

Allen thought for a second, then flipped open his planner. Nothing. He remembered that he wasn't even supposed to be back in New York yet from Jacksonville, North Carolina.

"That's funny, I don't have an appointment," he said.

"He says it's important, and that if you don't want to talk to him, he'll go to The New York Times with the information."

"Okay then, I'll be down." He got up from his desk and walked toward the door. Then he stopped, remembering he needed a pen and notepad. The whole thought of winning the Pulitzer was seriously debilitating his ability to function. So much for being a pro.

He went back to his desk and grabbed a pad and pen. In the reception area, a man in a suit awaited him, standing and looking about nervously. Allen smiled. Guy looks like a government agent, he thought.

"I'm Allen," he said to the man as he walked up and offered his hand.

The man stepped closer, shook his hand, and whispered, "Can we talk outside?"

"Uh, sure," Allen said glancing back at his secretary. Her face said, "Give me a break. Who does this guy think he is?"

Allen followed the guy toward the elevator. It opened before the guy could press the button, something that only rarely happened since their office was on the fourteenth floor. At best, a coincidence since Allen's floor was rarely visited. Two other men were in the elevator and neither moved toward the door. Now that was odd, Allen thought. Wonder why the elevator stopped if they weren't getting off and the button had not been pressed on the floor by either him or his new source?

A cursory glance revealed one wore a button-up blue shirt with khakis. He was smiling at Allen, real eerie like. The other person was hidden behind an outstretched New York Times, but the slacks and shoes screamed male. Allen hesitated to make sure they weren't getting off, then moved forward and got on the elevator with his visitor. They both turned to face the doors. The doors began to close and Allen felt the hair on his neck stand up. As the doors were inches apart, he thought of thrusting his hand in between them and running.

By the time that idea had crossed his mind it was too late. The doors closed and he heard the rustle of a newspaper as it fell. He knew he was in deep shit as he tried to turn. His arms were grabbed from behind by both men and he struggled to break free. He started to scream and his source covered his mouth, which he bit for all he was worth. The guy screamed, but then Allen felt something, at first he thought it was a knife, stabbed into his back. As a burn began to spread, he realized it was a needle and something had been injected into him.

“Stay calm,” the source said. “Don’t fight it.”

The elevator continued down the fourteen flights. The doors opened and two paramedics were waiting with a gurney. Allen felt his knees buckle and as he fell, arms propped him up. He tried to yell, but his mouth would not respond. The two medics were the last thing he saw as the walls began to spin and go black. He heard the source say, “Here he is, help him,” in an urgent voice to relieve any onlookers.

Allen didn’t know the other people in the building lobby who were watching and concerned. He heard a woman say “Oh my God,” but the paramedics were loading and strapping him down. They had it under control, so no one pulled out their cell phones.

Allen’s source and the other two men split up and disappeared in the confusion.

The paramedics checked his pulse as they rolled him toward the door and told everyone watching that Allen would be fine. No one that saw the incident bothered to call his office, the hospital, or the police.

CHAPTER 7

Allen Green awoke, dizzy and disoriented. His mind was groggy, like a hangover, but worse. He closed his eyes and tried to focus. Opening them again, he saw he was in a room without windows. An empty, concrete cell he realized as he came fully to. He was lying on a green military issue cot and the only light for the room came from a single bulb built into the ceiling and enclosed behind wire.

Belatedly, he noticed a man sitting across from him. The guy, who was built like a NFL linebacker, was in a metal folding chair reading the magazine, Muscle and Fitness. He wore blue jeans and his upper legs had that deformed look only big weightlifters with even bigger legs have. The inside of his upper legs, down by the knees, had huge bulges pushing inward against the jeans. It looked as if the thighbone on each leg had been snapped inward from the knee and was held in check by only thick cotton, as if each leg needed a brace.

The man's face even looked tough. His jaw jutted forward like the front of a train, blocky and solid. The face was narrow and sleek, and the nose thin. His eyes, small and intense, were brown, as was his hair. He looked up, bored. His eyes narrowed, seeming to imply how ridiculous it was he had to stand guard over Allen. "Glad to see you're up," he said. "I'll get Whitaker."

He walked over to an iron, windowless door, knocked three times and was let out. The door slammed, thick and heavy, like a vault. Allen tried to remember how he got here. It was hazy. He was pretty sure he'd left Jacksonville for New York, but not certain. He also thought he'd published the story about American snipers killing Soviet soldiers, but he was not sure now. He sat up and rubbed his eyes, which strangely had no sleep in them.

The door opened and the big guy that had been reading the magazine walked in. Another tall man followed him. This man wore business attire: gray slacks, white starched shirt complete with gold cuff links, suspenders, and burgundy tie. The tall man took a seat in the metal chair previously used by the linebacker. Allen took the well-dressed man to be Whitaker. Whitaker crossed his right leg over his left leg and looked like a CEO sitting for a good game of chess. He stared at Allen, mute.

Allen took advantage of the time. As a reporter, he was used to noticing small details and he had a feeling if he lived to see the outside world again, he might want to remember the face. Whitaker in a single word was handsome. He was tall and thin, but obviously in shape. He looked like he ran marathons. He was white, and the word "leader" seemed to be written all over him.

His hair was short on the sides and just long enough on top to comb to the left. His eyes, a light blue, seemed alert and sharp.

After what felt like at least thirty seconds, Whitaker rubbed his jaw and began to speak.

"Allen Green," he said. Allen could tell he was definitely Ivy League educated. "You have no idea what you've done, do you?" Whitaker asked.

Allen was still groggy, but wasn't in the mood to argue. "Where am I?" he asked.

"Allen, I'm going to be directing this conversation" the man said calmly. His accent and style screamed Ivy League education.

"Who are you?" Allen screamed.

Allen never saw it coming, as the big guy stepped forward and threw an uppercut into his solar plexus. He fell backward and his weight flipped the cot. His back slammed into the concrete and he hit his head against the floor. Stunned, he tried to shake it off, but before he could clear his thoughts, the man yanked him to his feet and sat him back on the now up-righted cot.

Allen gasped for breath, unable to breathe. Tears fell from his eyes, without him willing it. He'd never been in a fight, having lived a guarded, sophisticated life in the New England area. Hell, he had been an only child who had always attended the best private schools. He began to whimper as he tried to breathe.

Mr. Linebacker, maple-legs, sneered in contempt at his weakness.

"Allen, now you need to calm down," Whitaker said in the same sophisticated voice. He sounded as if they were chatting and sharing drinks at a wedding reception. "As I was saying," he continued, "You have no idea what you've done or the world of shit you've created with that little article of yours."

He said the word "shit" in a detested way, as if he had never wiped it from his own ass.

Allen sat mute and wiped the tears from his eyes, suddenly embarrassed. Ashamed.

"With just one article, at that," Whitaker said. "Thanks to your article, a double agent has been taken hostage and we've lost contact with five other agents in the field. Six field agents, Allen. Do you know how large a chunk of national security that is? Regardless if the Cold War is over, we can't have nukes proliferated, now can we?"

Allen's brain was clearing up and he was beginning to catch his breath. The article was coming back into his mind, and the way he was snatched from his office. He remembered the article, but could not figure out how it translated into six "field agents" being nabbed. Not being one who was afraid to ask a question, he asked Whitaker to explain.

"You moron," Whitaker said. "The double agent you said was arrested was never actually arrested. He was our most important double agent. And now he's gone, as are five others."

"Oh," Allen said. He didn't really care if a traitor was getting his toenails ripped off. Frankly, he just cared about getting out of there.

"Allen, we need you to think, and play this smart," Whitaker said. He grinned, a slight and controlled smile that was a bit awkward, if not creepy. "The choices you make now matter. You see, we have lots of collateral damage to clean up. Your choice is either a life of cooperation and silence, or a string of bad coincidences."

"You ever heard of protected sources or the First Amendment, asshole? Journalists never give out their sources. You should know that --"

The linebacker stepped forward and cocked his fist before being stopped by Whitaker, who grabbed his arm. Whitaker smiled as the linebacker stepped back, as if the man was just a dog that had got a little too excited.

Allen expected Whitaker to say, "There's no need for that." Or, "We don't want to have to hurt you." That's always what happened in Hollywood. Instead, Whitaker pulled out a small cell phone from his pants pocket. As he punched in some numbers, he nodded to the linebacker, who quickly left the room. Whitaker waited until Allen heard someone else answer the phone, and then Whitaker said, "Do it," before hanging up.

Mr. NFL Linebacker returned to the room, this time carrying a hand-held police scanner. He turned it on and it took several minutes of routine chatter before the connection between the phone call and police radio became clear. A dispatcher reported a fire at Allen's apartment address.

"You mother-fucker," Allen said.

Mr. Linebacker stepped forward and repeated his earlier punch, but harder. As Allen fell back again, he felt rather sure his sternum might have been cracked this time. Again he was hauled back onto the cot far before he was ready. He managed to say between gasps, "You know," deep breath, "nearly a hundred people," deep breath, "live in that complex."

"Allen, two-hundred and eighty million people live in the United States. You still aren't following that whole national security theme I mentioned earlier. More than likely, your most secret notes, e-mails, encrypted data on your hard drive, etc., was in your apartment, not at the office. And don't worry about the fire safe, you can be confident we have a firefighter looking for it. Oh, and by the way, at your office right now, a warrant has been handed to your editor and we are seizing your computer, files, desk and contents of your locker. We're also starting interviews with your fellow employees. You know Allen, you really shouldn't store pornography of little girls on your hard drive."

"You know damn well I'm not a pedophile," Allen screamed as he jumped from the cot. He never even got to his feet. A flurry of punches, elbows, and knees from the Linebacker left him in a heap on the floor, blood flowing from his nose, mouth, and a cut on the right side of his face.

On the scanner, frantic voices screamed for ambulances. Firefighters were trying to rescue people from the second floor, where they were trapped. The fire continued to grow in intensity and desperate calls to other fire stations were made.

"Now Allen, you being a divorced man with no kids, it'd seem we wouldn't have much leverage on you. But, we know you are kind of fond of Jennifer. Right?"

Allen flinched and immediately regretted it.

"I'm sure you know she's off today, but did you know

she's shopping right this minute on Sixth Avenue? Let's get down to business before another accident happens. First, where'd you get your information?"

Allen said nothing. He debated holding out. You were taught from day one in journalism school to never give out your sources. They were your leverage, your hidden weapons.

"Allen," Whitaker said, "this involves more than you and Jennifer. Those who stand up for you, your friends, your editor, and whoever else may be out there, their lives are going to get uncomfortable, too. And soon. Unless you help. You can stop this right now."

It felt like a nightmare. Allen had never believed in conspiracies. Yet now it seemed he was caught up in one. They indoctrinated you about a free press and the fact that these things didn't happen. But, the prick Whitaker sat there smiling, his hands clasped together on his knee. A real pompous ass.

"While you're thinking," Whitaker said as he dialed a number into the phone, "let's check on Jennifer."

"No," Allen said, not even meaning to. He was amazed at how easily he broke. He despised their strength. Relenting, he told them Colonel Jernigan's name and listened to their instructions for damage control.

CHAPTER 8

Whitaker made it to Jacksonville, North Carolina, where Colonel Russell Jernigan was, just three hours after his talk with Allen. Back in New York, Allen was now under surveillance and in the process of admitting to his editors that he had fabricated the entire story. They were doing damage control -- major damage control -- sending out a press release to announce the mistake, preparing a retraction for their magazine, as well as deciding how they would fire their once trusted reporter.

Within two hours, Whitaker knew Allen would be arrested by the New York Police Department for multiple child pornography charges. How that panned out would depend on Allen's conduct.

Whitaker wasn't sure if Jernigan was the leak or not. Jernigan was a coward, so it seemed odd he would dare talk about it. There was a good chance Allen Green had told him Jernigan's name to protect his real source, who would have known Jernigan's name, as well. That man wasn't a coward and he had a grudge.

Whitaker decided to play it safe. He opened his cell phone and called his boss in D.C. He'd have him get the FBI team stationed in Knoxville to take the other potential source into custody, too. Just in case.

CHAPTER 9

Bobby Ferguson carried out his earlier thought at the construction site and came home with a bottle of wine. His mood had changed though. After leaving the liquor store, he had driven east down Interstate 40 and got off at the Rutledge Pike exit. It was the most logical route of three possible ways he took home from his work site. Though he hadn't taken this route in three days -- instead choosing to vary his way home each day with other routes -- he was still aware of his surroundings.

And while keeping an eye on passing cars -- cars ahead of him and cars behind him -- he had noticed a green Honda Accord following him. It wasn't your typical undercover police sedan, but that's what really worried Bobby. If he was in charge of surveillance, he wouldn't use a typical police sedan.

The car was driven by a woman who had used her cell phone several times during the trip while behind him. She had followed him 6.7 miles after he noticed her -- he had managed to write it on his palm while driving -- before she turned into a service station. In the depths of his mind, he thought he remembered the same car and woman following him before.

If it was the same woman and car that he had noticed a few weeks earlier, then she had changed her pattern, because she hadn't stopped at the service station the last time. He needed to check his journal. And that thought preoccupied his mind when he arrived home, carrying the roses and wine but thinking of anything but a kiss from Anne.

Anne was in the kitchen, the water running, probably doing dishes. "Hi, hon," he said as he headed straight for his bedroom. He had to check his journal fast before he forgot even a single detail. In his bedroom, he laid the roses and bottle on the bed and opened up his underwear drawer.

He glanced behind him to make sure Anne wasn't there -- it was too far away to hear if the water was still running -- and pulled out a black hard back book. He flipped through the pages, toward the back, skipping over his hastily scribbled manuscript.

Each entry was dated and described every contact he observed, even those that didn't cause alarm. Because to not list those could hide patterns that became visible with disciplined note taking and review. At the top of each entry, a subject identified either a vehicle or person. Bobby had underlined these subjects.

He scanned page after page of vehicles and suspect descriptions. He flipped and turned, flipped and turned, and was just about to give up -- it had been long enough for Anne to come see what he was doing -- when he found it. "Green car." The entry was dated Oct. 5, which was thirteen days earlier.

It read: "Honda Accord, green, probably four or five years old. No identifiable dings, scratches, or bent fenders. Female driver. Blonde. Too far back for better ID."

It was the same car and woman. He was certain now.

"Bobby, what are you doing?" Anne asked.

He flinched hard, surprised. "Nothing," he said, turning and trying to play off the fact she had caught him doing something. "Just checkin' my shootin' journal to see how much powder I been puttin' in them one-hundred and eighty grain, thirty-aught six rounds," he said.

"Bullshit," she said walking toward him. "Let me see."

He pulled the journal back, out of her reach. "It's nothing, Anne."

"Let me see," she said, becoming angry.

"Damn it, Anne, I don't need this."

"Give it to me." She reached for it and grabbed it. It only took reading a couple of entries to confirm her suspicions.

"I can explain," he said.

She wasn't listening.

He took her by the arms. "Anne, I just proved it."

"Proved what?" she asked. She stood deflated and on the verge of tears.

He felt powerless, like a desperate man in a sinking boat. He had to get her to understand or, or . . . He didn't want to think about her leaving him. He started babbling in a last-ditch effort.

"Today, driving home, I saw this car. A -- a Honda Accord. Green. Anne, I remembered it and I checked this book to make sure and it followed me thirteen days ago. Look."

He grabbed back the journal to show her, flipping clumsily for the page the entry was on. He couldn't find it. He flipped back and forth. The pages looked familiar. Where was it? Then, he remembered to find the date. He didn't even hear her first few words as he searched for March 5.

"No," she said. "Let me show you something."

"But, Anne, not only was it the same car, it turned off at the Conoco service station to vary its pattern. It didn't do that the last time. You know thirteen days ago."

"Bobby, it's nothing. Can't you see?" She was getting too loud. "No one is after you. People have routines. I see the same cars on some days too. There's only one main way to get from Knoxville to here. You know that."

"Anne --" He didn't know what to say. Why couldn't

she see? "Look, think about it."

She cut him off. "Bobby, guess what I found taped under the sink yesterday?"

He remembered the .380 pistol he kept hidden in the bathroom and could see the end. Panic filled him.

"I was going to ignore it," Anne said. "I thought it was nothing. But, this is more proof. Proof that you are not well."

"I'm not going back to see no damn doctor," Bobby said, infuriated. It came out loud and violent, but he meant it.

"You're scaring me," she said, now crying. "Can't you see I love you? You need help." She was crying hard now.

He hated to see her cry. He hated to argue. He walked past her and went outside. To something he understood. The woods.

CHAPTER 10

Jack Ward was scared. Kneeling at the edge of the woods just 50 yards from the assigned possible exit point, FBI Agent Jack Ward watched a dark house, feeling comfort in the pistol he had pointed in its general direction.

He wasn't supposed to be doing this and couldn't catch his breath, he was so nervous. His hands shook and he tried to control them. Mosquitoes buzzed by his face and he shook his head from left to right to keep them off. He'd bring bug spray next time. And learn to bring camouflage pants to work, just in case he was ever needed again -- he had gotten his pressed, starched khaki trousers muddy getting into position.

He hated fieldwork, what little he had done. He was an English major and felt he would be better employed drafting reports, something none of the others could do worth a damn.

Idiots can't write, he thought. They probably paid tutors to do their writing in English courses they had somehow passed during college, by the way their grammar looked. Oddly, it never occurred to him that he could be used for an arrest, as any other FBI special agent would be. Like they said though, "Just for a night." They were short a man and this would go into his "been there, done that, got the T-shirt" file of bullshit FBI stories he told.

Their suspect had a long list of registered and unregistered weapons, including assault rifles. Worse, he had extensive military training and an anti-government view that left a realistic possibility of armed resistance. Although the night was chilly, Ward found himself sweating.

He wiped the sleeve of his blue nylon jacket across his sweaty forehead. The jacket was one of his favorite bureau possessions. It was blue and had "FBI" across the back in big yellow capitalized letters. It was like the ones he'd always seen in the movies, or on the news during police investigations. It had once gotten him laid and he wore it every chance he got.

A mosquito or something went in his ear and he shook his head violently before using a finger to dig it out. In the process, he nearly dropped his pistol from his sweaty hands. Shit, he hoped the entry team would hurry up.

In the front yard, a four-man stack of FBI agents dressed in black SWAT gear moved nervously toward the front door. The blue 1996 four-wheel-drive truck, license plate TRV-668, and 1997 red Lumina, license plate VUN-142, were both parked in the driveway. That meant both suspects were home.

The point man, distracted by having to cover the front door and the window beyond it with his submachine gun, never noticed a thick pine branch in his path on the ground. His stiff black boot landed squarely on it and it snapped loudly making every one of the agents flinch as if they had been fired at. The point man froze in his tracks, which caused the second agent to slam into him. The team lost its composure.

"Damn it, Vinny! Just go! Go!" The third man and assault team leader harshly whispered.

CHAPTER 11

The crickets stopped chirping. That was odd, Anne thought. She couldn't sleep, but rarely could after she fought with Bobby. The crickets had been driving her insane as she debated what to do about him. She really felt she should stick to her guns and get Bobby to go see Dr. Blevins again.

She wondered what had gotten the crickets to shut up. They were so loud and annoying. Must be something walking near them, she thought. Maybe a coon or possum or deer. Their rural home sat surrounded by game-filled woods. She lay there thinking about how she could help Bobby. He really had some problems, problems she had once thought she could solve. But, more and more, she just didn't know.

A branch outside snapped. It was loud and only something big would have done that. Her heart fluttered and fear gripped her. Damn it, why was Bobby outside pulling one of his "I'll sleep in the woods tonight" affairs. Reaching over, she pulled open the nightstand's drawer and pulled out a heavy revolver, yet another weapon Bobby kept throughout the house. Her hands trembled as her imagination took over. Could it be a bear? One had been seen weeks earlier, down from the Smoky Mountains. Or a burglar?

But why would someone break in at night instead of during the day, when both her and Bobby were working? Maybe they wanted to hurt her...

She slipped out of bed carrying the pistol and crept down the hall toward the back door, her nightgown sliding along the carpet. Calling the sheriff was not an option, since he was twenty minutes away and probably in bed. She tried to calm down. Bobby had told her the best thing to do in such a situation.

Then she heard them. There were voices right outside the front door. Her heart was beating so fast, throbbing against her chest so hard that it hurt. Her breathing was rapid, out of control. She wanted to cry or scream or run.

But, Bobby had once told her what to do in one of his too many "just in case" sessions. How was it she was supposed to position herself? Oh yeah, right here, Bobby had said. She knelt four feet from the front door and aimed the heavy gun. Looking down the sights of the pistol was impossible in the darkness. That thought scared her more.

Taking a couple of deep breaths, she remembered Bobby had said that cocking the pistol made it easier to pull the trigger and thus resulted in better accuracy. She adjusted her kneeling position placing her left knee forward and supporting her body on her right leg. She placed her left elbow on her left knee and felt comfort with the increased stability. She had always hated guns and now hated the fact she was comfortable with the heavy deadly machine in her hands.

CHAPTER 12

Outside the door, the first three FBI agents stopped about two feet from the door, holding their position with the first agent covering the door with his black German sub-machinegun, a Heckler and Koch MP-5. The fourth agent, the breacher, moved up from the rear of the file with a forty-five pound battering ram. Now in front of the door, he reared back and swung the ram as hard as he could, aiming just to the left of the door handle.

The ram smashed into the door with a roar, threw back the door, and set off a screaming alarm that Bobby, in all his paranoia, had installed without Anne's knowledge.

* * *

The door flew open and hit Anne's forearm, causing the cocked gun to swing right and fire. The powerful .357 magnum boomed, temporarily overpowering the 126-decibel alarm. With the door open and the alarm ringing, Anne's fear took over and she bolted for the back door.

* * *

Special Agent Price, the breacher, was spun around and thrown down by the 422 pounds of knockdown power.

The partially mushroomed, jacketed hollow-point bullet entered his quad muscle and smashed through his femur before exiting along with several bone fragments.

The SWAT team froze, panic taking over. None had ever been shot at, much less hit. And the damn alarm had them frozen with its overpowering sound. Then, training took over as one screamed, "Shots fired, officer down!" into his radio.

Now, everyone was trying to scream over the incredibly loud alarm. Suddenly, the first man felt a hand on his shoulder as the second man hurled a flash bang grenade into the room. The grenade blasted at over one thousand decibels and flashed with two million candle light power. The officers burst into the room behind the stun grenade.

* * *

Anne tore out the back door. An explosion behind her roared and lit up the entire house like a firecracker lighting up a barrel. She stumbled over a root, falling hard and dropping the pistol in the process. Scrambling to her feet she could barely make out people screaming over the alarm behind her. She had to get in the woods. Bobby was there somewhere. He'd protect her.

She saw motion off to her left in her peripheral vision. Someone was running at her pointing a pistol and screaming, though she couldn't hear what he was saying over the alarm. She raised her hands to show she was unarmed. She saw a flash and felt a searing, burning pain erupt in her stomach.

Lying back on the ground, she struggled to stand, but her legs would not move. As it dawned on her that she was paralyzed, panic took over. She screamed in an ear-piercing, heart wrenching wail.

Numbness began to spread and the world grew dimmer and the alarm seemed quieter. She lost track of time. Several people stood over her. She realized they were police officers and thought, how odd? Darkness seemed to overcome all her thoughts.

*   *   *

There was someone running out the back door. Special Agent Jack Ward screamed, "Freeze, Police," but, the person couldn't hear him. Actually, he could barely hear his own words over the damn alarm.

"I can't let someone get away," he thought. He began to pursue the "felon" racing out of the tree line, even if she wore a nightgown and looked non-threatening. "Stop! Freeze! Police!" he shouted as he closed the distance.

She saw him and a cold fear overwhelmed him. "Holy shit!" he thought. She was raising her arm, swinging it his way and he saw a gun. She was going to kill him, just like she had one of the members of the entry team. He'd heard it on the radio. He raised his pistol.

His hands seemed slow, as though they wouldn't respond, like his senses were inhibited by alcohol. As he pulled the trigger the sight picture remained locked in his brain and he knew he had made a bad shot, even for him. He never even got on target again before the woman fell from his sight picture.

CHAPTER 13

Again, Bobby heard the sound. This time there was no doubt in his mind. It was a gunshot, not quite as powerful and distinct as the first, nearly undetectable off in the distance. Countless possibilities ran through his mind. The shots were definitely from the direction of his home. He stood up from his rock perch where moments before the first shot, he had been debating how best to make up with Anne.

He was probably a mile from the house, but a steep ridge was in his path. The night was quite dark with only a quarter moon to penetrate through the trees. It would not be safe for him to run, but he decided to anyway, taking off at a brisk jog.

Limbs slapped his face as he tore through the night. Noticing a hole, he cut hard left only to find his feet sliding out from under him on the leaves. He landed hard on the side of his left leg. Groaning, he scrambled back to his feet, put weight on his left leg to test it, decided it would be okay, and took off again.

* * *

The scene at the house had changed. Flashing blue lights from five police cars lit up the landscape. There was a state-trooper vehicle, three unmarked cruisers with flashing strobe lights on their dashes, and the large armored FBI SWAT vehicle.

A siren roared in the distance as all heads turned in hope that it was the ambulance. It was not. The local county sheriff skidded into the driveway slinging loose gravel. He nearly jumped out of his car and shouted to the nearest body, which happened to be a woman dressed in an elegant skirt and blouse.

"Just what in God's name is going on here?"

The sheriff then saw Anne. Three people were kneeled over her. The three were standing now and someone pulled out a white sheet to cover her.

* * *

From inside the tree line, a sweating and out of breath Bobby Ferguson watched the scene. He nearly ran out of the treeline until his ears caught words of anger between the sheriff and some guy dressed in a suit. Bobby knew if Sheriff Bo Jensen wasn't privy to what was going on, it meant feds.

Then he saw the trio kneeling over a prone body. He recognized the nightgown and nearly burst from the woods, but a voice from the depths of his conscience, just a whisper thanks to years of tranquility, peace, and happiness, told him to stay put. To watch. No, to "recon the objective." He needed to size up what was going on -- "assess the situation." He saw the bleeding agent who'd been shot. She'd hit one of them, though he'd likely live.

Around the perimeter, agents began to put up yellow police tape. He then saw the white sheet get spread over her. He tried to control his anger, but a deep rage began to tear at him. His unpracticed, near extinct discipline, barely kept him from rushing out. To maul the assholes on his land. He felt the rush of adrenaline and the cold thoughts of a killer. He clenched his teeth and felt tears roll down his face.

No! He nearly screamed. She was his anchor. His foundation. He looked at the soft agents in his yard. In suits and fucking sedans. Those fuckers don't know war, he thought. I'll show them fucking war.

He hit himself in the face, hating the tears. Hating the situation. Hating the feeling of helplessness. If he'd had a knife, he'd have made a blood oath right there to Anne.

He shook his head, ripping dirt from the ground with his fingers. Got to control myself, he thought. I'm a sniper, not a maniac. I need to get somewhere and think this through. Find out who's behind it.

And with that, Bobby Ferguson, formerly Nick Woods, Marine Sniper that had bagged his limit of Soviet soldiers in the hills of Afghanistan, crept back into the woods and dark night air.

CHAPTER 14

Picking up Colonel Jernigan proved a cinch.

An undercover police cruiser with a North Carolina Highway Patrolman sat waiting on the tarmac for Whitaker and his henchman when Whitaker's plane landed. The cruiser pulled up right next to the taxi-ing jet and Whitaker and Tank, the man termed Mr. NFL linebacker by Allen Green, climbed in. The officer hit his lights and squealed out of the airport toward Camp Lejeune.

Not a word was said during the drive. The Highway Patrolman was rightfully intimidated and Tank was contemplating the upcoming action. He lived for the opportunity to hurt those that needed hurting. Meanwhile, Whitaker had too much on his mind to talk. The story by Allen Green was a potential catastrophe of Herculean proportions. He tried to plan the next steps, but there were far too many unknowns. As much as he hated it, it looked like he would be playing this one by ear.

The guard gates of Camp Lejeune broke him from his thoughts. The patrol car avoided the pistol armed Marines checking military IDs by turning into a driveway before it. The road led to the visitor's building parking lot.

Waiting for them in the corner of the parking lot was a Major in camouflage utilities and an enlisted Marine with two green military hummers parked behind him. Whitaker and Tank exited the vehicle without even a thanks to the trooper.

The Major nodded to Whitaker as the three approached. "Long time no see," he said.

Whitaker said, "You're right. It has been a long time, but we need to move fast."

"Sure," the Major said. "Follow us past the guards and then go wherever you need. We'll tell the guards you're with us. Stay on the base as long as you need. If MPs pull you over, call me on my cell phone. When you're done, leave the hummer anywhere you'd like, either on or off base. Just call me so we can retrieve it quickly."

Whitaker nodded, impressed. "I owe you."

The Major smiled, knowing a debt repaid by Whitaker took one far in life. It was worth endangering his career by breaking more ordinances and rules than he could name. But there wasn't time to get approval for something that would almost certainly be unnecessary. Whitaker and his friend wouldn't be partying in the hummer. They had a task, and then they'd leave.

The Major jumped in his hummer and Whitaker and Tank climbed in the other one. They got past the guards with no problem, which was quite a feat in the post-Sept. 11 world. The Major sped away and left them to their business, which he knew better than to ask about.

The whole interview with Colonel Russ Jernigan took less than two hours and was uneventful. Tank had driven Whitaker to Colonel Jernigan's office, where Whitaker had gone in and told Jernigan they needed to talk. Not asked, just told. Jernigan had willingly left without a scene, though he had looked a little pale and nervous to his fellow Marine officers.

They had driven Jernigan off base to a motel in Jacksonville. By that point, Jernigan had really begun to grow concerned. The complete silence during the trip hadn't help.

Inside the room, they had "questioned" Jernigan, which of course meant Tank got to throw some punches and spill some blood. As the pain and pressure began to build, Whitaker increasingly started to think Jernigan was either lying or hiding something as he continuously denied spilling the information to Allen Green. He was too nervous.

But then Whitaker's phone rang and the need for questioning ended. Whitaker learned by phone that the FBI had raided Bobby Ferguson's house the night before, or Nick Woods depending on which name you preferred, and he was gone. That made it certain who had talked to the press.

Whitaker apologized to Jernigan for the "misunderstanding" and headed back to the airport. He and Tank were headed to Knoxville. Jernigan, though bloodied and nearly at his breaking point, felt only relief he hadn't told them about the night at Leatherneck bar. They would have certainly killed him.

CHAPTER 15

Flying now toward Knoxville on the same private jet, Whitaker tried to control his anger. After hearing about what had happened in Tennessee, besides Bobby Ferguson being gone, he cursed himself for depending on FBI goons.

I swear they're really nothing but office personnel these days, he thought. His men weren't college educated, and he cared more about how much they could bench press or how tight their groupings were on the range than if they cussed or made fun of women or homosexuals.

The multiple shooting, one-left-dead raid at Bobby Ferguson's house had left a clue for the world, at least those smart enough to connect the dots.

Allen Green was smart enough, but he was under complete observation twenty-four hours a day. Besides, he'd been fired from The New Yorker and no one would hire him now. He now lacked "integrity" in the eyes of most of the world and many suspected, including the New York Police, that he'd started the fire (actually started by Whitaker's men) to gain more attention or notoriety or whatever the hell they thought he was seeking. Typical unsuccessful writer with a midlife crisis, they probably thought. Whitaker grinned at his own ability.

An undercover agent working for Whitaker had tried to

hook up surreptitiously with Allen for details of the story, pretending to be another reporter. He had posed as an editor for a British tabloid. Millions were offered, in addition to the thing most important to Allen. That if the story proved true, the parent company of the tabloid, a media conglomerate, would hire him on one of their respectable papers. And with a good salary. It was another chance for Allen. But, Allen wisely said "no," and in the process unknowingly extended his life.

So what was the threat? What was the possibility that Bobby Ferguson could do much damage to Whitaker's organization or the U.S. government? True, he could shoot better than ninety-ninety percent of the world, but he lacked any education, wealth, or elite friends. He'd left in his home every single weapon he owned and immediately Whitaker's computer geeks had contacted his bank and frozen his accounts, which were meager anyway.

So he had no money, no vehicle, no friends that mattered -- every single construction worker he worked with, even the woman, was under surveillance, just in case. Even stranger, his men had expected for a car to be stolen or a minor robbery or two to occur as Bobby made his way out of Grainger County, but it hadn't happened. Not a clue. Bobby Ferguson, or Nick Woods the sniper, was gone.

What would I do if I were him, Whitaker wondered. An all points bulletin had been issued nationwide for the name Bobby Ferguson, and his picture had been faxed across the country. If Whitaker had ever owned a conscience, he'd have felt like shit for distributing nationwide an APB that a "Bobby Ferguson" was a serial child molester, not a renamed former Marine that had honorably served his country. But, the child molester approach always garnered more attention from police departments and other agencies, as well as media attention.

Truthfully, Whitaker finally acknowledged, he was worrying too much. There was just too much against Nick

Woods. He was done. It might take a couple of days, or a week or two, but he'd be caught. He'd get pulled over or have some cop walking a beat rouse him from some alley and recognize him. He might hurt an innocent cop or two, but their radios would bring his death. And if they took him alive, Whitaker would make sure he didn't live long. Even if it had to happen in the depths of a prison. Nick Woods would be killed.

He laid his head back and closed his eyes. It had been a long two days, starting with publishing of the story, the questioning of Allen, the trip to North Carolina the next day to visit Jernigan, and now the flight to Knoxville. The stress was a small price to pay, he thought. It was nothing in the big scheme of things, which is what he dabbled in.

CHAPTER 16

Nick Woods was deep in the foothills, walking down a worn deer trail less than an hour after seeing Anne's murdered body, lying motionless in the wet grass. Nick tried to come up with a reason as to why his house had been raided by the feds, some plausible thought that was not based on his conspiracy theories. Maybe someone had committed a crime in Grainger County and they'd got the addresses mixed up.

Shut up Bobby, the old Nick said, returning. You know why they came.

But he didn't. He hadn't talked. He had told no one about the number of Soviet bastards he had bagged in Afghanistan. Then, it hit him. He stopped walking. Only one man outside the CIA other than himself knew the truth. Captain Russ Jernigan, if that was even his real name. That motherfucker spilled the beans, Nick thought.

Nick had always distrusted the man. For Jernigan, the entire episode in Pakistan had been a game. More than likely, Jernigan had never killed a man or he wouldn't have been that way. Or maybe he had, but he'd definitely never been on the losing end of a firefight where a friend or acquaintance didn't walk away. Or walked away, but only on crutches. Because Nick knew war wasn't a game. It wasn't about containment or falling dominoes when rounds were skipping rocks into your face and you were screaming for your mom.

He could hardly remember the details of Jernigan, what he looked like, or where he might be, but it didn't matter. Because now he had a target. He began walking again. He knew he needed time. He headed toward his cave.

He found the cave with ease, though he hadn't been to it in years. Back in the day, he hadn't gone to it much because it left sign. Disturbed the leaves and such. Gave clues to those interested. But, in the last couple of years, Anne had actually begun to win him over. And the medication. And the lying doctor.

"Bobby, there isn't anyone watching you," the doctor would say at every visit. "What makes you think that? You're just sick."

Nick had always thought the doctor was one of them. Paid to say that. Trained to know what to say that was most effective for veterans. In fact, Nick had thought for a long time that Anne was one of them, or sent or set up by them. Just to calm him. To keep him quiet. To make him soft. And, it'd worked. He'd changed from a murderous man intent upon finding out who had sold him and his partner out in Afghanistan, to a paramilitary nut on a hill content with being left alone, to finally a married man who shot for old time's sake and was just a touch paranoid.

Yet now he knew that Anne wasn't one of them. They'd killed her. The thought made him shake with rage, as did the fact he had ever doubted her sincerity. He paused to swallow down tears.

Get in character, Nick. They used to say it in the Corps all the time. You had to stay focused. Without emotion most of the time. Especially in war.

Standing outside the cave, he wished he had a flashlight. He wondered why he'd never thought of that. That he might have to find this cache in the dark. Then he remembered. Because more than likely, he'd be in the house at dark and he could have held off an army there. Held it off until he decided to retreat through his tunnel.

The thought of the tunnel underneath his house made him think of Anne.

If she had known about that -- God, she would have left him. He smiled. She was a hell of a fighter. Shit, she had to be to partially tame him. He closed his eyes and remembered her gorgeous face. Her passionate kisses. Her rage when he upset her. It took all Nick had to fight back more tears.

Alright now, Nick, get your head in the game and get in character, he said. You love Anne? Then put the murderous bastards that hurt her in the ground. Every. Single. Fucking. One.

With that thought, he got on his hands and knees and crawled into the black hole of his cave. It was damp, and stank. Reminded him of the smell that always permeated around Camp Lejeune in the swamps. Stagnant water and rotting wood.

He couldn't see a thing. His hands groped through damp dirt and he hit his head on a rock outcropping along the ceiling. He was scared shitless. Worried he'd grab a snake or run into a bobcat waiting at the end of the cave. His head went through a spider web, and he spit and knocked at his face, nearly stopping and backing out.

Hatred and training took over. He had to do this for Anne. And if it was meant for a copperhead or bobcat to be in here, then so be it.

The fatalistic instinct he'd always relied on during combat was returning. It kept you sane, making things easier. Play smart. Play the odds. But in the end, fate often decided where rounds struck and where targets were when they struck. And in the end, you kept moving as the bullets went by you or you died. Period. And once you understood and believed in fate, courage came easier.

Besides, with Anne gone, he had little to live for.

So he pushed deeper, fear keeping his heart beat at a dangerously high rate. After he'd crawled for what seemed like miles, but what he knew to be twelve feet, he found it.

An opening on the right side of the cave that was about a foot higher than the tunnel he now crawled through. This higher portal was designed to keep his equipment dry.

He'd spent years digging the tunnel with a Marine e-tool. It'd taken weeks to dig in the uncomfortable small space, but now it had finally paid off. He reached up into the side hole and immediately felt canvas.

It was a green military issue backpack, stuffed full of things he'd once thought he might need in a survival situation: a couple sets of civilian clothes, heavy climbing rope, duct tape, flashlight, extra batteries, a green wool blanket, an unloaded .45 pistol, three empty magazines, two boxes of .45 cartridges, and cash. Lots of cash in small denominations.

He dragged the pack out of the cave as fast as he could and took a deep breath of fresh air. Damn, it felt good to be out of that cave. In the darkness, he laid the pack upright and opened it. Thankfully, the straps appeared to be fine. He'd always worried they might dry rot, but apparently the semi-dry cave had worked.

Inside the pack, a green sealed bag met him. It was rubber and tied at the top by a wrapped and knotted string. The classic Willie-Pete bag, as Marines called them, the W-P standing for "water-proof." They were a Godsend for infantrymen. They helped your pack float if you needed to cross a deep river and kept your clothes dry regardless of how hard it rained.

Untying the strings, he opened the bag and found another identical one. Also sealed. He opened it and felt around inside the clothes and supplies for the pistol. He found it and pulled it out. It took longer to find the two pistol magazines and flashlight. Then he searched for a box of cartridges and finding one, began to load each magazine while using his mouth to aim the mini maglight. He was pretty sure he could load the magazines in the dark correctly, but he wanted to make certain he didn't load a round backward. That might be bad in a gunfight.

He'd left the magazines unloaded because he'd always worried keeping them crammed full of bullets might weaken the springs over many years. And if the springs were loose, then his gun might jam. And if your gun jammed, you died.

After loading the three magazines, he pulled one more cartridge out of the box and closed it. He put the box of cartridges back in the pack and turned the flashlight off. He then stuck the single round between his teeth and worked the pistol's slide back and forth. It slid easily and felt smooth. Dependable.

He then aimed it through the woods and pulled the unloaded gun's trigger. The hammer fell crisply. The function check completed, he fed a magazine in the pistol and worked the slide once more, feeding a round in the chamber. Then he dropped the magazine, pleased with its easy release, and took the round from his mouth. He loaded this last round into the magazine, giving him eight rounds of .45 ammo in a firefight instead of seven.

Finished, he checked the safety lock and then stuffed the pistol, now cocked and locked, into his waistband behind his back. Using his left hand, he stuck the two extra magazines into the left side of his waistband, bottom up so the lip at the bottom of the magazine would keep them from sliding down.

He picked up the flashlight and used it to look in the pack for his money. He found the thick envelope within seconds. It was a nine by twelve mailing envelope, encased by three plastic bags. It held $10,600.

He'd started with $200 in twenty-dollar bills hidden in his house after he was discharged. Then, he'd set aside a twenty-dollar bill each week for ten years before finally stopping with Anne's help. He took out one hundred dollars and put it in his wallet. He put the envelope back in the pack, at the bottom, and sealed the whole thing up. He figured anyone trying to rob him would ask him for his wallet, not his pack.

He wished there was some food in it. He was hungry after the late-night run and movement through the woods. But, he'd decided not to put food in it on purpose, even sealed military issue MRE's for fear that animals might smell them and chew into his pack. Well, that's what he had money for. He hoisted the heavy pack and welcomed its weight, for its contents were his only chance of getting away. And the weight brought back old memories of long night marches.

He adjusted the straps, bounced up and down to get it seated, and then adjusted the straps one last time. He placed the flashlight in his left front pocket and adjusted the pistol on his right hip. He was ready. He headed off through the woods.

He saw the highway about an hour later. He thought it might be about that long because he hadn't looked at his watch at either the cave or immediately following the shootout. He'd been debating whether to take the road since taking off from the cave. The argument between the sheriff and the FBI led him to believe there wouldn't be roadblocks all across the county. This had to be an illegitimate operation or why wouldn't the sheriff be involved? And where were the other squad cars and investigation vans?

So he figured the roads weren't blocked, but that likely they were on his trail. And if he were them, he'd have some dogs following, too. An inexpensive yet effective operation. It wouldn't draw much media or public attention. But, if they set up roadblocks and stopped every resident on every major road, then the newspapers and TV news would be going nuts in no time.

His decision made, he walked up on the road. He had to hope the next car or so going either way wasn't a police officer. But, he had to get out of the county fast and that meant taking bold risks. He was sort of surprised they didn't have a helicopter after him yet. They must have been nearly certain they'd get him in the house. Hadn't planned any other contingencies. Damned fools, he thought. They just saw his truck and moved in. They wouldn't last long in war, where a thing called Murphy's Law had put many a man in the ground.

Headlights illuminated his path. Coming from behind him. He kept walking. He knew from his experience in giving rides that you never picked anybody up that was looking for a ride. So he kept walking, but let his shoulders sag some, real tired-like. He added a bit of a limp, too. The car flew past him without slowing or swerving out of the way. Nick wasn't even sure if it saw him.

Then he saw headlights approaching from his front, from way off. There were three sets of them. Two cars and one truck passed without a thought. Then more lights appeared from behind him. He resumed his tired, weary gait.

The front vehicle was slowing as it approached. He could tell by the squeal of the brakes that needed to be replaced. It went past him, its right signal warning the car behind it to slow down. It was stopping.

It was a truck. A Ford, mid-eighties. Rust visible along the corners of the fenders. Nick sped up and caught the look of the man in the truck. He looked old. Probably sixty. Sure that the man was okay, and not some agent, Nick dropped his pack and hoisted it into the bed of the truck. Depositing it with relief -- he needed to do some serious training because he had grown soft in the construction business -- he readjusted his pistol in the darkness and climbed into the truck, thankful country folks were so warm hearted.

"Howdy there," the driver said.

"Howdy."

"Where you headed?"

"West," Nick said with a smile.

The old man, his face covered with grisly, unshaven gray hairs grinned back. "You running from something?" he asked good-naturedly.

Nick tried to read him and decided to play it honest. “Yep. You might say that, but don’t you worry. Just need to get away and think awhile. Me and my wife are having some problems.” It was an answer not too far from the truth.

CHAPTER 17

The old man got him as far as Rutledge, a small town barely twenty miles from his house. A pitiful distance away really, but outside immediate danger for sure and probably far enough away for Nick to consider himself safe for the night. Nick debated handing the man some money and possibly asking him to be quiet. To never mention this to anyone. But that seemed too much. It would only increase the man's interest. Might convince him that Nick was a real criminal. So in the end, Nick had opened his wallet, careful to keep it tilted so the man couldn't see in it, and said, "Partner, I owe you, but I'm a little short on cash."

The man smiled, full of wisdom, and said, "I've been there son. I've been there."

Nick tipped his head in a grateful nod and closed the door, which squealed loudly. Unfortunately, the old man had dropped him off at a gas station. Thankfully, it was empty except for someone at the counter, but that was still more attention than Nick needed. He figured the feds would have someone out asking questions tomorrow. And you just didn't see many men with packs and on foot out this way in the country. At forty miles, it was just too far from the interstate for any real traveler making his way by foot.

Oh well, thought Nick. He shouldered his pack and

began walking up the road. He looked down at his watch and saw it was eleven thirty-three. He was tired. Drained. Too much emotional and physical exertion combined with his old construction routine -- early to bed, early to rise. He walked along the road, west and when he got far enough that he was certain the gas station attendant couldn't see him, he ran off the road and through a field toward some woods.

Reaching the woods, he pushed into it fighting limbs, brambles, and vines. It was a thicket, much thicker than the open woods behind his house. He pushed about fifty yards deep and began looking for a place to call it a night. He found enough room to lay down finally, an old deer bed, and unpacked his poncho liner. He laid down. He'd forgotten about his pistol and the magazines until the ground pushed them into his back. Groaning, he removed them and laid them by his side.

He fell asleep within minutes.

CHAPTER 18

Nick had no idea where he was when he awoke. It was daylight. He was deep in a carpet of trees, wrapped in his blanket. His mind tried to unravel it all and then he remembered. He sat up, sad now. Alone, with Anne gone, he felt the forces of misery press against him.

She'd been with him for those perfect eight hours of sleep, his exhaustion having pushed the thought of her death from his mind. Damn, he was going to miss her for a long time.

He cursed himself for letting her in and for being the cause of her death. For letting her convince him his paranoia was unneeded. Damn it, he could have kept her alive if he had been stronger. He'd argued for putting in a gate at the end of their driveway. Sensor detectors along his property. Even fencing in the property to let a few Dobermans or German shepherds roam about freely.

He unwrapped himself from the poncho liner and sat up. He saw the pistol by his side lying on the ground, its magazines lying next to it. He pulled his legs from out of the blanket and groaned at the feel of sweaty socks. He'd left his boots on through the night like a dumb-ass recruit, and his feet had gotten sweaty. Already, his feet tinkled, the burning pain of athlete's foot just around the corner.

Before doing anything, he looked around him and

listened for a full two minutes -- he used his watch as a guide. Nothing. Quickly he took one boot and sock off -- his right foot -- and allowed the foot to air out. He picked up the .45 pistol, feeling safety and power in its heft. With adept ease, he dropped the magazine then removed the eighth round from the chamber. He laid both on the ground and extended the pistol toward a large pine. Aiming, he pulled the trigger, dry firing it. He worked the slide and repeated the dry firing, this time with his eyes closed.

He was trying to feel the trigger pull. Learn when the hammer released. To get really familiar with the very unfamiliar pistol he hadn't fired in years. He dry fired it thirty times, feeling somewhat better about his skill with it.

The old 1911 .45 was no different than the thousands that had been used against the Germans and Japs in World War II. They had the knockdown power of a bulldozer and had been used far into the Korean and Vietnam wars, though now they were being phased out by 9 mm Berettas, because Berettas had more safeties, held more rounds in case you missed, and didn't kick so hard, which helped the women and fags, Nick always believed.

Fucking Army's been in the shitter for a long time, he thought.

He laid the pistol down, pulled out a fresh pair of socks from his pack and covered the bare foot with a clean sock. It always felt so good to put a clean, dry pair of socks on. One of the few joys of being in the field as an infantryman. He then put his right boot back on. Rebooted, he then untied and removed the boot and sock on his left foot. As it began to air out, he picked the unloaded pistol up again.

Again he pointed toward the pine and acquired it in his sights. He chided himself. Damn it, don't look at the target (or tree in this case). Focus on the front sight. He lowered the pistol then raised it quickly aiming at the pine. This time his eye focused on the front sight and kept the pine fuzzy, or unfocused. He knew, as all good marksmen know, that the secret to accuracy was a focused front sight, with both the rear aperture and target out of focus.

It was a damn difficult thing to learn and even more difficult to master. And if you were really good, you'd remember the advice when you got the shit scared out of you in a firefight. You would notice the front sight and not what your target was doing when you pulled the trigger.

Nick had had both occurrences happen. Better things had occurred when he'd barely noticed his target and remembered to focus on his front sight. So, he sat there and practiced aiming, role-playing various scenarios. He remembered the saying, the more you sweat in peace the less you bleed in war. They used to say it daily in the Marine Corps. And Nick believed it. After all, he was living proof of it. Just ask a few Soviets who had managed to "meet him" and survive their time with him.

He finished practicing. These days, few understood the importance of practicing without firing shots, or dry firing as it's called. Of learning not to anticipate a gun's kick. Of having to imagine a shot being fired. No, it was way more fun to shoot fast and with one hand on a range with live rounds. And less work. It took less time in the hot sun or wet rain to fire 30 rounds than it did to dry-fire sixty times, and then fire 30 rounds. These days, it was more fun to play Nintendo or some damn thing than train for war. He knew. He had talked to young men that had served since he had been discharged. Why on earth the officers and sergeants allowed men to play video games in their rooms was beyond him, but he'd heard it from enough men to believe it.

He put a clean sock on his left foot and quickly tied his boot. It seemed like déjà vu playing the one boot game. Another old infantry trick. It was a rule a wise man never broke. One boot took less time to put on than two, and you always had to anticipate contact with the enemy at any time. With that thought, Nick took a quick look around him again. Still nothing.

He debated doing some push ups, but held off until he was where he could shower. He'd have time for that. He packed up his poncho liner and cinched closed his pack. Now, only his pack, pistol, and magazines were lying at his feet.

He picked the empty pistol up and held it at his side. He then performed a close-encounter drill, which involved stepping back with his right foot, while pushing an imagined person too close to him back with his left hand and leveling his pistol at the target while keeping it close to his side. It was one of the few instances Nick would fire a pistol single-handed. He practiced the movement fifty times, this drill more important in his mind than focusing on the front sight.

Finishing that drill, he placed the empty pistol in the small of his back. He checked his surroundings again and satisfied he was still alone, he slowly moved his right hand and withdrew the pistol, aiming it. He replaced it and withdrew it again, this time a little faster. He did this drill one hundred times, because it was by far the most important. He could never be too fast on the draw, though he could damn sure be too slow.

By this time, small beads of sweat covered his brow and his right hand burned in a few spots, the classic early warning of blisters. He reached down to the side of his pack and grabbed his canteen. He took ten good swallows -- he counted -- and replaced it. Ten swallows, they'd always told him. You could run, fight, or swim after ten swallows without puking or cramping. Any more, and you were pushing your luck.

Nick didn't feel like doing the last drill. He was hungry and imagining a couple biscuits for breakfast, but he immediately cursed himself. You little bitch, he thought. This ain't the ARMY, which he always remembered stood for "Ain't Ready for the Marines Yet." He could hide his pack and go up to the store once the lady he'd seen last night was gone.

With that thought, he began his next drill. He aimed the unloaded pistol at the pine, mentally fired, BOOM, then took a knee and fired twice more, BOOM, BOOM. Again, he thought. He did it, "firing" a single shot at his target before taking a knee and firing twice more.

He only did this drill ten times. He knew he should do it more, but the tactical side of him reminded him that he needed to stay at least partly presentable. Not sweaty and stinky. He already needed to shave and his shirt was starting to look, well like it had been worn for two days and slept in one night. He still resisted the thought of reaching down in his pack and changing into a new one. He was in the country and few would care. Many in the country either farmed, or hunted, or fished, and looks wasn't something folks in the country worried much about.

Resuming his training in the middle of the thicket, Nick began to think his way through a firefight as he was currently armed. It would be close and few liked that, even him. Hell, that's why he was a sniper.

But, still, it'd be close. They would either get the draw on him or perhaps he would get lucky and recognize them before they had pulled their pieces; either way, he could do the last drill, firing a single shot quickly at the nearest one's chest, half-aimed, before dropping to a knee and firing two well-placed shots. Ninety percent of the time, Nick would go with that option. In cities, there likely wouldn't be any cover so he would just engage. One quick shot, followed by two controlled shots from the kneeling position.

Yet there could be cover, so he thought through that. Perhaps it might be a vehicle. Step one, get down or race behind it. Then return fire. Few could hit a nearby target that was running laterally. Normally, even he wouldn't try. He could also use bystanders. Feds would worry about hitting them. He wouldn't. There was also concealment. Concealment could be anything from thin desks to couches to walls. Concealment didn't stop rounds, cover did. But concealment caused most untrained people -- even cops -- to hold their fire because they couldn't see their target.

Look for cover and concealment, he thought. Cover and concealment, he said again, reinforcing the idea. The two bastions infantrymen sought. The two things that could keep you alive on any day of the week. Satisfied with his morning pistol work, he reloaded the pistol and placed it and the magazines in his belt.

He'd cooled down while he thought through shooting engagements. Now he needed to practice his hand-to-hand. The thought made him instantly realize he was without a knife. He'd fix that soon. Find him a good single-hand folding defender. A Benchmade if he could find one, but a Spiderco would work.

Before starting, he checked his surroundings. Then he began, all of it nice and easy. He practiced various blows that at best would be considered dirty by most if used in a fight. He practiced eye gouges, shots to the nuts with low kicks and knees, throat punches, elbows to the temple, and double-hand slaps to the ears. He hated those.

Then, he practiced joint manipulation, at least that's what they'd called it. He never liked the term. Breaking arms, ripping shoulders out of sockets, and snapping fingers like they were freshly harvested snap beans seemed to be a bit more than mere joint manipulation. But, he didn't know. He was just a simple man and some piss-ant, college-grad liberal could hardly title a section of a manual, "Fucking another man up with your bare hands."

He did all his moves in slow motion. He had barely practiced them in years, Anne having convinced him he was paranoid, maybe even sick.

Nick had always believed mastering hand-to-hand combat was about having mentally been in every possible situation a fight could end up in. It was hard to think when blades were flying and punches were connecting, and damn if a person didn't do some stupid stuff in a fight.

But, as he'd become trained in fighting, he'd found that if you had envisioned certain instances, you usually would react right.

So he began practicing his blocks, beginning with the counter to the overused right hand sucker punch. He went through his blocks, doing each ten times without exception, though in slow motion as he had his attacks.

His stomach growling reminded him of his hunger and he nearly didn't finish his regimen.

Nick, he thought, there are a lot of people not training right now. Cops, feds, and CIA soldiers -- your pursuers and true threat. If you plan to own them and survive this war, get back to work. They'll wish soon that they had been training when they were hungry, too.

So Nick began working on the ever important aspect of range in a fight. He practiced his footwork. Circling, stepping back and even stepping forward to jam an opponent. He then practiced his head movement and body movement to avoid someone's punches.

Though he hadn't watched his time, either when he began or as he went along, Nick spent close to two hours in his training. By the time he'd finished, his whole body felt shaky from lack of food and muscles that had softened with limited use.

But, the time had kept Anne off his mind and made him think about pain, murder, and death. He'd believed for most of his life before he met Anne that force was one of the most important influence in the world. It was simple. Effective. And had conquered and dominated peace since the beginning of time.

But, having finished mentally maiming or killing a few hundred imaginary opponents, Nick began thinking about Anne again. Her smile. The feel of her bare skin when they lay in bed at night. She'd lived her life trusting too much. He remembered how exasperated she'd been when he taught her to fire a pistol. Looking back, he realized she'd probably let him teach her just so she could be with him, sharing in his one love besides her: Guns.

Nick swallowed. He knew he wouldn't cry. That Nick, or Bobby Ferguson, or whatever the fuck he'd been when he was with her, was dead. He realized he'd probably never cry again. He had never cried while he was in the Corps. Even when he lost his spotter in Afghanistan. They made you into a machine. He realized he'd never really lost that spirit. Maybe for a while, when he was with Anne, the machine in him had had a governor put on it and a granny behind the wheel who refused to slam down the pedal, but he had always had it.

He'd always been a machine since his first day at Parris Island, though really it began before then. From his time on the gridiron playing high school football, he had always had an affection for toughness. No, it was not toughness. It was maleness. It was saying what you thought. Taking a good ass whooping instead of wisely backing down. It was pride.

Maybe a more accurate description of his time with Anne was like having a chip loaded into a powerful car that forced it to act completely differently. To change gears easily and not get the RPMs up so high. Either way, it didn't matter now. He had people hunting him and he'd have to turn into the machine of war he'd once been yet again. No, he'd never fancied being prey or running much. It was about force. That was life's simplest common denominator.

He had once heard that everyone has a plan until they get punched. That was true, he knew. He had seen it happen to those wannabe karate types, and even big as shit men who had easily won every fight they had been in. So often, their confidence got shattered once that first punch knocked a couple of teeth down their throat.

And with that thought, he retraced his steps from last night. He had some hunting to do. The deck was stacked against him big time and it was a long shot, but he'd made a few long shots in his day. Someone, or some group, had come after him with a plan, and now it was time to strike back and remind them that two sides could bring pain. That once you start a fight, you lose full control of what will happen. Your opponent can move and strike back, and that's precisely what Nick Woods would now do.

CHAPTER 19

It was dark and Nick was in the woods again. The day had proved uneventful. He'd left his pack in the woods, bought some food at the gas station following his two-hour morning practice session, and gone back into the woods to eat. He'd stayed there until after five, confident at that point that if there were roadblocks or patrols, likely undercover feds, they'd be giving up or at least in less force.

Everyone has to sleep, eat, and shit at some point. And usually with manhunts, you went all out in the beginning, pushing your folks until they could barely stand anymore, then you started thinking about rest and long-term capabilities.

At five, he'd grabbed his pack and headed for the gas station again. Upon arriving, he'd hid it in some bushes and stood outside the building, leaning on it waiting for the right person. That person had showed after twenty minutes and six cars filling with gas.

Again, it was an old man and again the man drove a truck -- neither were uncommon in Grainger County. Nick had approached the senior and offered him sixty dollars to drive him to Oak Ridge, better known as "The Secret City" and home to the Manhattan Project. The man, who relied on social security, had quickly agreed. So just like that, Nick grabbed his pack, threw it in the back of the truck, and jumped in.

This man had been a real talker, unlike the one from the night before. He'd lost his wife to cancer and his only son had moved to the big city (or "seety," as he called it) and rarely visited. The big seety was just Knoxville, and hardly a true big city, but Nick had listened respectfully. Nick had answered some of the man's questions, making up shit as he went. But mainly, he kept the man talking about himself or his son. Above all, Nick knew it was important the man not find anything memorable about his situation, and part of how he kept that from happening was by making certain his situation didn't seem too strange. Thus the need for Nick to talk with the man and not act like he had something to hide.

Thankfully, keeping up this pretense and conversation with the man was no challenge, so as Nick had been throwing out worthless horseshit to the man, he'd been thinking. Unless he was totally mistaken, he figured that in some media outlet somewhere, the story involving him and his spotter's work in Afghanistan had been published.

Besides just stocking up with war supplies once he got to Oak Ridge, he knew he needed to find his target. He had Colonel Russ Jernigan already. Now he needed the name of the bastard who had shot Anne. You couldn't hunt without a plan and you couldn't plan without a target.

He had the old man drop him off at a shabby motel. Nick didn't even see a name for the place, just a red lit vacancy sign in the window of the office. Perfect. He handed three twenty-dollar bills to his driver and then looked at him real serious.

"Sir," Nick said. "I'm going to be real honest."

The man looked worried, more than likely preparing for the worst. Was Nick some kind of criminal, Nick could see him thinking.

"I've had some trouble with the law and I'm running from the police."

The man's face tensed and Nick could feel him taking in his features, etching them in his mind for when he had to describe his passenger. Shit, Nick thought, maybe this idea had been stupid. Well, he couldn't give up on it now.

"Basically, a man I thought was my friend got to fooling around with my wife. I found out about it and well, you know, had words with him, so to speak. It was a little worse than I planned and he had some injuries. My wife kicked me out and the law wants to throw me in the pen for assault charges," Nick said, looking down, overwhelmed by his "predicament."

The man looked relieved to hear such a trifling story. He had worried Nick had killed someone. "Sounds to me like he had it coming. It figures that a man who'd cheat on his friend's wife would try to deal with his problems through the courts. Gutless bastard. You just hang in there, son. God will take care of you," the man said.

Nick met the man's eyes. He nodded thoughtfully.

The man seemed to buy Nick's acting.

"Sir, you have a good day," Nick said. And with that, he grabbed his pack from the man's truck and headed into the office of the complex.

CHAPTER 20

Back in Washington, in his Pentagon office, Whitaker sat with his legs propped on his desk. He was pissed. It had been two days since the raid and they hadn't found Nick Woods.

While he didn't know where he was, what he did know was that Bobby Ferguson was dead. Some of his men had tracked Bobby after the local and state police had cleared out and found the trail leading into his cave. And in the cave were drag marks, heavy drag marks. So, Bobby had reverted back to the old Nick and in retrieving his cache become the highly touted Nick Woods. Sniper legend among CIA insiders. Unknown Marine among the military community.

Now, Nick had been alerted. And, he had disappeared. Just like that. As soon as Whitaker had received the call from the FBI reporting that Bobby wasn't at home, he had scrambled his forces. Every available person in his organization not already assigned, even those that had recently entered retirement. Thirty-one of his undercover people, nineteen men and twelve women varying in age from twenty-two to sixty-six, had closed in on Grainger County.

They'd sat in restaurants, driven around, asked clerks in gas stations about a friend that had broken down and was traveling on foot, every known trick. Waiting for the call that Nick had been spotted by these undercover agents were three eight-men strike teams parked strategically throughout the county in undercover work vans. Whitaker's boss had assigned the FBI to the light work, since they were definitely involved now, to watch friends, family, every known acquaintance of Nick's. Whitaker didn't expect Nick to make such a mistake, but he had to play it safe.

Still, nothing. From anyone.

Besides the bad news that Nick Woods hadn't been at home, a woman had been killed and the media were asking questions about the quickly planned raid that reportedly caught some FBI agents off guard. That infuriated Whitaker. It presented a definite dot on a map. In his line of work, there were always dots. No, not dots, small blips. The blips were always scattered, separated by hundreds if not thousands of miles. They spanned counties, states, and continents and seemed unrelated.

Allen Green had somehow connected a few blips. Somehow figured out that American troops had straight up gone after and killed Soviet troops. He'd brilliantly connected the blips, or dots. And even somehow figured out that America had then sold out its own men and given away their location to the Soviets. Of course, he was wrong about the sniper's death and other minor details like the fact that the mole was killed, but that was to be expected when you were dealing with small blips on the radar screen without the context of being able to put together the whole picture.

Allen Green presented a great threat. He was a respected journalist and no doubt had friends and colleagues that would never be convinced he invented the entire story, or was a pedophile. After all, how could a man with such a record of integrity truly be so worthless. His friends were reporters and eventually it'd start to wear on them how they'd misread this man's character, and eventually they'd decide that they hadn't misread Allen Green's character; that something else was going on; something much more devious.

This was exactly why Allen Green was under surveillance by CIA agents not under Whitaker's command. Not to mention, tech folks were tracking e-mail traffic among media personnel in New York and phone calls made by Allen. Eventually, as time went by, Allen would have to be killed. Of that, Whitaker was certain.

That was the lesson from this situation.

Whitaker had failed to eliminate Nick Woods when he was in Afghanistan. After Nick Woods had completed his primary mission of taking out the majority of an elite Soviet Special Forces team, they had sent him and his spotter on worthless ops so that false info could be handed to possible moles inside the CIA in the hopes that they could ferret them out.

It had worked after several missions. They had soon found their mole -- a huge victory in itself -- and leaked the coordinates of Nick and his spotter. They had hoped the Soviets would tie up the loose ends of Nick and his spotter, and the Soviets certainly tried. They went after the two Americans like madmen. More than a hundred troops. Mortars. An entire operation just to get two men. The Soviets had bagged Nick's spotter and wounded Nick, but he had escaped their cordon and worked his way back to the embassy in Pakistan.

Whitaker was nearly certain Nick had known he had been sold out. As part of every op, Nick and his spotter were given coordinates of where to be picked up. Not just one set, but many in case they couldn't get to the primary pick up point, or in case the primary pick up point was compromised by the enemy.

But, Nick had avoided the three primary points and two other alternates, all within ten to twenty miles of his mission site, and traveled more than a thousand miles to Pakistan over a period of weeks. Of course, Whitaker had leaked each of the pick-up points to the mole, hoping the Soviets would bag Nick at one of them and end the mission for good.

Whitaker had been so certain that Nick and his partner would be killed or captured that he hadn't had anyone watching the embassy. He'd closed down the operation and sent all his forces back to America figuring that there was no way that Nick or his spotter would get away from the battle-hardened Soviets. Not when the Soviets had the specific location of the two men.

But letting down his guard and making that assumption had proved a huge mistake. Weeks later, Nick showed up to the American embassy in Pakistan dressed as a civilian. He made a demand to the Marine guard at the door that he wanted to meet with the American ambassador, and by the time a leak in the embassy informed Whitaker of the situation, he could hardly have Nick picked off.

Thankfully, Nick had been smart enough to create a credible story of being a missionary kidnapped from Pakistan and dragged into Afghanistan before finally escaping. Whitaker had helped Nick handle the messy details of the story and helped Nick with a new identity -- Bobby Ferguson. He'd also worked with some friends in the Marine Corps to fabricate the death of Nick Woods in a training accident, along with his spotter. Whitaker had been forced to do this because killing him with so many witnesses and embassy staff around was impossible; especially given how on guard Nick Woods had been. It was as if Nick had known he and his spotter had been sold out, and he trusted no one.

The press never caught wind of any of this. The press had always cared little about missionaries and their religious zeal, so Nick's story had proved brilliant at several levels. Quite impressive for someone untrained in the art of covert operations.

Whitaker had always debated when to take Nick out once he returned back to the states. Nick had understood he'd been thrown into something over his head, and had gone along with giving up his old life. Nick Woods was dead and his family would get the $200,000 in life insurance they were due. He agreed to never go near his hometown again -- at least for ten or twenty years and then only in disguise -- and to begin his life anew under the name Bobby Ferguson.

Nick had been told by one of Whitaker's handlers that he must go along with this new identity in order to avoid Soviet KGB agents eventually finding and identifying him.

"The Soviets still want your hide for all the men you killed," the handler said. "Not to mention you helped turn the tide of war against them nearly single-handedly, so they'll be looking for you for years and years. From now on, you're Bobby Ferguson. Make up a false back story and youth and forget all you know. That's your only hope of survival. We can't protect you from the KGB. We'll try, but ultimately only you can."

Whitaker knew he had to take Nick out at some point. It had to be done, he knew. But it wasn't that simple. Nick was a nut, and he was good. And Nick knew -- somehow -- what Whitaker hoped he wouldn't: That his greatest threat wasn't the KGB, but the CIA hoping to tie up a loose end.

Initially, Nick had placed dynamite all through the house. All primed to go off and there for the sole reason to cause a scene, because Nick was smart enough to know that he couldn't possibly stay alive. You couldn't live forever if expert killers were after you. No one kept their guard up that well.

But, you could cause a scene and Nick had been smart enough to know that if a house exploded, they would come. Local law enforcement. The media with their dangerous cameras and questions. And, they'd find numerous bodies in the house with weapons that weren't solely Nick's and weren't used by police agencies. Everything from laser sights to explosive shotgun shells.

Whitaker had debated taking Nick out on the road in a classic "hit and run" or something, but Nick had approached the sheriff and told him there were people sending threats to him. So, if he'd died within the first few months, there would have been at least an investigation by the sheriff, which wasn't a problem. But, if the Tennessee Bureau of Investigation got involved, it could have gotten ugly. Especially, if the FBI decided they would provide assistance. And who knew how many documents Nick kept in safe deposit boxes that Whitaker hadn't known about. Nick was crazy and they knew by his behavior that he was doing everything in his power to prevent his death and ultimately take down the men behind the death of his spotter and best friend in Afghanistan.

So they'd waited for Nick to take his guard down. To stop carrying two pistols and a knife. To stop watching his mirrors as he drove to work and living a life utterly without pattern. Even driving to work, Nick changed his patterns. Sometimes he would go in to work two hours early and on other days, he would show up ten minutes late. He even took different routes, one of which added 24.6 miles and thirty-three minutes to the commute. The man was a nut. A hard target. Psychotic. But, above all of that, he was just good.

So, they had let him be while keeping him under surveillance in case he tried to leak the story. Then something totally magical happened. Nick had met Anne. They had watched the two with interest and Anne had saved Nick's life. She had tamed him and made him into nearly a normal man, one that could be taken out, no doubt. But, Whitaker had changed his mind in one of the few instances of sympathy he'd ever had.

Whitaker decided that Nick had served his country well by turning the tide of the war in Afghanistan, being used as a pawn to stop a dangerous Soviet Special Forces team, discover a painful mole, and then finding out the real truth of how he'd been sold out, but still remaining mute. A true patriot, if ever there was one.

For sure, Nick could have started probing and looking for who had set him up, but he hadn't. He'd understood that he'd been caught up in a game much bigger than himself. Much, much bigger. Or perhaps, he never did anything because he realized how little he could achieve. Or maybe he couldn't confirm well enough in his own mind that he'd been sold out. Either way, Anne had finally closed that door for good by falling in love with the distant, stern man, and wearing down his crazy behavior.

But, now Whitaker knew he was in a world of shit. Nick's single guiding force, his rudder in life, had been brutally killed. Whitaker had no idea how the death of Anne would affect Nick. Currently, three of the nation's top psychologists were evaluating that type of behavior in a "hypothetical" situation. One that mirrored Nick's quite closely.

Worse than not knowing what Nick would do, several FBI agents were asking questions internally about the extremely odd last minute assignment they'd been given. One of their men had been hit and was wounded bad. And these men had no reason to keep quiet. Whitaker imagined every one of them getting phone calls from media outlets literally at that moment. All Whitaker needed was for one of them to explain to some reporter how odd the raid had been. How none of them had heard about their target and how the place hadn't been scoped by some snipers to make sure Nick, or Bobby Ferguson as they knew him, was inside.

The director of the FBI had called and reamed out Whitaker's boss. The director wasn't happy about the embarrassment the raid had caused to the FBI. He'd have to get over it, though. And he would once he received a package later that day that had some great photos of the man in them.

CHAPTER 21

The office was close to what Nick expected. A near empty desk dominated the room, sitting in the middle of it. It was one that had likely been from Wal-Mart's greatest line of prefabricated furniture. It was now dinged and dusty.

In front of the desk sat two guest chairs. They were green vinyl and cracked from overuse. A piece of notebook paper was taped to the desk. In black magic marker, the message said, "If not here, use phone to call 421-6539." An arrow was drawn pointing to the left and sure enough, a phone was behind a big vase-bottomed lamp.

Nick grabbed the phone and dialed the number.

"Yeah," someone answered.

"Hey, my name is Nick. I need a room."

"Okay, I'll be down there. Give me a few minutes."

A man appeared about ten minutes later. He was young, early thirties, quickly getting fat. He looked like he had two days of growth on his face and his black hair, though moderate in length, hadn't been cut in more than a month, judging by the curly neck hair that came up over his collar. He popped a cigarette out of a pack and lit it, blowing smoke toward Nick like he didn't give a shit.

"Well," he said.

"I'd like a room. My wife and I are -- Well, she threw me out. I may need quarters for six weeks or six nights. I don't know. What's the going rate?"

The man looked at Nick's clothes, trying to judge his worth. Nick looked rough in his soiled filthy blue jeans and shabby face. Before he could take in more, Nick said, "Look, all I've got on me are these clothes and this pack. Times are rough. I lost my job two weeks ago. I can go eighty a week, and you'll hardly know I'm here."

"Eighty it is then. But, the maid only cleans rooms once a week, on Saturday, from as early as ten in the morning 'til as late as four in the afternoon. At some point during that time, Greta will be by. You better be there. She's not bonded and has taken some stuff in the past. If you're not there, she cleans anyway, and more than just your room. Be there. For eighty, you get the room with the TV that doesn't work."

"No problem," Nick said.

"And also, this is a rough joint. Lots of problems with loud neighbors and fights and shit. The last thing I need or want are the cops here. They've been threatening to close this joint down for years. You call the cops, you're out on your ass. No questions asked."

"I wouldn't want it any other way," Nick said, opening his wallet and forking over $80, enough for one week.

* * *

Unlocking the door, Nick saw the room was serviceable. The carpet was drab and pocked with cigarette burns. Thankfully, the door had a deadbolt and chain lock. That was probably because of the crime problem that the manager had mentioned, but Nick didn't care. He was a big boy.

The sheets and blanket on the bed weren't fit for a dog, stained and smelling of sex or some other God-awful stink. Nick ripped them off, even the mattress liner and threw them in the corner. He'd buy some sheets. The room had a chest-of-drawers, with the nonworking thirteen-inch TV on top, a cracked mirror over that, a nightstand next to the bed and of course a bathroom. He braced himself before entering it.

Going in, he was glad to see that it was clean, though it was sixties in design. He hit the handle on the toilet and it flushed. Good. He turned the shower's hot water on, and it worked. He just needed to buy some shower shoes, just in case. He now had his command post. Now, it needed to be stocked.

Using a worn phone book, he called a cab and headed to the grocery store. He bought lots of nonperishable items and picked up a newspaper called The Oak Ridge Observer on his way out. He needed to look through its classifieds. At a minimum, he needed a car and other handy things, like a rifle.

After returning, he dropped off the groceries, called a different cab and headed to Wal-Mart. There, he bought shower shoes, sheets, and other necessities such as hygiene gear. He also bought some shorts and cheap running shoes. He'd be doing some running now that he could shower. Arriving back again, he showered and shaved and washed his jeans and shirt in the sink, hanging them on the top of the shower to dry. By then, it was late and he was tired.

Fighting drowsiness, he forced himself to do fifty pushups and then some quick pistol work, working on his draw and the immediate action drills again. He was getting quicker in his drop down after the first shot and this pleased him. He also went through some of his hand-to-hand moves again. His upper body felt stiff from the earlier work, so he went even slower, watching himself in the cracked mirror for openings and mistakes.

Finished, he put the new sheets on the bed and set the alarm clock for seven a.m. before lying down to sleep. Thankfully, it was just after nine so he'd get plenty of rest.

The alarm rousted him roughly. He clicked it off and debated closing his eyes and nodding back off. He didn't have anywhere to be, but he had things to do. Hell, Anne's killer was out there. Both the direct one and all of those indirectly responsible. He stood and went to the bathroom to piss. Finishing, he walked over to a pile of plastic grocery bags. He riffled through them and found the bag that held a six-pack of Coca-Colas. They were warm, but he didn't mind. He stripped one from the plastic holder and opened it.

He walked back to the bed and sat, relishing the morning soda and the caffeine it provided. He took about ten minutes to drink it, the whole time procrastinating. Finishing it, he really lacked an excuse. So he dug through the bags for his new shorts, white socks, and running shoes.

He got dressed and grabbed his keys off the nightstand. He felt naked without his pistol, but knew that there was no way he could take it with him on the run and keep it hidden. So he went to his pack, jerked some duct tape off the roll and taped the pistol and two magazines and envelope of cash from the pack to the bottom of the top drawer of the chest-of-drawers. Satisfied, he left the room and locked it.

His shorts lacked pockets, so he took off jogging with the keys in his hand. His legs felt a little sore from all the walking two days ago and the leg work involved in throwing kicks as part of his hand-to-hand training, but the morning was cool and the run energizing.

It'd been probably two weeks since he had run, but he felt pretty strong. He'd always been a flaky runner since getting out of the Corps, running only two or three times a week for about two or three miles. Maybe as much as five miles on a really good day. But today, as he passed what he felt in his mind to be the two-mile mark out from his room, he kept going. This was for Anne. And probably a lot of others that some piece of shit man had hurt or would.

Nick didn't have a clue who he was, but he knew his type. Probably the son of a military father, or maybe State Department. He'd be the kind of guy that so bought into the argument of service that it was scary. No doubt, he probably thought everything he did was an acceptable loss, or worse, "necessary." But, he also probably dug the power trip. Nick knew that the old saying that "power corrupts and absolute power corrupts absolutely" was true. He'd seen it too many times.

The guy, or maybe a woman though he didn't think it likely, was probably in D.C. or perhaps Quantico. He'd have to be in one of those places to be in the intelligence loop. Probably either a former Senator or Congressman, or at least an aide, with time both in the military and CIA. He'd be formidable. Nearly untouchable.

But, no man was completely safe from danger. Especially if the predator didn't care about his own safety. Nick pushed himself harder at the thought.

Once he got back, he showered, and stretched out his legs, certain he'd be sore tomorrow after such a hard run. He put on a clean pair of blue jeans from his pack. The jeans were a little wrinkled since they had been rolled up tightly in the pack, but they were fine. Nick pulled on a clean T-shirt and his hiking boots, which bore a dusty look from all the mud he'd gotten on them the night he'd gone into the cave.

He then called a cab. He needed a ride to a grocery store where he could pick up vitamins, supplements, and protein shakes. It was a decision he'd regret.

CHAPTER 22

Allen Green's life was finished. He was unemployed, after the magazine fired him for "making-up" his big Afghanistan story. The child-pornography charges were public record and just as he'd published stories about police charges in his day, always making sure he included the words "alleged" and "charged" to keep from being sued, so too had both the local and national media widely reported his story. He had attained one of his life dreams: he was now a celebrity. Unfortunately, it was not how he had wanted it.

Allen had no one to confide in. He refused to go around Jennifer because he didn't want Whitaker's goons watching her and knowing how much he cared for her. They might use her for leverage. She'd left three messages for him and he'd yet to call her back. It hurt, but he knew it was for the best.

Though it hurt to not talk to Jennifer and tell her the truth, the pain paled compared to the actions of his "friends." Every, single, one, had abandoned him. Not a single call from them. At work, everyone had looked the opposite direction and avoided him as he had boxed up his belongings. They were all a bunch of gutless sell-outs.

It'd only been three days since the events spun out of control and it seemed like a year. His arraignment for the child porn charges was thirty-seven days away. Allen figured that just about the time the media moved on and stopped reporting his story, the arraignment would come and they would all be back.

The child porn charges were bad, but the media were crucifying Allen in all of the journalism trade publications. He was a disgrace to the industry, not because he looked at kiddy porn, but because he hurt the profession with his lack of integrity. He was a liar. He was the equivalent of scum. There was even talk that maybe some management at the magazine should be held responsible and forced to resign. This caused Allen to smile. Fuck them. None of them had backed him. He hoped they fell on their ass, too.

Allen understood the quote by Benjamin Franklin during the early days of America's independence. Franklin had said, "We must all hang together, or surely we will all hang separately." Apparently, his management was not well versed on history. Worse, they didn't understand common sense.

During the hell of the last three days, a single thought had drowned all the pain and disappointment. Revenge. Allen didn't know who was behind this, but he had obviously stumbled on to something or this wouldn't have happened. He hoped they underestimated him. It sucked fighting the temptation to start immediately by getting on the phone and on the Internet to start trying to nail down the truth, but it was necessary. They were watching him far too closely right now.

No, he would let them get lackadaisical. Start to trust him. Drop the charges. And then, he'd either make a break for it or start clandestinely checking around. They'd taken everything away from him and in doing so had created their worst enemy: A man who had nothing to lose.

CHAPTER 23

Nick Woods nearly lost it in the grocery store. He had walked back to the magazine aisle and walked by a Knoxville News Sentinel, the main newspaper for the Knox area. The shooting at his house several days had made the front page, above the fold. The headline read: "Agent wounded; woman killed in raid."

Nick had read three paragraphs before finally pulling himself from it. His breathing was out of control and his anger was nearly uncontrollable. There was a large picture of his house and two smaller pictures; one of Anne and the other of some agent. At first, Nick figured that the picture was of the head dick in charge of the FBI, but back in the cab as he read the story with better focus, he found out the picture was of the man who had killed his wife.

The paper said the FBI agent pictured had been suspended and that an investigation was underway because Anne was unarmed when he killed her. Nick lost his bearing at that point.

In the back of the cab, he crumbled the paper and began slamming his head on the back of the headrest in front of him. The cabbie had said, "Hey man. Stop. Calm down. You alright?"

Nick wasn't. All he said was, "Those bastards," as tears rolled down his cheeks.

Back at the motel and back under control, he had uncrumpled the paper and finished the article. An FBI agent had killed an unarmed woman. It was unforgivable, in Nick's eyes. The man had probably had on a bulletproof vest. He'd known about the raid. About everyone's assignments during the raid. He would have had the opportunity to ask questions before the raid. To get comfortable with the plan. He should have been role-playing all of the what-ifs as he waited behind the house.

Anne had been surprised, outnumbered, and scared. For Christ's sake, she was a woman. The reporter from the News Sentinel had dug up more facts on the agent in the three days since the shooting. The agent had missed the last three monthly required range days. And before that one, he had missed the two prior to it as well. One out of six required days on the range in a two-year period.

It was this fact that really wore on Nick. He had always hated hunters who didn't respect the game they hunted. Who didn't have properly sighted rifles. Who took poor shots at running deer and didn't fret about wounding animals and tracking them down, often armed with dogs and shotguns.

This was the exact same situation, except it involved a human. And not just a human. Nick knew veterans who hadn't been serious enough, but this was not an enemy and a declared war. It was an American citizen. And it was a woman. And it was Anne -- his wife.

CHAPTER 24

Whitaker walked into a crowded room. It was a rented conference room at the Marriott Hotel in Knoxville and his troops were assembled. Tank -- his big-ass right-hand man -- was with him, as he always was.

Whitaker wasn't in a good mood. Senator Ray Gooden had called less than an hour earlier and questioned and threatened Whitaker for nearly twenty minutes -- an incredible amount of time for his boss, who was on the Senate Armed Forces Committee, to talk to him. Usually all direction from Gooden came through various aides, since Gooden purposely kept his distance from Whitaker. Whitaker understood he was the fall man in case this whole unit and its various operations were ever exposed. This was Gooden's project, and Whitaker was merely one of several men to lead it. He wouldn't be the last, not as long as the crusty old Texas Senator was kicking.

Whitaker's troops watched as he ambled to the front of the table. They knew that Whitaker ambling was not normal. Definitely a bad thing. Whitaker normally "advanced" places, never walked. And definitely never ambled.

They were all concerned about what he was about to say, though likely some would deny it. He was likely to tell them to double their efforts or some other crap like that.

They had all heard stories about his service in Vietnam. How he had arrived as a brand new lieutenant and had nearly been fragged within three days. A record by all accounts. He volunteered his men for everything. Patrols. Ambushes. Guard duty.

When they were not behind their rifles, he volunteered them for working parties. They burned shit. Filled sand bags. Cleaned machine guns on the line. All because he said they lacked discipline, and America had a war to win; and apparently Whitaker had decided he'd win it himself.

They hated him. Before his first contact, he had told the men and squad leaders that any man who didn't pull his share of the load during a firefight would find himself on every dangerous assignment Whitaker could find. He had said that if they were not naturally brave, he would make them brave.

Those who despised Whitaker were put on point during patrols. The one that hated him the most and had thrown the frag, a guy named Jones, lost his leg below the knee.

Jones had been leading the platoon across an open field one day, mentally and physically exhausted. Whitaker had kept Jones on point for six straight hours. If Whitaker's superiors had known that, they would have likely court-martialed him. But they didn't and never would because no one dared cross Whitaker. So, Private First Class Bill Jones, a wily veteran with just thirty-two days left in 'Nam, stepped on a mine that even a green replacement would have seen. But, Jones didn't because he wasn't paying attention. Not that any man could have been after six hours on point.

Even worse, Jones was dizzy with exhaustion from being put on the ambush squad the night before by Whitaker. Jones had also worked double duty the day before that, filling sandbags while the platoon was in the rear at a firebase, supposed to be resting. He was practically a heat casualty when the event happened.

So trudging along, fighting the urge to turn and gun down a boot lieutenant, Jones had stepped on a mine pitifully hidden by a nine-year-old Vietnamese boy.

Some in the platoon swore Whitaker smiled when the blast threw blood and bone into the air like a geyser. Whitaker had simply called a medevac helo and then had the audacity to tell Jones as he lay on a poncho stretcher, "Son, your country appreciates your service."

Strangely though, they eventually grew to respect Whitaker, though he was a mad man. They became better than the other platoons. Even tighter, because they had to endure more. He actually became a good leader, finally learning to take care of his men and not to volunteer them all the time. None dared smoke dope and they began to buy into Whitaker's philosophy: that a badass platoon that fought daily would take less casualties in a firefight than a shitty one that made one bad contact with the enemy.

Whitaker's platoon was lethal in combat. They would pursue the enemy with an intensity befitting the best Special Forces troops. They walked a bit prouder because they knew they bore a heavier load and twice their platoon, leading the company as usual, wasn't ambushed because of their intensity and alertness. Instead, the Vietcong had ambushed trailing platoons that were walking and talking, some even wearing headphones. Eventually, soldiers were requesting transfers to Whitaker's platoon. Safety came with the lethality dished out under Whitaker.

Whitaker flourished. He fought the war politically in the rear even better than he did in the bush. Before long, he went from a platoon with twenty-three men to a company with more than a hundred men. He returned to America after his tour was up, but missed Nam and couldn't handle the hippies.

Frustrated, he returned to Vietnam. He did work in Saigon in intelligence. He re-enlisted and extended his time and finally got to fill in as a battalion commander. The power was incredibly addictive, though Whitaker was only battalion commander for three weeks. Seeing there were few opportunities for command and knowing for sure he was not cut out to do the many years required to become a battalion and eventually a regimental commander, Whitaker began seeking other avenues.

He eventually finagled his way to working intel directly for Ranger teams, Long Range Recon Patrol teams, and even a few CIA teams. He had left the Army shortly after that and had been in the shadows with the CIA ever since.

"All right people," Whitaker said, finally stopping his ambling. He now stood at the head of the conference table. He never sat when he was in this kind of mood. His erect figure helped remind them of the chain of command, which way it went, and exactly where his position on it was.

All thirty-one of his undercover people were in the room and his three eight-man strike teams were present as well. All wore civilian clothes, but were packing heat under coats, in brief cases, and in ankle holsters.

Looking around the room at his people, he said, "We are changing plans. Forget the restaurants and the gas stations. Start checking out the motels, and maybe the hotels too, though I think he'll stay in low-budget motels to conserve his cash. Also, start pulling badges and drop the you-are-looking-for-your-friend story. We're pulling out all of the stops on this one."

His troops listened and tried to hide the concern. Whitaker's change of plans concerned them. None of them wanted to find Nick Woods alone, but then again they couldn't call for back up with every possible confirmation made by some motel manager. So they would inevitably knock on some door and a very dangerous, super paranoid man would answer.

Whitaker understood this. Even knew this, but was willing to lose someone or several of them just to locate Nick Woods. Once he was located, Whitaker's strike teams could move in and they would get him. And if they couldn't get there fast enough, the locals could cordon off the area and finally kill him after losing some men.

It was win-win as far as Whitaker was concerned. National security trumped concerns for his people. It was no different than taking a hill. You knew you would lose a few, but you took the hill. And holding a hill allowed you to dominate terrain. Dominating terrain allowed you to win a war.

Killing Nick Woods was a national priority.

CHAPTER 25

Nick Woods had been busy. He spent the day going through the classifieds of the local weekly paper, The Oak Ridge Observer. He had found a car to buy, as well as a used rifle. He had made phone calls about likely vehicles, narrowed it down to three, and then taken cabs out to look at the vehicles and talk to the owners.

He settled on a 1982 Chevy Caprice. It was green, ran fairly well, and wasn't too eye-catching, being neither a complete piece-of-shit nor a shiny brand new vehicle. If he was lucky, it wouldn't draw the attention of cops or potential witnesses. More importantly, it was a heavy, well-built car that could be used to drive through a roadblock if necessary. It cost him twenty-five hundred dollars, which he paid in cash.

Next, Nick began looking for a scoped deer rifle. There were lots of them listed. After all, it was east Tennessee, and deer season was underway. He narrowed it down to deciding between a .30-06 and a .308. He went and looked at both and finally bought the .308.

The .308 was a Winchester Model 70 bolt-action rifle. It cost him $400, including the mounted scope. He left the farmer's home and went straight to Wal-Mart, where he bought five boxes of shells. One hundred rounds. It was a start. He left Wal-Mart and bought five more boxes of .308

shells at a gun store in west Knoxville, as well as some targets.

As the day was ending, he drove the Caprice to a large field and began sighting in his rifle. It was way out in the country north of Oak Ridge, in Morgan County, and he knew the gunshots would not alert anyone. However, he was worried some armed angry farmer might pull up. He didn't know how he would handle that. He just took his chances and his chances paid off. He shot thirty-four rounds and got the rifle sighted in. More importantly, he got some-what comfortable with the rifle and its trigger. He picked up all of his casings and target sheets before leaving and headed back to his motel room. He needed a shower.

After the shower, Nick hit the rack. In the morning, he would go to the public library, first thing.

CHAPTER 26

Nancy Dickerson was tired. She had been driving from shitty motel to shitty motel for the last eleven hours, following the change of plans ordered by Whitaker. She had only slept five-and-a-half hours the night before. The search for Nick Woods was taking a serious toll on her thirty-five-year-old body.

Today, every stop had been the same. She would walk into a motel's office, show a real FBI badge (though she wasn't a real agent), and then show a picture of Nick Woods. There had been seven "possibles" already, which was understandable since she was stressing to each manager that Nick Woods may have changed his appearance.

She had knocked on all seven "possible" doors with the manager standing by her side with a key. Each time her adrenaline had been pumping and she had kept her hand on the heel of her nine-millimeter pistol. Each time, a man had answered and it had not been Nick.

More than three hours ago, her search brought her to motels in Oak Ridge. She really wanted to call it a day and get some rest, but Whitaker had explained this guy was spying on the U.S. and had some top secret information he was trying to get out of the country to China. It was vitally important, he had said, and she believed him.

It had to be. They had flown her from Los Angeles to take part in the search. And beginning today, she and the other cohorts of Whitaker were flashing FBI badges, an action only taken in the most extreme of circumstances. This man -- Nick Woods -- had to be one of the worst enemies America could possibly have.

CHAPTER 27

Nick woke up rested, though sore. After drinking his morning Coke, he jumped in the Caprice and drove toward the public library. He needed to do some research on the FBI office in Knoxville and he figured the library was the best place to start. Nonetheless, he worried there might be some video cameras in the library.

The library was just down the Oak Ridge Turnpike, a busy road with two lanes going both directions divided by a median lane. On both sides were fast food joints, banks, and other assorted restaurants. And across Nick's path far too many times for his own sanity were traffic signals. Red light after red light. One would turn green, he would speed up and then have to stop at the next one. Over and over.

Nick, having lived in rural Grainger County since his time in Pakistan, and having grown up in the country, was being pushed to his limit by the traffic, which by any other city's standards was inconsequential.

Some drivers were old and in no hurry. Others were on his bumper as if it was his fault they couldn't go faster. Still others were on cell phones and completely ignorant of the other vehicles sharing the road. None of this was good for an armed and annoyed vet.

But soon, the library appeared. It was on the left side of the road and part of Oak Ridge's Civic Center. Nick pulled into the median, waited for a break in oncoming traffic, and then darted in front of an approaching UPS truck into the ample parking lot of the library. He debated leaving the .45 in the car, but decided he would live and die, win and lose with it on him. So, he kept it in the small of his back under a loose untucked T-shirt.

He walked through a set of glass doors and immediately panicked. Just inside the doors was a set of gray security sensors. Nick didn't know if they were metal detectors or the sensors that detected if books were being stolen without being checked out and de-magnetized. Nick stood there stupidly, debating the issue.

A man and woman heading for the doors stopped and watched him. A library staff member behind the checkout desk stopped typing on a computer and looked up. Nick decided to go forward and if it went off, so be it.

He took a step, looked down at his watch to play off the awkwardness and went through the sensors. The sensors remained silent and Nick walked over to the magazine reading section. He wanted to map out the place while sitting down. He had already stood out too much.

He grabbed the day's paper and sat in a wide, plush chair. The FBI raid on his house was not on the front page, as it had been the day before. Nick decided to thumb slowly through the entire "Nation/World" section just to make it obvious he was not looking for the raid story, which he was now confident would be in the local section of the paper. While flipping, he glanced throughout the library and made sure there were no cameras. He didn't see any.

A story grabbed his attention. The headline read, "Reporter that broke story, now ridiculed." The story was short, obviously the follow-up to a follow-up to a much bigger story. But, it named Allen Green, the reporter from the New Yorker magazine, and gave the gist of what happened. This reporter named Green had uncovered a massive story involving Nick and his spotter's actions in

Pakistan, gained immediate fame, and then resigned after admitting it was false. He was now charged with storing and distributing child pornography. His arraignment was nearly three weeks away, the story said.

Nick stood and went to the library staff person behind the desk. He asked for past newspapers. She pointed to a stack he hadn't noticed. The articles from the two days before shocked Nick. The reporter had most of the facts right about America's actions in Afghanistan. The major exception to this accuracy was that Allen Green had written that both the sniper and spotter had been killed after having their information leaked.

Now everything made sense, Nick thought. This shit-hot reporter broke the story, and Nick (unaware since he didn't keep up with the news) had carried out his "regular" work routine. Some covert unit had immediately jumped on the ball and moved in to kill him and his wife. Just like that. Stop the collateral damage. Except that Nick had been fighting with Anne and had stormed out of the house hours earlier. Something they couldn't have expected.

Nick Woods knew he needed to get to New York to find this guy. A small picture of the reporter was in the article from the second day. He looked around and not seeing anyone, tore out the picture and the name. One thing was for sure, this guy would die in some accident soon if Nick didn't get to him.

CHAPTER 28

Nancy Dickerson pulled up to one of the roughest joints she had seen yet in Oak Ridge. Why does the city let them keep operating this thing, she wondered. She walked into a shabby office.

A repulsive man sat behind a dusty, cheap desk. He was in his early thirties, needed to shave and wore a dingy T-shirt. Chest hair came up and out of his T-shirt like bushes growing across a fence. Everything in her wanted to hurry up and get home and get some sleep.

Nancy pulled out her FBI badge and gave her pitch for the umpteenth time this day. She was an FBI agent in search of this man. Yes, he might look slightly different. The man took it all in and pulled out a cigarette. Nancy watched him. Surely, he wouldn't light it inside --

A lighter appeared in his hand and he lit the cigarette. The man blew smoke in Nancy's face and said, "That man is here."

"In town?" Nancy asked.

"No. In this building," the man said as his eyes took in her breasts. "In fact he's back from some errands. I just saw him go in his room about ten minutes ago."

Nancy wasn't buying it. But, the faster she checked it out, the faster she could get away from this pervert.

"Grab the key and let's go check it out," she said.

CHAPTER 29

Nick Woods was in his room packing up. He had decided to cancel his physical training and pistol drills for the day. Also, his dry-firing practice with his rifle.

Now, nothing mattered but time. Some man he'd never met named Allen Green was hours, maybe days from dying. It all depended on the media. If the media stopped writing about Allen Green's story, then they would move in and kill him. No doubt about that.

Nick stuffed his dirty shirts and blue jeans into his pack. He wished he would have hand washed them the day before and allowed them to hang dry across the shower rack. Well, he could wash them in New York somewhere. Of course, it just hit Nick that he didn't know how he was going to get there. You're a damn fool, he thought, cursing himself. He had been in the library with hundreds of maps and internet access and had left without charting a course.

You need to stop acting like a greenhorn, he thought. He stopped for a second and debated going back to the library. He could, or he could just hop on one of the interstates heading north, either I-81 or I-75, and get a map later. Shit. He was losing his composure. He bent over to cinch down the pack when he heard footsteps at the door. And then a knock. And then, "FBI, open up."

It was a female voice. He didn't move, afraid to make a

sound. His hand grabbed the .45 behind his back and pulled it out. Maybe she would go away. Probably just checking every door.

No way, he thought. He had not heard her until just then, so she hadn't knocked at the door either to his left or right. She knocked again, harder. He heard a male voice say, "I just seen 'im go in there."

He heard a clicking sound as either a key or pick was inserted. He looked at the dead bolt on the door. Fuck, he hadn't bolted or chained the door in his urgency to get packed and headed to New York. He started toward the door, thinking maybe he could get behind it or hold it shut, or some other silly shit since he was totally panicking now.

The door swung open before he could get it locked and there stood a woman. Her hand on the butt of a pistol. Her eyes said she recognized him immediately and her hand began to pull out the pistol that was on her right hip.

Nick, still moving toward her, screamed as he raised his pistol. Scared. "ARGH," he screamed! He didn't want to die. There were probably ten men waiting to rush in. He dreaded the bullets that would soon rip into his flesh. He had been shot before and knew the pain.

He fired at her without aiming.

The round caused her to scream, too. She flinched. Nick's recent practice of his drills took over as he immediately stopped and knelt, taking a kneeling position without willing himself to. Thankfully, his eyes focused on the black front sight of his pistol as the gun fired on its own, it seemed. The big .45 hit her in the chest and threw her four feet back and onto the pavement. He knew her being thrown so far back meant only one thing: bullet-proof vest. And vests stopped .45s easily since .45 rounds were so wide, compared to nine-millimeter rounds.

On her back, she raised her head and brought the pistol in his direction, her left hand moving up and molding to the pistol in a good two-hand grip. At least as good a grip as is possible after being surprised and suffering a broken rib and cracked chest bone. She was well-trained. And tough.

Nick, seeing he better get his mind back into the present, focused on the front sight, keeping her head centered and the pistol fired again. He saw the results. Her face lost about one-quarter of the oval outline of it, from her right eye outward, similar to how an ax will knock a chunk out of a tree. The power of the slug knocked her head back to the ground and she was dead before it slammed into the pavement.

Nick rushed the door ready to charge a team while they were still stacked against the outside wall, though he now knew, since he was finally thinking clearly, that no team would be there. Otherwise they would have led the way. But, there was a man. He had heard him.

He turned the corner and the fat, stinking manager he'd met just days earlier stood there, motionless and pale. The man had his back to the wall. Completely frozen. As if he had turned when she tensed, but then had been unable to run once the shooting started. Nick grabbed the side of his head with his free hand and drove the pistol into his ear on the opposite side as a wake up call. Oh, that hurt, Nick knew, as he pulled the side of the man's neck toward the gun.

The man yelped in pain and tried to recoil, but Nick pushed harder, lodging the fat pistol's barrel deep in his ear. "Get the fuck in the room, motherfucker," Nick said. His voice surprised him. Reminded him again of his past. Sounded evil.

The man didn't comply, which is normal when a bullet rests perfectly aimed about two inches from your brain. The man thought any movement might cause the gun to fire. Nick jerked the pistol away and kneed the man in the balls as hard as he could. The blow destroyed the man and he turned from a tense man afraid to move to an inflated doll, willing to go anywhere. Nick grabbed a handful of hair and dragged him toward the door across the ground. He shoved him into the room and the man fell and curled up in the fetal position, groaning and holding his nuts with both hands.

Nick ignored the manager and still standing outside the room, looked around, scanning the parking lot. Nothing but a few scattered cars and drape-covered windows. He saw no one, though the shots had been so loud. Probably people were still too scared to look out. He stuffed the pistol into his pants and rushed out to the agent. He grabbed the pistol from her still warm hand and threw it in the room. Then, he grabbed her legs and started dragging her toward the room.

She was light, Nick thought, as he noticed her gray dress, more of a suit really, was still meticulous except for the blood stains. The shot to her chest had brought no blood, thanks to the vest. And the headshot had blown most of the blood back. Pulling her legs, he saw her panties, which were light blue.

It never ceased to amaze Nick the shit you would see and remember at the craziest of times. Behind her, a trail of blood led to the pile of brains where her head had hit the pavement. Though even a 10-year-old playing detective could have seen the mess from a half-mile away, it didn't matter. He had to move fast and didn't have time to clean it up.

Inside the room, he slammed the door and locked it. The man had righted himself and sat against the wall, terrified. Too scared to even crawl toward the pistol Nick had chunked into the room. Shit, that was stupid, Nick thought.

Nick debated killing him. The man had seen him. He brought the pistol up, infuriated the man had dimed him out. Had been so stupid. Well, the manager had earned this death.

The man brought his hands up and closed his eyes, as if his hands could stop the bullets that would soon tear through his body as easily as a sharp fishing hook goes through a man's finger. Nick lowered the pistol and the man slowly opened his eyes, relieved. The guy actually smiled. Nick walked over to his pack and dug out some rope. The man stood and extended his wrists to be tied, a willing prisoner. A jubilant, God-is-alive, please-show-me-my-cell, attitude written all over his face. He looked almost happy, as if the stiffening female body lying near his feet was nothing out of the ordinary. Must be Stockholm syndrome, Nick thought.

Nick knocked the man's hands out of the way, grabbed the man's shoulders, and spun him. The man willingly turned and went to put his hands behind his back -- it was the way cops bound prisoners after all.

Nick looped the half-inch wide rope over the man's head and as the rope fell to his chest, Nick jerked it up and back. The man made a sucking sound of surprise as the rope burned into his neck. Nick, trained in the art of garroting, turned his body and shoved his back against the man's back.

In a smooth motion, he bent forward and pulled the rope tighter, lifting the man off the ground with the rope digging into his throat. All that fat weight against the rope around a soft neck. Oh, the guy was struggling now, the weight heavy across Nick's right shoulder.

The man was kicking and jerking in spasms of panic like a man flailing in deep water, unable to swim and having swallowed too much. His fingers desperately tried to dig under the rope and his fingernails carved deep gashes into his neck. Nick pulled forward hard with his hands and felt the man's full weight on his back now, versus just his shoulder. The man kept kicking and gasping. Nick knew if you ever had someone garrote you, your only chance, assuming it was not piano wire, was to have a weapon, preferably long and sharp and easily accessible. Even with that though, few survived the surprise of feeling something wrapped around their neck.

Instinct made you try to free the rope so you could breathe and it was hard to ignore the pain and oxygen deprivation to grab a weapon. The mind simply thought of dealing with the immediate concern, unable without tons of training to correctly solve the dilemma. This man had neither weapon nor training. He lasted a little more than twenty seconds, though Nick didn't let him down for at least three minutes. He wanted to do more than make the man pass out.

Nick finally allowed his body to slide to the floor. He realized how hard he was breathing, as well as how bulged out the veins were in his forearm. Well, the man had been a heavy sack of shit.

For a second, he thought about making the whole mess look like a drug deal gone bad or something. No way, he thought. Just run.

He stuffed the rope back into his pack, grabbed the envelope full of cash from beneath the top of the drawer, and closed the pack. He grabbed the rifle, slid the bolt back far enough to see brass, which meant there was a round in the chamber, and closed it. Hoisting his pack, he reached for the door and stopped.

Shit, his pistol wasn't topped off. He had fired what, once, twice? Fuck it, no time. He opened the door and scanned the parking lot. A woman was watching from an open door some thirty feet down. He aimed the rifle at her and she screamed as she ducked inside and slammed the door.

The cops were probably on their way, but he didn't need her to see what he was driving. He unlocked the green Caprice, threw the pack across the seat, and laid his rifle, stock down, in the floorboard of the passenger seat.

He turned the key and the engine roared to life -- thank God for small favors. He backed up quickly, slammed it into drive and sped out of the parking lot. A police siren could just be made out and he quickly headed for the busy Turnpike of Oak Ridge.

Would they have his vehicle description? Probably not, though the lady he'd aimed at may have seen it and could now be calling it in. Would dispatch have that distributed yet? Not likely.

It didn't matter. He wasn't going to jail. He'd kill until someone put him down. As he drove down a neighborhood street, he found the thought hard to believe. He had been a law-abiding citizen just days ago. A man who'd served his country honorably and with valor. Now, he had killed an FBI agent for doing her job and was thinking he would do likewise to any cops who got in his way.

He wasn't sure anymore about honor. Maybe he was losing it. Maybe he just wanted to survive.

But, they could never say this was his fight. They landed the first blow and had no reason to go after Anne. Somebody needed to pay, and if it was pawns carrying out orders, then so be it. Pawns could pay as well as kings and queens.

CHAPTER 30

Whitaker heard about the shooting about fifteen minutes after it happened, the best he could figure. An aide told him the Oak Ridge Police Department had responded to a "possible shooting/armed white male menacing residents" call at 11:32 a.m. The police had arrived and quickly discovered the bloody mess in the parking lot.

The officer had noticed the drag marks toward the room and had run back to his car, calling for back-up as he raced to the cruiser. He had immediately opened the driver's door, unlocked the shotgun, and hefted it out of its console mount. And when the next cruiser arrived two minutes later, he was still kneeling in the opening created from the cruiser's door being open, his shotgun aimed at the door.

By then, dispatch had notified the two officers that a white male had been seen leaving the parking lot in a boxy, large green car. Make and model unknown. An All Points Bulletin was then put out. The two officers had finally approached the door and tactically entered it, their guns and flashlights looking like a real threat, unless you had had some military training under your belt.

They discovered the two bodies, one female and well dressed and the other fat and unkempt, passed over them to clear the bathroom, and then called for ambulances. Seconds after calling the ambulances, the officers changed the call to a non-emergency code for the ambulances. These two were dead, no doubt about it, and there was no need for an ambulance to kill anyone in their rush to the hotel.

The two officers then left the room, careful not to disturb anything. It was now a crime scene and every piece of evidence needed to be undisturbed. The first Oak Ridge detective who arrived found the FBI badge and immediately called the FBI office in Knoxville to tell them they had lost one of their own.

This came as quite a surprise to the FBI Special Agent in Charge, since every member from his Knoxville office was sitting in a full command briefing with him.

He immediately canceled the briefing and they scrambled, some working the phones and some heading for Oak Ridge. The FBI leader made his first call about the situation to his boss in D.C., who immediately called Whitaker's boss -- Sen. Gooden. Whitaker's boss denied at first that any operations were ongoing in Oak Ridge, but then asked why the FBI Director was asking, suddenly interested.

The FBI Director had said, "Sen. Gooden, so help me, if you are doing something down there using real FBI badges, I'll have two hundred Washington agents flown in and you want be able to pass gas without us knowing it."

"Now, now," Gooden said. "I've got nothing going on."

"You better hope not," the FBI Director said before slamming the phone down.

Sen. Gooden had immediately called Whitaker, and as Whitaker ended the call, he calculated what to do. No doubt he had lost someone. He really had two options. He could flood the area in search of Nick Woods or call back the troops. Disperse them so things didn't get more complicated.

He knew he had to go with the latter option. The exposure already was too great. Shit, he thought. Now he would have to go on the defensive against Nick Woods. Of course, Nick could get caught by the locals or feds, but he doubted it. Nick had avoided hundreds of Soviet troops and native Afghans after having his location passed to them. And that was in a country where he couldn't even speak the language.

Yes, he would have to go on the defensive and wait for Nick's first move. He could try to role-play what Nick would do, but where would that even begin. Even he didn't know what he would do if the roles were reversed. Nick wouldn't know who the enemy was, so what could he do?

Irritated, Whitaker dialed the number for one of his team leaders. He would release the retired ones and send his regulars on vacation or something. Just as long as they got as far from East Tennessee as possible. And fast.

Whitaker cursed himself for not immediately knowing who was in the Oak Ridge area. A good commander would know that. He thought it was Nancy Dickerson. She was a pretty good agent. Pretty good for a woman, anyway.

But, you needed women because men never suspected a woman to be tailing them. Or to put a pistol in their face. They were a great tool. Or usually were. But Nancy hadn't proved a threat to Nick. That was for sure.

The exposure wasn't much of a threat. She, like everyone else, would have legitimate paperwork to prove she was a bounty hunter. Furthermore, she had three printed fact sheets for real east Tennessee fugitives. So, the locals and feds would think that some crazy bounty hunter was out searching for some con while impersonating an agent.

Not that rare of an occurrence actually. The chances the feds would connect much larger dots were small. Small, that is, if all of his agents got out of the area without getting caught. One more armed "bounty hunter" carrying an FBI badge would make the situation something more than a coincidence. It would spell disaster. The thought made Whitaker's stomach rumble.

CHAPTER 31

Nick Woods drove south down the Pellissippi Parkway, away from Oak Ridge. He kept his speed right at sixty miles per hour and his eyes darted from the rear view mirror to as far forward as he could see, looking for police cruisers coming up behind him or roadblocks up ahead. Would there be roadblocks? He wasn't sure. Perhaps. He'd killed an FBI agent.

Should he see a roadblock, though, what would he do? That was the great question. He could turn around, which would only lead to a pursuit by cruisers and a pretty quick and certain death. He could take his chances of just driving slowly through, hoping they wouldn't recognize him, but that wouldn't work. They would have his vehicle description by now.

He knew what he would do. He would stop as soon as he saw it and either engage them with his rifle -- guaranteed death for them, as well as him in the long term -- or grab his pack and head for the woods that paralleled the interstate.

Running would only work for so long. Knox County had several helicopters, Nick knew, since Grainger County (where he'd lived until just a few days ago) got the same news as Knoxville; and since the helicopters had been a source of controversy regarding their cost in recent months.

Besides, all the tracts of woods were small and enclosed by residential subdivisions or developments. He wouldn't get far or be able to stay hidden long.

No, his only chance would be to take some quick shots at the two or three officers blocking the road and hope to kill them before they got on their radios. Of course, other drivers would see him and they would have cell phones. Realistically, he didn't have many options if there was a checkpoint.

He hoped he didn't run into any, and for a moment felt thankful Afghanistan had lacked such pesky devices as cell phones back when he and his spotter were running for their lives.

There weren't many vehicles on the road going south, the direction he was going. That worried him. Worse, none of the vehicles he saw were green. Shit, he had picked a bad color in his zest to find a cheap, heavy car. So, even without a roadblock, he might get spotted by some alert cop driving the opposite direction north and responding to an all points bulletin out of Oak Ridge.

He needed to get to Knoxville. Fast. With its horrible traffic and immense size, it would provide him at least some safety.

CHAPTER 32

A car moved north along interstate I-81, near Harrisonburg, Virginia.

Rain and a slick pavement kept most drivers from pushing the speed limit or passing except when absolutely necessary; yet nearly all passed one northbound vehicle.

It was a boxy, green Chevy Caprice. One of those harsh cornered cars that looked like it had been designed by engineers using Legos. The underside of the rear panels and the metal around the trunk latch bore bubbled paint and spreading rust, which was causing the paint to chip and flake. The back window was cracked and the car's interior head liner sagged from the ceiling.

Nick Woods sat on the cigarette-burned front-seat of his $2,500 Caprice. He didn't notice the traffic that rode his ass before swerving over and angrily passing. His mind was on Anne.

It amazed him he hadn't thought of her more in the past days. But then again, when had he had time? He had either been running or hiding, or buying necessities, or doing research, or working out the entire time.

And now he had nothing but time. Hours and hours of it. About thirteen or fourteen, he guessed. He had already decided what he would do once he got to New York. He had initially thought he would look the guy's address up and just call or stop by, but that seemed suicidal once he thought about it. Hadn't he himself said they would be watching Allen Green?

His second thought had been to recon outward in. Once he figured out where this guy lived, he could work his way in looking for patterns. Eat at a deli for a couple of hours "working" to solve a crossword puzzle, in which he wrote out the descriptions of possible agents in the margins. He could sit at a park bench, walk by the home randomly, ride by it in cabs, find out who "they" were. But, he realized this plan had two major shortcomings.

One, it would take too long. It would take days and days, and maybe a couple of weeks, to find out the opposition and their observation posts.

The second major problem was they would likely discover who he was during that time. Surely, they had pictures of him and knew to be looking for him, just in case he came looking for Allen Green. And after giving up on plan two, he had racked his brain for more than an hour and a half before a simple plan emerged: he would hang a note on Allen Green's door.

Well, it was a little more than that. He would go print a shitload of door advertisements and would put these on doors throughout the neighborhood, except on Allen's door, he would pull from the bottom of the pile and put a contact note in light pencil in the margin; top left corner to be precise. Light enough so agents watching with binoculars from across the street couldn't make it out.

Nick figured that if he started five blocks away and went five or six more blocks past Allen's house, they wouldn't be suspicious. And as the plan became more etched in Nick's mind, and his confidence in its success had put him at ease, his mind had begun to drift.

It quickly drifted to Anne. Shit, he missed her. He'd give anything to be sitting on the couch with her watching some dumb-ass reality show on TV -- even if it included some gay singer with silly-looking hair.

He remembered how soft her lips had been the first time they had kissed and how it had felt the first time they had got carried away. And while she had been so lustful in bed, she had been so sensitive most of the time. She always loved for him to hold her as she went to sleep each night, especially after sex. It always grew old to him in a hurry, his arm quickly going numb beneath her, her curves turning him on again, the closeness making it too hot under the sheets.

Damn though, what he would give to be able to hold her now though.

He remembered their last moments on that last terrible night: a bad fight. Their fiercest. He had hurt her. His last sight of her, she had been her crying. Devastated. Worried about him.

He gripped the steering wheel with all his strength. He then realized he didn't even know if, or where, she had been buried. Those motherfuckers, he thought. And that was the real question. Who were those motherfuckers?

Actual FBI agents had raided his home. That didn't make sense. He was hardly a criminal. So was someone high up in the FBI behind this? That didn't seem likely. It seemed more likely that someone with real power had used that power to get the FBI to assist in some quick damage control.

Not that Nick thought very many FBI agents would purposely kill an innocent person, but they would apprehend and turn over people. They did it all the time. To U.S. Marshals, to local and state police, to the Justice Department, to the Department of Defense.

Nick didn't know who was behind it, but he was for damn sure going to find out or die trying.

As he continued northbound, toward New York, and as the rain picked up and started to pound his car, Nick realized how cold his car had grown while he was lost in thought. He shivered, then reached down and slid the thermostat knob from the blue and white colors on the left side of the dash to the right, toward the red.

CHAPTER 33

Whitaker was now in Los Angeles, having called off the search for Nick Woods after the death of Nancy Dickerson. After all, how did you find a guy who had to make it through Afghanistan and parts of Pakistan unnoticed, during the middle of a war, all without a translator, and several hundred Soviet troops pursuing him by tank, truck, and helicopter? And that was after leaking Nick's precise location to one of the Soviet's best battlefield commanders.

So, after Nick got away from gunning down Nancy Dickerson in Oak Ridge, Whitaker had reluctantly called off the search. No doubt local authorities would eventually get lucky and run into him. There was still the "wanted" child predator alert on him distributed throughout the country. Besides, there was more Whitaker had to worry about than just Nick Woods. His first and foremost mission was fighting the war on terror, which was the real work of Whitaker's group these days.

In fact, two of his eight-man strike teams -- he had a total of five, three currently in the states, two overseas -- were right this very minute inside Pakistan searching for Osama Bin Laden. They were doing what only his unit could do -- enter countries clandestinely and operate invisibly. If they were caught or killed, no problem. They had no way of being tied back to the U.S., since they used non-U.S. weapons and carried various French, Italian, and German papers. Politically and legally, American troops couldn't operate in Pakistan, an ally ostensibly assisting in the war on terror. But the pressure from Pakistan was too little on al Qaeda, so Whitaker's teams had been called in on one hot and one cold lead regarding bin Laden's location.

They appeared to be a group of mercenaries, or some other clandestine group from a European country. The real beauty was the fact that not one cent of funding for Whitaker's unit was found anywhere -- not even from the CIA's undesignated fund. No reporter could ever blow their cover. No Congressman could ever find out through an audit or Inspector General report about them.

That was because Whitaker's unit was entirely funded from its own efforts, which resulted mainly from illegal drug running. Which, of course, was why Whitaker was in L.A.

A local competitor, some gang offshoot of the Crips called the Hands of Death, had been growing and somehow bringing in enough cocaine to actually cut into Whitaker's profits by 36 percent in the LA area. Of course, that was totally unacceptable. So, he was out here reconning the situation, driving around in a shitty part of town. Checking out the competition.

He had lots of options. The easiest option would be to give a tip to the cops and let them clean house on the competition. Problem was, the competition had corrupted a few police officers to work for them, just as Whitaker had. So that option wouldn't work, since the Hands of Death would clear out of wherever the cops might raid long before the officers ever left the station.

Another option was to call the Los Angeles Times and provide a tip about some of the collaborative efforts between the cops and the Hands of Death. Unfortunately, that option left open the possibility that the hysteria from elected officials following the press vendetta would cost him some of his informants on the police force, as well. Strike two.

Which left one option, as Whitaker saw it. It was also why he had brought one of his U.S.-based, eight-man strike teams to L.A. with him. His boys were going to spill some major blood in L.A. Really shake the place up, while also getting in some great and very realistic training.

And Whitaker being Whitaker, he wanted to take part in it. He'd always pick being behind a rifle to being behind a desk.

CHAPTER 34

Nick Woods hesitated before stepping out of the elevator. He was nervous, like a useless gun-shy hound. Gun-shy fitted in this case.

Nick stood in unfamiliar territory, and he knew it. He hated New York, its people, its maze-like feeling, its utter lack of green, its dingy vertical look. He hated the subway and all the trash, both the discarded kind and the breathing kind.

In fact, Nick had not run into anything yet, that he didn't consider trash. There were too many blacks and Mexicans and Puerto Ricans. And too many rich, stuck-up white people. Elite, better-than-you types that really pissed Nick off. He had to get back to the damn South and fast.

But, he had to find Allen Green, so he would keep dealing with it. Besides, he had his .45 and a couple extra magazines, which might put a dent in cleaning the place up, if it came to it.

Nick focused again on the task at hand, took a deep breath, and walked out of the elevator. He took in the surroundings. A secretary sat behind a desk. Looking at her, he thought about turning around. But, what other option did he have.

He had discovered the apartment listed in the phone book as Allen Green's address was burned, but not before designing, buying, and distributing a couple hundred damn flyers. Now, he really hated the fact that he had raced out of the library in Oak Ridge like a stupid, boot recruit. No doubt he could have found a side story in the newspaper mentioning the suspicious fire of the esteemed-turned-infamous reporter's apartment.

Now here he was, on the floor listed as the address of The New Yorker. West 42nd Street in Manhattan, to be exact. He knew Allen Green didn't work here anymore, but where else could he turn?

The make-up plastered woman behind the desk was staring now. He finally moved forward.

"Can I help you?" she asked.

"I'm looking for Allen Green."

"He doesn't work here anymore."

"Well then, I need to speak to one of his good friends."

She squinted at him, looking disgusted. She'd been about as condescending to him after hearing his Southern accent as she could have possibly been. Bitch, he thought as she picked up a phone. She dialed some number and asked a "Mike" to come to the front desk.

Mike showed up a couple minutes later. Nick knew he wouldn't get along well with Mike. Mike had curly, long hair and some kind of designer glasses with really small lenses. Lenses barely larger than his eyes. He also had a notepad and pen in his hands.

Nick hesitated, his paranoia returning, but then realized this fag couldn't possibly be anything other than just a reporter. He for damn sure was too soft to be an agent waiting to take Nick out.

"Did you need something?" Mike asked, his voice too educated for Nick's tastes.

"I called you, didn't I?" Nick said.

"You sure did, but I'm busy, so if you don't mind?"

"Lead the way, hoss."

Mike looked at Nick's tight Wrangler blue jeans and shook his head in disgust. This guy had definitely strayed too far north of the Mason-Dixon line. He better have something good to say, Mike thought, as he led him through the cramped and crowded newsroom.

Nick took in Allen's old work place. Cubicle after cubicle dotted the interior, like islands. The cubicles were low, maybe four or five feet high, and heads popped up and shouted across the room intermittently. Nick figured it would be stressful as all get out working here.

Mike stopped off at a glass room and stepped inside. Nick followed and Mike shut the door behind him. A conference table and ten chairs made up the room. In the corner was a shoulder high tree of some kind growing out of a basket. Amazingly, the room was well insulated from the noise outside in the newsroom once the door closed.

"What's your name?" Mike asked, opening up his notebook.

"I don't know that you need to know that," Nick said.

Mike groaned and dropped his odd-sized notebook on the table. "Look, we're not going off the record. I only do that with people I know, that I approach because I have to."

Nick shrugged. He'd need to do some good acting here. "Sorry. I'm not taking."

Mike looked intrigued, like he was on the verge of giving in, but --

"All right," Nick said. "You win, but not today. You get me Allen Green's address or phone number, I don't care which, I'll talk to him alone and get him to vouch for me. If he doesn't, then you'll never see me. If he does, well, we'll talk I guess."

"This better be good," Mike said.

"Well, I'm not sure what you consider good, but when you get what I've got to tell, it'll be worth the wait."

Mike picked up the pad, wrote down something, and tore off a sheet. "Here's his number," he said pushing the paper across the table. "Call him and then call me." With that, Mike reached into his shirt pocket and pulled out a business card. He slid that across, too.

Nick accepted both, nodded, and said, "Thanks, Mike. You've been most helpful." He tried to hide his smile, but couldn't. He had scored a major accomplishment, having finally found a way to get ahold of Allen. He needed to find a pay phone. Fast.

Nick found one seven and a half blocks away, inside a stuffy, stinking section of the subway. He dialed Allen Green's phone number, after checking to make sure the phone he had picked up was clean from shit or ear wax. He assumed it was a cell phone number since Allen's home had burned, but he didn't know New York numbers. He looked around him for anyone suspicious around him. No doubt, things would soon get dicey.

It rang three times before it was answered.

"This is Allen," Nick heard.

"Allen, hi, uhh, how are you?" Nick said. "Look, I need to meet you."

"I don't even know who you are," Allen said. "Who am I talking to?"

"Uh, I can't say over the phone."

"Then I'm not interested in whatever it is you called me about. Besides, I'm not in the news business anymore."

"Look, this is really important."

"I don't meet strangers," Allen said. He hung the phone up and thought back on the experience of meeting a "source" who had brought a couple of friends for a friendly elevator ride. Not to mention a couple of paramedics. Damn, they were good.

Nick listened to the dial tone in the phone. Shit. Allen had hung up on him. He should have planned the phone call better. He reached in his blue jeans pocket for some change. He only had a dime and a nickel. Well, he would be forced to think about what to say this time, since he needed to get some change. He hung the phone up and stepped from the booth.

On the other end of the call, Allen Green remembered

Mr. NFL linebacker and Whitaker. They had broken him so easily. Whitaker asking for a radio and giving a command. Someone or several someone's already waiting at Allen's apartment to burn it down. The fire being reported over the radio minutes later. Then, it hit Allen. They were professionals.

But, whoever had just called had hardly been a professional. He had been a tongue-tied idiot, and a Southern one at that. At least that was how he had sounded. It might have been an act by someone who was not a tongue-tied idiot, but couldn't Whitaker and his thugs come get him whenever they wanted anyway? Pick his locks, or show up dressed as a cop and arrest him?

Allen punched the menu button on the cell phone and looked at the number on the caller ID. He punched the talk button and hoped he hadn't waited too long.

Nick had made it close to twenty feet from the pay phone when he heard it ring. At first, he thought nothing of it. Then, he realized it might be Allen. He ran back to it.

"Hello?" he said, somewhat stupidly.

"Hey, it's Allen Green. I've changed my mind. Let's meet."

"Okay. Well, that's great. I don't know the area so you'll have to pick somewhere. And it needs to be really public, lots of people around, if you know what I mean."

Allen did, but he played it off. "No, I don't know what you mean. Well, how about O'Mally's diner. It's just off --"

"No," Nick said, "I'd rather meet at a busy bus stop or somewhere near the subway."

"Okay, let's meet at Luzio's. It's a pizza shop just a half a block from the sub station on 46th street."

"Done. I'm on my way," Nick said, digging out his recently purchased map of New York City.

CHAPTER 35

Whitaker drove down a waste barren street, deep in one of LA's ghettos. He was still preparing for the strike against the rival drug-running gang called the Hands of Death.

Empty warehouses with graffiti-covered walls flanked the street and Whitaker shook his head in disgust. A plastic bag blew across the street in front of him. Spray-painted dumpsters and trash-covered alleys seemed to be the only noticeable landmarks.

This was the new frontier, Whitaker thought. It used to be the oceans for centuries until men like Columbus broke them, and then later, the Wild West, which Calvary troopers and unflinching, gritty sheriffs tamed. Then came outer space, but man had conquered it as well, putting a man on the moon and a space station in the air.

Some said outer space hadn't been conquered, that the U.S. should now try to put a man on Mars. But, that was all bullshit, Whitaker knew. The real frontiers resulted from lost ground, where once developed cities had turned to business-deserted, drug-infested inner cities.

The days of negotiating with the likes of Sitting Bull and Geronimo had been replaced by worried mayors giving pandering political speeches to strong majorities of minorities -- blacks, Hispanics, even whites; all uneducated, all unmotivated, all driven toward violence to feed their families instead of education or self-improvement. These people would riot and burn and loot what few valuable buildings they still had, given the smallest reason.

Whitaker felt very much alive, with every sensory gland screaming out warnings, as he drove down the deserted no man's land of L.A.'s ghetto. No different, he thought, than it was a good hundred and fifty years ago. He was the lone gunfighter riding through town scoping out the enemy, his posse just behind him.

He had passed three groups of thugs, each standing on street corners. These were the black type, not Hispanic or white. Not that it mattered. They were all scum, Whitaker knew. Armed, the men had eyed him and his black BMW with suspicion. Even Whitaker, the daredevil that he was, knew he was pushing his luck.

Whitaker was certain they were all members of the Hands of Death. He figured they were packing pistols, maybe an automatic Uzi or two among them.

But, he was armed, too. Underneath his right leg, a fat Glock pistol lay. It was packed with seventeen rounds of hand loaded nine-millimeter ammo. The rounds, crammed to the limit with powder like some mid-Western silo stuffed full of corn, dangerously pushed the limits of safety as to what could be fired without his pistol exploding like a small grenade. But, Whitaker trusted his unit's hand loader, one of the best in the country. More important than safety, he wanted the additional knockdown power of the super-powerful bullets, as well as the higher magazine capacity of the smaller nine-millimeter round.

He was watching the last group of thugs in his rear view mirror when his cell phone rang. Few had his number, so he answered it. "Yes?"

"Sir," a woman said, "Sherlock Holmes reports a likely contact between their target and Lone Wolf. Please advise."

Shit, Whitaker thought. Sherlock Holmes was the code name for two agents keeping an eye on the reporter Allen Green back in New York. The two agents, a man and woman, were pulling murderous twelve-hour shifts, taking turns relieving each other while everyone tried to guess what Allen Green would do. Thankfully, the shifts had been boring and mundane to date.

But that must have changed, since the term "Lone Wolf" was the code name for Nick Woods.

Shit, shit, shit. There was no way the two strung-out agents could take down Nick Woods. Not likely anyway. Nick would have selected the rendezvous and have it scoped out to his advantage. It was routine sniper procedure. But, damn it, he couldn't let the two get joined together either. Allen and Nick together, if working in collaboration, would pose the most serious threat that Whitaker's un-named unit had ever faced.

He had no strike teams within range. Two of the eight-man teams were still in Pakistan and one was prepping for the bloody raid planned for tonight, against the Hands of Death. The other two were off training. One doing desert training in the Mojave Desert, and the other practicing building assaults in a rough part of Seattle.

Who else was available? He thought there might be a retired member of his unit in upstate New York, but that old man probably could not make it to New York City in time. For that matter, the old man could probably not make a successful hit on Nick. It didn't matter. There was a chance of success and unfortunately, freedom demanded a heavy price. He would order an immediate hit on both of them.

"Sir, are you there?"

"Yes," Whitaker said impatiently. He practically screamed.

Distracted, he never noticed the stop sign he ran or the black and white police cruiser that pulled out from an alley between two buildings. The car immediately flipped on its flashing lights, which caught Whitaker's attention.

"Shit, got to go. I'll call you right back," he said, slamming shut the folding cell phone before his agent on the other end could reply.

Whitaker's heart was throbbing, his hands shaking. He knew running was not an option. Too many other cruisers and helicopters in L.A., not to mention he didn't know the area. He pulled the car to the curb, easy-like. No, his only option would be an ambush. A brutal, cowardly ambush.

The officer watched him warily from inside his cruiser once they were both stopped. He bent his head to the side and said something into a radio. Whitaker was not worried about that. His license plate was authentic, as was the car's registration. Both to a retired U.S. Army officer. The retired officer got paid good money for the small risk of letting Whitaker borrow his car while he was in L.A. Whitaker would warn him to report the car stolen as soon as he took care of this piece of business.

The officer got out of the car, remarkably slow. Wary. Standing behind the opened police car's door, he looked about him, eyeing the thugs from the Hands of Death standing on the corner behind them two blocks away. Satisfied all was well, he shut the door.

The officer was Hispanic, and young. Probably early twenties. Of course, that made sense. No veteran officer in their right mind would be patrolling this part of town. They'd have earned safer patrol zones.

The police officer was slim and wore thick black leather gloves. His short-sleeved shirt revealed strong arms, not like a body builder's, but more like a runner or soccer player. His belt had the usual pistol, pepper spray, radio, and extra magazines. He left his baton and shotgun in the car.

The officer looked about again as he walked toward the car. His eyes remained hidden behind reflective, aviator sunglasses. That would make it more difficult for Whitaker. No doubt about it.

The cop approached Whitaker, his body closely hugging the car providing practically no target. Damn, he was good, Whitaker thought. Who knew, in a different time and place, Whitaker might have recruited him.

By now, Whitaker knew a conversation followed by a distraction and a deathblow in the form of single round was impossible. This guy was just too good. Had probably been patrolling this part of town long enough to know that you didn't think about sex or football or anything when patrolling this area.

Whitaker braced himself. This was the hardest part. One of them was going to die, or at least get hurt bad. Fuck it, Whitaker thought as he grabbed the door handle and swung the door open.

The officer, the consummate professional, was raising his hand, but not his voice. "Sir, please stay in the car."

Nothing uncommon happening here, the officer thought. He had control of the situation. Besides the man was white and well dressed.

But, something very uncommon was indeed happening.

Whitaker's shoes hit the pavement and he stood, but his movements were slow and smooth, very non-threatening. His left hand, purposefully visible.

Then, things changed, the officer realized, everything moving too fast to do anything about it.

Whitaker twisted to face the man frontally and now moved at a speed that screamed death. The officer, now only three feet away, finally knew he was in serious trouble. His right hand was reaching for his pistol on his gunbelt, while his left moved toward Whitaker to shove him off balance.

Whitaker ignored the hand and fired one-handed, his right hand holding the pistol low near his beltline and out of reach of the officer. The shot connected, hitting the officer low in the belly, but not penetrating the bulletproof vest or knocking him down. It did stop both the shove and the draw of the man's pistol. Instead, the officer's hands clutched his stomach and his body tried to comprehend the extreme blow. The mind-shattering pain. The boom louder than a freight train blasting by. The ringing ears and fear of death. The sudden reversal from complete calm to calamitous catastrophe.

Whitaker fired again from his hip. The round hit in the chest area, twisting the man and knocking him backward. Whitaker's pistol extended and he aimed this time, firing four shots into the officer's back. The shots were fast, machine-gun like, and the officer had no trauma plate to spread the shock along his back. The vest also probably couldn't stop that many shots that close together.

Whitaker didn't care whether any had penetrated. As the officer jerked painfully and further lost his balance, Whitaker kept shooting, walking the rounds up into the neck and back of the head.

The man jerked with each shot and landed hard on the pavement, his head leading the way. He jerked and shook from spasms on the ground, like a snake with its head cut off. Whitaker did not believe in taking chances. He aimed at the man's head and fired, hitting low and to the right. The man still jerked in spasms, so Whitaker aimed still better and fired another round into his head.

Whitaker's ears rang, a loud, annoying, but familiar, whistle. He hated shooting without earplugs in. His hands shook badly. Uncontrollably. He looked around, eyed the thugs two blocks away and calmly changed magazines. He climbed back into the car and drove off, refusing to squeal the tires. Behind him, the thugs from the Hands of Death looked on, impressed by the well-dressed white man in the BMW.

Whitaker regretted having killed the cop. There were not many of his killings he regretted, and he was already certain this one would be the worst. Thankfully, he had mentally prepared himself for it.

The arguments were many. His unit's mission was too important strategically speaking for the country, when compared to what one good cop might accomplish. Not to mention, the cop's death would only improve the police force, make them train harder, play it safer.

Crime-wise, no doubt the death would create outrage and the community would rise up with the cops, determined to exterminate the vermin responsible for the man's death. That was good, except it would hurt his own drug trafficking efforts. Of course, he could shift his boys and focus in some other city for the short term. The crackdown might even break the Hands of Death for good.

He was four blocks away now, and certain he would get away. Probably in another two or three minutes, dispatch would radio the officer inquiring why he hadn't checked in, as was standard for even routine traffic stops. They would scramble their forces moments after that and dispatch would know his license plate.

No sweat, he thought, opening up his cell phone. He would just have to ditch the car and call his unit for a quick pick-up.

CHAPTER 36

Nick Woods beat Allen Green to Luzio's and selected a table near the back. The place reminded him of a Waffle House, a small rectangular restaurant with a long bar. The only difference was this bar had stainless steel vertical ovens behind it instead of an open grill and used green as its primary color, instead of yellow.

Nick's waitress was a voluptuous Italian girl, probably in her early twenties. In a "Luzio's" branded white tee shirt that fit way too tight, and with her hair up in a young, youthful ponytail, she was hard not to lust over.

She took Nick back to a time before the brutal murder of Anne, before the horrors of operating in Afghanistan, before the Corps. Back to his high school days, when the place to go was a small ice cream shop in his home state of Georgia. There, it seemed some young hotty had worked at the local burger joint since the beginning of time. They rotated through, usually just a summer or single school year.

It felt awkward thinking about sex. It was a slap in the face of Anne. Shameful.

Nick remembered her body lying in the wet grass that night. The agents standing over her, finally covering her with a blanket that seemed to come from nowhere. They probably each carry one, Nick thought. He tried to clear his head. He didn't need to be thinking about Anne or the waitress. This meeting with Allen could likely be one of his last actions. It could turn into a modern day Alamo, with feds in suits firing wildly as they overran him.

Well, he had eight rounds in the pistol, and two magazines of seven to add to the tally. Who knew? Perhaps a huge gunfight would get enough reporters chasing after whatever organization was behind this thing and maybe, just maybe, they would crack the nut. It would be a small victory for Anne.

One thing was for sure. Nick wouldn't have picked Luzio's to meet at. It had only a single entrance/exit, which was about midway up the wall from Nick. Three sides of the building contained windows. All it would take was for one good sniper -- no, actually just any half-assed wannabe cop with a scoped rifle -- to pop a good shot off from one of the windows in a four-story apartment building across the street. It wouldn't take long for them to find Nick. He was one of only two white males in the place. Four other males were Italian and one other older male was black. Oh yeah, you have really put yourself in a pickle on this one, Nick, he said to himself.

He glanced down at his watch again. It had been twenty-three minutes since the phone call. Frustrated, he took a sip of his Coke -- it definitely wasn't a time to be chugging a beer. Or even sipping one for that matter. He needed to be sharp.

He saw Allen walking toward the entrance. He knew it was him before he could even make out his face. Allen Green walked fast and looked about from left to right like a felon still wearing an orange jump suit. He walked in, looked around uncertainly and focused on Nick. Nick waved him over.

Allen Green had not changed much from the picture that Nick had of him from the newspaper clipping. He had long hair that was parted to the left, though carelessly. It was brown with lines of gray intermingled. Nick guessed he was fifty. Sitting in front of him, Nick realized how small he was. Probably five-seven, maybe one hundred and sixty pounds. His hands looked soft and his fingernails were round and even, almost manicured-like. He wore khaki pants, a button up long-sleeved shirt and a dark suit jacket over that. He wasn't the kind of guy Nick would strike up a conversation with back home, that was for sure. Too much like a lawyer or preppy, metrosexual. Nick preferred to hang around men who wore jeans and work boots.

* * *

Allen realized as soon as he walked in that Nick was the man that had called him on the phone with such a Southern twang. This guy, whoever he was, was straight from the movies. Tall, lean, and serious. He wore dark blue jeans, the kind way out of style, straight from the eighties. They were probably Wranglers, if Allen had to guess. The man's blonde hair was short, almost like a tuft on top, and even shorter on the side. Definitely the preferred hair cut of cops and soldiers.

The man's blue eyes could have been handsome, but they were too grave and biting. His tee shirt showed a strong build and his forearms, covered in thick blond hair, would have made even Popeye jealous. The man had to be a mechanic or something, given his forearms. His hands were sitting on top of each other, but Allen figured they were calloused like sandpaper.

"Hey there, have a seat," Nick said, though he immediately realized it had sounded too country. He extended his hand.

"Allen Green," Allen said, trying to match his grip, but failing miserably. "Lying journalist and child molester. What can I do for you?"

Allen saw that the man still looked serious. As if he didn't even hear the joke. "I'm not going to beat around the bush," the man said. "There's some mean folks that intend to kill you."

Allen tried not to show anything. "Maybe I should order something to drink before our discussion gets too serious," he said.

"We don't have time for that. We need to be leaving right now."

"'We,' you say?"

"Yeah, 'we,' if you got any sense."

"Please explain."

"Look, that article that you wrote? I know it was true."

Allen was intrigued now, but still cautious. Perhaps this was a test, to see if he would admit the article was true, only to be killed later by one of Whitaker's thugs. He had been warned after all, by Whitaker himself.

"How's that?" Allen asked. "Even I admitted I fabricated the entire thing."

"Because you wrote about me, that's why."

"Really? What part?"

Nick looked about him and leaned forward. "Does the name Nick Woods mean anything to you?"

Allen nearly gasped. He knew his face paled. There was no controlling it. Nick Woods was the name of the sniper who had died in a "training accident." That was a fact only Allen, his editor, and his publisher knew. They hadn't published the name.

"Alright, I'm listening."

"Look, we don't have much time. Read this."

Nick threw the article on the table that summed up the raid on his home. Allen picked it up and began reading. He finished it so fast that Nick wondered if he had read it.

"I'm not sure," Allen said, "what this has to do with you. Who is Bobby Ferguson?"

"I was Bobby Ferguson until you wrote your article."

"I don't follow," Allen said, still skeptical.

Nick looked toward the door and eyed a young man that entered. He was young and wearing a jacket. No obvious bulge indicating a pistol, but he glanced toward their table.

"Look, I don't have time to explain. I pulled off those missions you wrote about, was sold out, and managed to escape back to Pakistan, where I made sure lots of people saw me, including the media. Thankfully, I was smart enough to make up the name Bobby Ferguson instead of just telling the truth."

"But, didn't your family see your face?"

"Look, mister. My family doesn't keep up with the news the way they do in other parts. Now, we need to go, and quick."

"Exactly why did you come here?" Allen asked.

"To warn you."

"No, what's the real reason?"

Nick sat there thinking. What was the real reason? Was it to warn this guy? Not totally. Nick realized his being here had more to do with getting his help than warning him.

"I'll shoot straight," Nick said. "I need your help. I don't think you had child porn on your computer and I know for damn sure that article was true. I lived it. But, I'm betting you've been visited by some nasty fellows. And, I'm betting they fucked with you, just like they fucked with me. My wife is dead and I'm hoping you got vengeance on your mind, because I intend to do some hunting."

Allen never said a word, just smiled, a bit eerie-like for such a soft, liberal type, Nick thought.

CHAPTER 37

Whitaker pulled off into an alley, driving deep toward its rear, not stopping until the bumper hit a dumpster roughly.

He dialed his team leader's number on his cell phone.

"Yeah," the man answered.

"Where the hell you at?"

"We're about three mikes out," the man said, "mikes" being the military term for minutes.

Whitaker punched up his GPS navigational system. "I'm at 369458," he said.

"We'll be there in seconds, boss."

Whitaker slammed shut his phone, pocketed it, and ran toward the alley's entrance. He withdrew his pistol from beneath his jacket, and kept it by his side. Reaching the entrance, he glanced up and down the street. Nothing. No screeching police cars racing toward him. No sirens yet.

Up the road, a white Land Rover came tearing around the corner, its back tires fishtailing as the driver whipped it around. The sports utility vehicle raced up to him and screamed to a halt. Driving the Rover was one of his best drivers and Tank sat in the passenger seat with an M-4 submachine gun across his lap. It had a second magazine taped upside down to the thirty-round magazine already loaded. Sixty deadly rounds ready to go.

Jumping into the back seat, next to the eight-man assault team leader, who also had an M-4 muzzle down between his legs, Whitaker could not keep from smiling. His men would have gone to any length to pickup their leader.

"Good to see you guys. Let's get the hell out of here," he said.

The Land Rover accelerated and as it wove its way out of the hotspot, and as the team leader searched various police frequencies on a scanner for the upcoming blitz, Whitaker forgot about calling headquarters back to tell his agents to move in on Nick and Allen. And while it was an oversight to be expected under such stress -- he had just wasted a cop, after all -- it was still a missed opportunity.

CHAPTER 38

Nick was back in his big Caprice now, with Allen up front next to him. Nick had wisely stored the car, with his gear and more importantly his rifle, before entering New York City. He figured finding parking would be a hassle and besides, the police were likely on the lookout for the green Caprice since he had killed an FBI agent at the cheap motel in Oak Ridge.

Following their meeting, he and Allen had flagged down a cab and rode straight to the storage site. Nick figured traveling in one of thousands of other identical yellow cabs was a safer proposition than being caught on camera boarding trains and subways together with Allen.

Nick had convinced Allen that he didn't need to return to his apartment, and once they were in the privacy of the Caprice, Allen had told him his story. Of how some man named Whitaker and a huge giant of a man, built like a NFL linebacker, had scared the shit out of him inside of some concrete cell. Had forced him into admitting he had fabricated his article. Of how they had placed child pornography on his computer.

As the story had been told, Nick recognized a deep anger in the soft-spoken, often satirical remarks of the New York man. It occurred to him that they had taken just as much from Allen as from him.

Nick's future had been with Anne. A few kids. A family. Stability.

It was the same with Allen. They had taken his credibility, which was just as necessary for his future.

Allen had nothing now. He couldn't write news articles and continue his career. Worse, they had likely taken his Pulitzer Prize, as he had just finished painfully explaining. And with that loss, came the loss of time off for a couple of novels. Allen's dreams were over, just as Nick's were. And given that Allen was a cynical, divorced reporter dedicated to his job, there wasn't much else out there for him.

Now, they were both quiet in the Caprice, just watching cars and buildings slide past. Both were brooding, thinking about their losses. It was growing dark and they had been heading basically south, in a round about way as was necessary around New York.

"So, where are we going?" Allen asked.

"To Knoxville, or its outskirts."

"Why?"

"Because I need to say hello to a certain FBI agent."

"The one that killed Anne?" Allen asked.

"Yep," Nick said.

"You intend to kill him, right?" Allen asked, still unable to read Nick yet. Still not sure if saying "hello" meant spilling blood or just saying "hello."

"You betcha."

"You think he did it for money?" Allen asked, a nosy reporter again.

"Nope," Nick said.

"So, it was an accident?"

"Nope."

"It wasn't an accident?" Allen asked, incredulously. "You're saying some paper pushing FBI bookworm wearing khakis and dress shoes purposely killed your wife, so he could get suspended, get his picture in the paper, and deal with a shitload of scrutiny?"

Nick took his eyes off the road and looked over at Allen. He went back to driving, and then said, "I do not believe Anne's death was part of the equation. I think those agents were just supposed to pick us two up. I would have likely been killed in some kind of jail fight or such, you know some convicted killer would have shanked me to get some years knocked off or to gain some perk. They would have left her alone, I think."

"So, let me get this right. An FBI agent, who is scared shitless and just doing as he is told, accidentally kills your wife. And for that, you intend to kill him?"

"That's about the sum of it."

"You, a man who has served in the military and faced danger, know how shit can happen in the heat of battle. You intend to kill a fellow service member, a man just doing his job?"

Nick said nothing and Allen wrongly assumed he was making headway.

"Don't you see it was an accident?" Allen asked. "And have you forgotten that she shot one of the other agents? He had every right to believe she was armed."

Nick kept driving.

"I would have shot her, too," Allen said.

Nick turned and looked at Allen, his eyes focusing on the wily reporter in the growing darkness. Allen met Nick's look and saw something for the first time in Nick's eyes that said, "Do not fuck with me." It scared him.

But, then Nick's eyes softened, back into the soft blue eyes that made him handsome. Then, Nick smiled.

"You wouldn't have shot her, sport," Nick said, his voice as calm as it had been before the look.

"Bullshit. It was dark. He was scared."

"You wouldn't have shot her because you are a professional. You respect your discipline. You're one of the best. That's how you got your story. You worked for months on it. Maybe years. That's why you should be getting the Pulitzer. If that man would have paid his dues on the range, he would have realized there was more to the job than drafting papers. But, he didn't and she is dead. For God's sake, he was supposed to be a professional. He was wearing a bulletproof vest and he should have been in the woods behind that house at least one hour before the raid went down so his eyes would have been adjusted to the darkness. But, he didn't. He didn't do any of that, including owning up to his mistake. In the military, if you accidentally kill someone from friendly fire, you get punished. This man is getting nothing."

Allen sat there trying to counter Nick's argument. He had some points, but enough to justify cold-blooded murder? Hardly.

"What if we --"

Nick interrupted Allen. "Look, you are a pampered, pansy-ass. You were probably raised by excuse-making liberals. Had to grow up among them, I bet. On top of which, you're a Yankee. This man killed my wife. If he hadn't, she would be in some jail or more likely already released. Either way, jail or free, she would still be living and waiting on me, once I get this business taken care of, which believe me, I will. But, she isn't. She's dead. She's dead because some limp dick who got beat up in high school thought joining the FBI would make him tough. He joined, made it, but didn't respect the game. You saw the article in the paper. He didn't pay his dues on the range. If he had, and if he had been more competent, my wife would be alive."

Nick paused as a police cruiser passed going the other direction. Sure it wasn't stopping, he continued, "At a minimum, the man is guilty of negligence. Negligent homicide will get you time, even by your liberal judges up here in New York. Whether you're driving a car at one hundred miles per hour, or whether you get in a bar fight and pull a knife. You got the education, you probably know how many years someone would serve for negligent homicide."

Nick paused again, looking toward a parked car that he initially thought was an undercover police vehicle.

Convinced it wasn't, he said, "Look, in the South we handle things differently. If you are on the school grounds and someone steals your pencil, you dot his eye. Now, you can call this revenge or whatever you want, but it's going to happen. Now, if you want, I'll let you out. But, I intend to bury this man and then bury Colonel Russ Jernigan, who doesn't know how to keep his mouth shut."

"In case you forgot, I was the one who got Jernigan to talk," Allen said.

"You were just doing your job, trying to tell a story that arguably Americans need to know about."

"I started this whole mess, in case you forgot. I am arguably responsible for Anne's death."

"You really think that?" Nick asked, looking over at him. "You're wrong. This was started when someone assigned me and another good man to go pull off a dangerous mission for our country in a foreign land we weren't supposed to be in. Whether that was right or not, I don't know or care. I take orders, or at least I used to. I never complained. I did my duty. So did my partner. And so did Colonel Russ Jernigan. But, Jernigan dropped the ball. He sold me out when he talked to you. At a minimum, he is guilty of dereliction of duty and conduct unbecoming of an officer. He let out our nation's secrets and look what that did."

"I tricked him. I got him drinking to loosen him up. Never even told him I was a reporter. I really pushed the limits of respectable journalism. Trust me on that."

Nick looked over at Allen and smiled. "You damn liberals got excuses for everything, don't you. You all think it's not a thief's fault that he steals, it's the environment he's in. A murderer shouldn't be executed, it's not his fault he was raised in a bad environment. Our prisoners shouldn't serve hard time, they should be trained and educated and readied for the outside world."

"Okay," Allen said, deciding to not argue about politics with such a simpleton. "You kill this agent in Knoxville, then you kill this Jernigan guy because he talked to me. Then what?"

"I'm not real sure," Nick said. "I figure you can help me on that, but I'm thinking then I come back and nab the FBI special agent in charge in Knoxville. I'd like to have a little chat with whoever he or she is and find out who gave the orders to raid my house."

"And, if it's the director of the FBI?"

"Then, I'll take a trip to Washington."

"You don't really think you could get close enough to kill him, do you?"

"Who said anything about getting close? Have you forgotten already I'm a sniper? One of the best this country ever produced?"

"But, that breaks your chain. That doesn't even get you whoever is behind this," Allen said.

"Yep, that's why I need your head, and your sources, and your research skills. And your determination," Nick said, looking Allen in the eyes again.

"Why don't we just publish the truth? Hide out somewhere. I know lots of reporters. I can get you interviews. We'll put you in front of lots of cameras. Get an investigation started. Put you in the witness protection program."

Nick looked over at Allen again, and grinned. "First of all, whoever is behind this was able to pull off an FBI raid on my house on short notice," Nick said. "They will find me and you, regardless of who is hiding us. But, even if they couldn't, we'd still lose. You are smart enough to know that every operation has a fall man. I'm betting this one would, too. So, we shut down one unit or organization, or one tier of it. We still don't take out the brains of the operation and another unit or operation pops right back up. Doing all kinds of bad deeds."

Nick kept quiet for a couple of minutes. He rarely

talked as much as he had, but he knew he needed to get Allen on his side.

Allen looked over at Nick. He tried to read the strong face. "I'm not sure I'm buying that you need to kill this FBI agent who got the shit scared out of him and has probably hardly slept since killing your wife."

Nick looked at Allen, started to speak, then fell silent. He thought for a few minutes to try to work out an argument. The silence became uncomfortable for both men. He debated turning the radio on, but had no idea what kind of music Allen liked. Didn't feel like asking.

"Well?" Allen asked.

Nick looked over at him again. Damn, this guy was going to get on his nerves. "Okay, you win. It's not totally about Anne. Your FBI agent who is hardly getting any sleep is going to die because he's a pawn. He's caught up in something much bigger than himself.

"I'm going to use him to make an example of him. You see, snipers operate out of fear. If you start killing men, you begin to get inside the enemy's head. Which is why all too often, a couple of snipers, who should be overrun by a large group of enemy troops, rarely are. Why, you ask? Because of fear. If ten men think they are going to be the next to die, and even if only one of the ten will die, usually, they won't budge. They sit frozen with fear once they see someone's melon split wide open just a couple of feet away.

"That's the difference between regular combat and sniping. In combat, there is chance. Sometimes, even luck. So ten men attack even ten other men. Maybe even twenty men. Why? Because there's a chance each may live. Hundreds and thousands of rounds are fired and few men are hit and still fewer die. There's luck involved and fate. Really, it's percentages. You know, we got to take this hill or beach and we'll probably lose twenty percent. Well, that twenty percent is never you, so you fight even though your scared shitless.

"That's not the case against a couple of snipers. Each of the ten knows damn well that the sniper will kill one of them. No chance involved at all. It's all calculated, practiced skill. Science, if you will. A shot will be fired and one man will die. No doubt about it. He won't be wounded or maybe just lose a leg or arm. No. Somebody is going to take one through the chest. Or maybe the head, depending on the range.

"So, your agent is going to die. And when he does, somebody who is responsible for killing Anne is going to say, 'Oh shit. Nick Woods is alive, and he's hunting.' And this somebody will try to rally his troops. Tell them they have every edge. Nothing to fear. All that bullshit. And then another guy, Colonel Russell Jernigan is going to die. And then it's going to begin to eat at them. They are going to sleep less. Start to think this shit isn't so fun when you're on the losing team. And their leader will try to rally them, but it will start to seem fake. Like he's trying too hard to rally them or maybe he hasn't ever had to rally them before. And then the threads of the organization will start to unravel. Hopefully, this man will start to make a few mistakes, too, or at least some moves we'll notice."

Allen didn't know what to say. He found the logic convincing, as much as it pissed him off. Still, he didn't think the agent needed to die. He debated his options. He could get Nick to let him out and then send a warning to the man.

Nick, glancing over at Allen, had a guess or two about what he was thinking. "Hey, partner," he said.

Allen looked back at him.

"You're still not sold, so let me give you two more reasons. If that still doesn't cut it, I'll let you out and you can live on the run. Or, face up to those child pornography charges. Serve some hard time. Maybe get fucked in the ass a couple of times by some big nigger in the penitentiary.

"The first reason you need to help me is because you

know now. You can't plead ignorance. While I know ignorance is bliss, you and I have a moral responsibility to stop whoever is behind this group. They're evil. Plain and simple. Almost certainly operating without Congressional approval, maybe even without the president's. And, as you know, you got to fight fire with fire, so we're going to have to do some evil things, too. Some things that probably aren't right.

"That's your high ground moral reason. But, there is one more. This business we are about to conduct is going to feel good. Believe me, revenge is sweet. Why do little twerps, finally pushed to the limit, pull out a knife and stab and stab and stab, even after the only thing under them is a corpse growing colder? Whether it's some bully or their mommy or daddy? Because, it feels good to finally get even with someone who's done you wrong. Why do some veterans stay in, never want to leave? Because after you have faced death, regular living gets to be a bit boring, to say the least.

"Don't you see, Allen? It's too late. The bully has already clobbered you. Bloodied you good. He picked you. Decided to let you have it. He fucked with you. He'll fuck with Jennifer and anybody else you care about, too. Now, the choice is yours. You know you got to pick up that knife and start stabbing him, or he's going to keep coming back. Some asshole named Whitaker will watch your every move until the day you die. He will threaten you and be in your head every second of the day. You're going to be miserable. He may even make you do something against someone else, because he owns you now. You're going to have to stay away from Jennifer, and from your writing and reporting. So, I'm saying, 'Pick up the knife, Allen. Don't be the bitch on this one.'

"Let's go do these guys. And, I promise you this. Whether we win or lose, live or die, it's going to be fun. And I'd rather die as a man standing up for himself than let fear rule my life."

Allen met Nick's eyes and felt pretty sure he was looking into the eyes of either a lunatic or one of the best combat veterans the country ever produced. Either way, the half-nuts country boy from the South had convinced him. He was in, and he was certain it would be the ride of his life.

CHAPTER 39

Allen and Nick sat camped out at the Holiday Inn in Knoxville. Allen had taken off for the public library, intent on doing all the necessary research on the FBI office in Knoxville. Nick had said he needed to do some calisthenics and weapons drills. Allen only vaguely could guess what that was.

Inside the library, Allen made short work of his research. Like any decent reporter, he began with a phone book. A cursory search revealed the FBI office was located at 710 Locust Avenue and its phone number was 544-0751. He jumped onto a computer -- there was no line this early in the morning -- and went to mapquest.com.

He found directions to the office and then printed satellite aerial photos of the surrounding area. It was too easy.

Back in the room, Nick had showered following a brutal workout. He knew at some point he would have to get Allen involved, for his own sake, but that could wait. Until at least after this hit. Now clean and cool, Nick was in the floor, lying down. He was dry firing his rifle, getting comfortable with the trigger and scope of the rifle he'd bought out of the classifieds section. He was practicing his seventy-third practice "shot" when there was a single knock on the door -- the signal that it was Allen.

Nick took no chances. He lay down the rifle, pulled out his .45 and got behind the bed. "Come in," he said.

Unlocking the door and coming in, Allen hastily said, "Alright, damn it. Put that thing down. No one is behind me."

Nick smiled and holstered the thing.

"I found the mother lode," Allen said. He dropped off some printed papers.

"Great," Nick said, picking them up.

"I had an idea, too," Allen said.

"What's that?"

"We need to do an interview with the local paper after the shot."

"Say what?" Nick asked.

"Yeah, we need to do an interview with the local paper after the shot."

"I'm not following."

"Trust me. It's the power of the press. You have to at least acknowledge that we could fail. That we could be killed without finishing the job, right?"

"Right."

"Exactly. We need to get as much of the story out there as we can in case that happens. This murder will give our story further creditability."

"Yeah, but it will get our faces out there, too."

"Oh, come on. Our faces are already out there. You've got a nationwide all points bulletin on you, or the alias 'Bobby Ferguson.' And, I'll have the same on me when I don't show up for court on those child porn charges here soon. Not only does this provide some insurance in case we fail, it will also hinder our enemy's movement. Think of it. Ten or twenty of the nation's top reporters asking questions at the Pentagon and at military bases around the country. Regardless of how ridiculous the story, the reporters will start digging. Believe me, I know these reporters. Even something this outlandish, will draw interest. And once that many start digging, then it'll be impossible for the group to blackmail that many people."

"Maybe," Nick said, coming around to the idea.

"One other thing."

"What?"

Allen pulled out a printed sheet of paper from inside his jacket. He threw it to Nick. "That lady you killed, the FBI agent who came to your room in Oak Ridge."

"I don't want anymore details. I'm not happy I had to do that," Nick said. "But, that's the way my hand was dealt."

"No, you can sleep well at night," Allen said. "She was a fraud."

Nick unfolded the paper quickly, scanning the printed news article. The article quoted several FBI agents who said Nancy Dickerson was not a FBI agent. Nick's relief was obvious. "Damn, she was one of them," Nick said. "Yep," Allen responded.

Two hours later, Allen and Nick were still in the hotel room. Allen lay on the bed reading a novel by Tom Wolfe. The near perfect phrases from Wolfe never ceased to impress Allen. Allen was a fine writer, but Tom Wolfe was great.

Across the room, Nick was kneeling in front of the motel's cheap chest of drawers, looking over the aerial photo Allen had downloaded from MapQuest. He was studying the picture, looking for the right answer, finding trees, rooms, and parking garages where he could shoot from. It had taken him more than an hour, broken up by sets of pushups and sit ups, but he had found the best answer.

It was hardly perfect. Just a parking garage located what looked to be two hundred yards away. Nick did not know how high the walls in the parking garage were, but he guessed them to be about four feet high. The simplest proposition would be to park, walk up to the wall, and wait until FBI agent Jack Ward left the building.

Nick could leave the rifle leaned against the wall, hidden behind his body except for the most alert passerby who might be in the garage. Nick would just look like someone getting some fresh air to most. He could smoke a cigarette for an added effect.

That was all fine and dandy, Nick thought, until he had to make the shot. Then he would have to heft up his rifle and get behind the scope. Now, that wouldn't require an alert passerby to see an armed man about to shoot somebody.

Well, that option wouldn't work. At least, not within the safety parameters Nick demanded. Sure, if the timing was right, he might be able to take the shot with no one seeing him on the second level of the garage. But, that would require some luck. Actually, if Jack Ward left the office after five, as Nick suspected he would, then it would require some divine intervention to have no one on the second floor, either walking to their car or driving down to the first floor exit. Too many people left work at five for Nick not to be noticed.

A better idea hit him. They could steal a van, one of those eighties models, full size with hardly a window on either side. It could be backed up to the wall, a back window removed and Nick inside it taking up a good kneeling position in the safety and concealment of the van. He could take the shot and have Allen play chauffeur as they left the parking garage.

Relieved, he stood. His knees hurt from his long study of the photo. No more playing rag head, Nick thought, remembering Pakistani Muslims, young and old, bowing five times daily on their knees. Age and arthritis seemed to have no bearing on their joints. Well, they did on Nick's.

The recent intense running hadn't helped much. Speaking of which, he remembered he hadn't ran in what, two, three days? He'd have to take care of that. Maybe have Allen drop him off downtown so he could run through what was now his AO, or Area of Operations.

"Hey, Allen," Nick said.

Allen looked up from his novel, lifting his head the slightest bit in the look of a "yes?"

"I got something you can do," Nick said. "I need you to take me downtown and drop me off. I'm going to do my run for the day, as well as check out this one location from where I might shoot from. While I'm doing that, I was wondering if you could get a map and find three routes from, uh, from …" he couldn't remember the name of the garage. He walked over to the printed "MapQuest" photo. "From the James White parking garage to some mall inside of town. You pick one."

"Okay," Allen said. "But, why a mall?"

"Because it has a huge parking lot there that stays relatively full. My green Caprice shouldn't be noticed."

"Well, I can just look at the map and pick three routes. And, didn't you already work out today? Why do you need to run?"

Nick realized Allen had a lot to learn about the craft of war. He remembered he should be patient, since he needed Allen and since his last argument with Anne might have been different had he not blown up and left her side on that fateful night.

"Look," he said. "Yes, you could pick out three routes from the map, just as I could. But, the map only tells you so much. You know, distance and size of the road. You may pick what you think are the three best routes from the map and then find out there's traffic lights or busy intersections on one of them that you didn't know about. Hell, there may be construction and a two-lane road may actually only be one. So, what I'm asking is for you to pick five or six routes from the garage from where I'll take my shot to whatever mall you choose. Once you've picked them, I want you to drive them all and narrow the list down. Once you've narrowed the list down to three, I want you to drive each of them several times, until you're comfortable with them. Until you know them. Then, start driving the side routes of them."

Allen nodded, thinking Nick did indeed make sense on some things.

"And," Nick said, "I'm going to run because I need to, and because I want to see the shooting site. You know, do a little recon."

Allen smiled, pulling a cigarette out from a pack. He lit it, sitting on the bed thinking. "How will this end up working?"

"We'll steal us a van, one of those old full size ones that doesn't have windows. We'll park on the second or third level, which ever is best for the angle of the shot, knock out the back window and back it in so that I can see the front of the building. You can be napping or whatever in the back with me until around five or so when he leaves. Hopefully, I'll be able to ID him quickly and get a good shot off. Then, it's up to you to get us out of the parking garage on whatever route you pick. Just remember, traffic will be a bitch at five, since it's rush hour."

Allen blew out a lungful of smoke. "What if he enters a side door and thus doesn't leave out the front door? Or what if a crowd is exiting at the same time and he's among them? You know, maybe you won't be able to get off a shot. And frankly, I'm worried about the five o'clock thing. That's a maximum number of people out driving and walking about. Lots of eyes and ears are going to be open and we're going to be leaving in some piece of shit van that will be missing its back window?"

Nick hadn't considered that. "You got any better ideas?"

"Not right now," Allen said. He stood, walked over to the sink and ground his cigarette in it. He rinsed off the black stain from the white porcelain and dropped the cigarette into the small hotel trashcan. Lighting another one, he thought of a better idea.

"I got it," he said. "Let's call him from a cell phone and

ask him to come down to the front of the building."

Nick nodded. That was good. Why hadn't he thought of that? Allen was trying not to grin too much, using his cigarette as a prop, but the sides of his mouth gave him away.

"That's a damn fine idea," Nick said. "Plus, that allows us to control the timing of the shot, we can do it in the morning at about ten or so, and it will keep him standing still, as he looks around for whoever called him." Now smiling at Allen, he said, "You're going to go a long way toward keeping my sorry ass alive."

"As long as you do the same, we'll call it even," Allen said.

Nick walked over to his pack and pulled out a worn, gray tee shirt to run in. Across the room, Allen was sitting on the bed, ignoring his Tom Wolfe novel and watching Nick. He watched as Nick pulled his shirt off. Allen was trying to size Nick up, to look at his build and muscle density and the way he moved, trying to judge him like a gambler would a fighter about to step in the ring.

Nick had a wiry, lean build and moved cautiously, in a smooth way, like he was carrying a tray of full wine glasses at all times. Allen figured it was some kind of sniper thing, since the toughest men he knew generally fell into two categories. The thick weightlifters -- cops came to mind as an example -- moved like elephants, puffed up and massive. While the small, gangster types strutted around like roosters, staring down and sizing up those around them with complete disrespect; fully confident the pistols and Mac 10s they were packing would protect them.

But, Nick was different. His manners and movements were more like those of a priest; no, a monk. One of those Shaolin types. A humble, easy going look that always appeared balanced and smooth. It was the kind of look and attitude that wouldn't get many looks from other men or cause many fights in a rough bar.

As Nick turned toward him and pulled the gray shirt

over his head, Allen saw a thick line of scar tissue on Nick's right shoulder. It was at least four inches long and had the rough look of being done by some miserable army doctor. Hell, Allen had seen smaller scars on men and women who had lost limbs during vehicle accidents and had them reattached. He guessed the scar came from a gunshot wound that had been followed with lots of reconstructive surgery. One thing was clear, there was no scar tissue on his back, which meant the bullet had lodged in Nick. Probably had to be dug out, Allen guessed.

And as Nick's shirt came down over his arms, Allen saw just a glimpse of a scar on Nick's chest. It was round and about the size of a quarter. As the shirt came down over the wound and Nick began to take off his tight Wrangler blue jeans, which showed a smattering of jagged, healed wounds on both legs below the knees (mortar round, if Allen had to guess), the quarter-sized wound began to take shape in Allen's mind.

He began to see it as a snake, albeit a short one, curved and sliding across Nick's chest. Then, he remembered the location, centered where many cons plant chest tattoos. And as Allen began to convince himself it was some kind of marking or tattoo, the snake idea began to grow weaker and weaker until he was sure it had never been a snake. But, it was definitely something, Allen just couldn't figure out what.

Yet as Nick began to tie his running shoes -- he had already put on his running shorts -- Allen realized what he had seen. He tried to argue himself out of it, but the harder he tried, the more convinced he became. The image on Nick's chest was burned into his mind now and it infuriated him. The symbol -- one of Hitler's second most recognized symbol after the Swastika -- represented evil and Allen began to feel a deep anger flare up. It would be simple to just let it slide or forget about it, but he couldn't. No New Yorker would. Hell, what was the worst Nick could do? Beat him into a pulp? Kill him?

I don't have much to lose anyway, Allen thought.

Nick was folding his blue jeans and stuffing them into the pack, when Allen finally found his voice.

"What was that on your chest?"

Nick stopped and looked up at Allen. "What?" he asked, having not heard the quivering statement Allen had said.

Allen thought Nick was being a smart ass. Shaking, from both fear and rage, he managed to stand, a small, diminutive man in his 50s. "I said, 'What is that on your chest?'"

Nick didn't understand what was going on, but he knew the little nut needed to quit reading whatever the hell was in that book he had. The man's tone and accent really pissed him off and he wasn't afraid to beat a small man's ass, if he had to. He'd give the twerp a chance to cool out. "What do you mean what's on my chest?"

"That symbol you've burned into your chest. Don't deny it. I saw it, you racist motherfucker," Allen said, spitting a little and looking quite pathetic to Nick. Then he remembered.

"Oh, this?" he asked, pulling up his shirt and showing off the burned scar, the ***SS***.

"Yeah that," Allen said, practically yelling.

"What about it?" Nick asked, still perplexed.

"Oh come on, you stupid bastard. You know what."

"Uh, no, I don't," Nick said.

"Bullshit, where's it come from?"

"Oh, Germany."

"No shit," Allen said. "And what's it stand for?" he asked, no longer an eloquent liberal from New York.

Nick now finally understood, but Allen's assumptions really pissed him off. "You know, you're not nearly as smart as you think you are. You think this symbol is some kind of racist trash, don't you?"

"No fucking shit," Allen said. "There's a few million Jews who can attest to that."

Nick looked down at the symbol again, the straight distinctive lines, ***SS***, and still felt proud of the tattoo. "Listen here, you liberal, left ass mother fucker," Nick said, about to lose control. "I've never even met a Jew. The symbol stands for Scout Sniper, the term the Corps uses to refer to its snipers."

He shut up for a second and calmed himself before continuing. "I was a sniper, so I burned this in my chest, just like most other scout snipers in the Corps. Why this symbol? Because the German military revolutionized the art of warfare, conquered half the world, and extensively used snipers. And as they began to lose the war, their army provided an example few can match.

"The Marines to this day study the German's tactics of World War II. Their Blitzkrieg tactics, their squad sizes, their delegation of command. And for me, having this burned into my chest reminds me … I don't know, it reminds me I need to be the toughest man on earth, that I need to be training at all times 'cause if I don't, I'll pay for it. That even the best can lose, as Germany did."

Allen was at a loss of words. It was such a simplistic reason and probably true. He knew he should just apologize, but he was still too mad.

Nick stepped closer and slapped Allen easily on the face. "Hey big boy, thought you were going to go to the mat with me there for a second."

Allen smiled, embarrassed, still scared, still mad. He tried to figure out a way to apologize, but Nick cut him off.

"Come on, let's go," Nick said. "You've got some driving to do and I need to do a little run."

CHAPTER 40

Whitaker was back in Washington in Senator Ray Gooden's office. It was only the third time Whitaker had reported to his superior's office. Doing so was risky for Senator Gooden, since a fall man in a conspiracy needs to remain distant from the real leaders.

Whitaker's mood had changed from giddiness following his easy escape out of LA after gunning down that officer to being livid at himself for forgetting to call back to headquarters to order the hit on Allen and Nick. Now that anger was growing into a sinking feeling of fear. Allen Green and Nick Woods -- their unique talents combined -- were worthy adversaries.

Senator Gooden sat behind his magnificent, boat-sized, mahogany desk reading a stapled packet of papers. He seemed unaware Whitaker was standing in front of his desk, at a modified parade rest -- feet spread about a foot apart, hands clasped together behind his desk. Whitaker had been in the position for nearly ten minutes, and that was after a thirty-plus minute wait in the reception area.

Oh yeah, Senator Gooden was pissed, Whitaker knew.

Gooden was a small man. About five-five, maybe a hundred and fifty pounds, he sat in a small chair to understate this fact. He was well into his sixties, though he still had a full head of hair. It was gray and combed to the left, the classic Washington look. He wore circular glasses and was always meticulously dressed and groomed.

Today, his coat was off and Whitaker could see a gold cuff link on his right shirtsleeve. Just above his left wrist sat a sliver of silver from a watch. Whitaker knew it was a Rolex, no doubt a gift from some corporation. Yep, Senator Gooden's friends were many. And his enemies were dead. Either politically or physically.

In fact, the mysterious death of a democratic opponent for Texas senate had mired Gooden for years. The opponent had been more than twelve points ahead in every poll with the election just two days away, when his plane had crashed soon after take off following yet another successful fund raiser. An investigation found faulty wiring, which oddly had not been found in a preflight inspection conducted just two hours prior to take off.

During that campaign, four major newspapers had endorsed his opponent. Since then, the number had continued to rise, regardless who his opponent was. Senator Gooden was hated. By the press. By his opponents. By much of the people across the country, just not in Texas.

And yet he kept getting elected. Everyone knew how dirty he was. He had taken illegal campaign contributions. He had twice been investigated by the Senate Ethics Committee for conflict of interest. But, with every opponent since candidate Bob Kile, who died with his wife, four aides, and two pilots in a fiery flash just outside of Houston, Gooden had easily been re-elected.

The tactics were as brilliant as they were barbarous. Nude pictures of daughters or wives showed up to media outlets. Strange investigations by the IRS were launched. Unexplained endorsements for the Republican Gooden would emerge from Democrats who had spoken poorly of him. Gooden believed a little dirt and leverage could win any political battle. To date, he'd been right. And even with all the ugliness in his past, he was as powerful -- or more so -- than ever.

And while Gooden was ruthless as a Texas politician, it did not compare with Senator Gooden, the defender of democracy. There was Whitaker's illegal unit to fight terrorism, set up by Gooden.

There were years and years of history of illegally funding struggling minority groups around the world with weapons and money. The mujahedeen in Afghanistan, when the Soviets were there and before it was legal U.S. policy. And the Northern Alliance against the Taliban following the Soviet departure. The Kurds in the Middle East. Most surprisingly, the Chechens against the now democratic Russians, until the Chechens had resorted to terrorism in Moscow. Gooden still believed the Chechens should be funded to keep the Russians from becoming a U.S. opponent again.

Whitaker knew enough dirt on Senator Gooden to bury him, but he didn't have the guts to spill it. Senator Gooden was no different than a mob boss. He would get you, even if he were in the confines of prison. He finally laid the paperwork down and locked his fiery eyes on Whitaker.

"Good afternoon, Senator," Whitaker said.

"The hell it is," Gooden said, cutting him off before he finished his sentence. "You want to tell me what happened in California?"

"As you know, we had a little situation."

"No shit. And why did we have a situation?"

"Because --

"I'll tell you why. Because you had to go out there on some kind of damn stunt. Had to lead the troops, huh? Great. Now your face is on a video tape courtesy of the Los Angeles Police Department."

Whitaker swallowed hard. The thought of a camera in the police car never crossed his mind, though he knew they were standard in the police departments of major cities. Shit.

"Give me a report on Nick Woods. I assume you've

found him?"

"Unfortunately, we haven't."

"Unfortunately, I know that," Senator Gooden roared back sarcastically. "I think there's something else you want to tell me about that situation, isn't there?"

Whitaker wondered how Gooden's intel was so good. Were there other units like Whitaker's under Gooden's belt?

"I asked you a question," Gooden said.

"As a matter of fact," Whitaker said. "We've lost Allen Green."

"No shit," Gooden screamed. "Don't you think I would have liked to have known that?"

"Of course, but I've -- "

"I don't want to hear it. You can't find Bin Laden. You can't keep a tail on Allen Green, some stupid, gay-ass liberal writer from New York. You go off like a cowboy and waste a cop, and still don't take care of the Hands of Death -- the very reason you went out there. My accountant says your funds are getting preciously thin, and those Hands of Death thugs continue to steal from you guys. My patience is wearing thin, Whitaker. You're quickly coming to a point where I'm leaning toward ending your command."

CHAPTER 41

In Knoxville, the weather was clear. Still a bit cool, but sunny and beautiful. Nick sat inside a once plush, 1970s full-size van, watching the building where FBI Special Agent Jack Ward worked through the scope of his .308 rifle.

The window of the rear door of the van had been knocked out the day prior and Nick and his rifle were about five feet from the opening, deep in the shadows of the curtained van. Nick knelt in the seat of a captain's chair with the rifle laying across the back of the seat for support. It was a shitty position, with Nick's head cramped against the top of the van, but Nick was only shooting 260 yards.

With the building's doors sharp in his scope, all he could do was wait. Two days had passed since his spout in the motel room with Allen over the Nazi symbol burned into his chest, but that was long forgotten. Though he knew he was only moments away from taking the shot, he found it hard to concentrate.

Behind him, Allen was smoking his third cigarette in five minutes. Allen kept thinking of all the things that could go wrong. Someone could walk by the front of the van and look in, Allen thought. Or, the employee waiting to take their parking ticket might not be in his booth when they made a break for it after the shot. He'd probably be taking a piss, Allen thought. Well, it didn't really matter now. He had already called Jack Ward from a recently purchased, disposable cell phone.

And there you had it. Allen Green, only child raised wealthy by a dope-smoking mom, was about to take another serious step back from his climb to the top. He'd already dropped from award-winning journalist to accused child molester. And now he was about to become a co-conspirator in the brutal assassination of an FBI agent that was involved in a controversial shooting. Allen figured that profile would warrant a short, sharp obit in The New York Times, which oddly enough had always been one of his goals.

Usually only about three or four people had short articles on them in the Times following their death. Famous politicians, scientists, sometimes writers. Allen wanted to be one of those writers.

Well, he thought, if you can't make it in the front door, go around to the back. The satire did little to cheer him.

Nick, still behind the scope, was far from worried. He had that feeling you get before you knock on the boss's door to ask for a raise or to say you aren't going to work another Sunday or Friday night. He knew he needed to carry out this shot, but it was like finally knocking on the door. You had to face the boss.

Nick figured he could pass on shooting Jack Ward and live the rest of his life on the run. Maybe find him a cabin somewhere. They'd probably stop looking eventually. But, like the cruel bastard of a boss who pushes some employees too far, Nick knew he had to go through with this confrontation. After all, this boss was responsible for Anne's death. Yeah, he'd knock on the door alright. And if he got fired, so be it.

Any doubts he had about knocking on the door were completely erased when special agent Jack Ward stepped through the glass doors and onto the sidewalk. He looked pissed, turning his head from left to right to meet whoever it was who had just called and demanded to meet him outside. Alone.

Nick knew the insolent piece of shit had twice told Allen on the phone that he was in "Administration" and anyone with a tip about a crime needed to talk to "Investigations." Only after Allen insisted he would only pass along documents to Jack Ward had the man finally relented. A real coward, thought Nick.

Nick knew the type. Ward didn't care about winning the war on drugs or crime. He was in it for the paycheck or bragging rights, or both. The eight-power scope brought into grand detail the fat face and soft body.

Nick pushed the analysis of Jack Ward out of his mind and began to focus on killing the son of a bitch, the sissy who had pissed his pants and murdered Anne.

The fears of meeting the boss were gone now. In fact, at that moment Nick didn't care whether he lived or died. All he wanted to do was to extract revenge on the disgrace before him. He'd teach others like Jack what happened when you didn't go to the range to practice your shooting skills. If Jack Ward's superiors wouldn't punish him, then Nick would. He clicked off his safety.

His .308 was loaded with Remington Express ammunition, which fired a 168-grain bullet. Unfortunately, the rifle was zeroed at 100 yards instead of 200 -- shooting in the farmer's field hadn't allowed for anything longer. And the difference was huge. Instead of the bullet dropping only 8.8 inches at 200 yards, it now dropped 14.7 inches, according to Remington's figures printed on the box.

Worse, Nick was using an average scope. With a military scope, he could estimate the range, twist a range finder on top of the scope and aim where he wanted to hit. Today, he'd be aiming high. It was going to be a sloppy shot, but it had to be done. And Nick was still certain he could hit Jack Ward. In fact, the pressure was on him to make a good shot so everyone would know a sniper made the shot, not some dumb ass hunter with top-notch gear.

Nick was guessing what a 14.7 inch drop would be on Jack's fat body. He also needed to hold a bit to the left to counter a light crosswind blowing to the right. Nick put the scope's crosshairs on the top of Jack's head. He figured the bullet would hit him high in the chest with the drop, and with a velocity of 2,143 feet per second, the seventeen hundred plus foot pounds of energy (or knock down power) would be more than enough to do the job. Even through a vest, though Nick had a feeling Jack Ward wouldn't wear such an uncomfortable thing unless he had to. After all, Jack worked in Administration.

Nick shifted his crosshairs to the left, about an inch above Jack's eyebrow. Jack was standing with his hands on his hips. He swung his head to the left, looking for whoever called, and Nick lost his point of aim. Jack then swung his head to the right. He was getting impatient and Nick began to worry he would bolt back inside. He began taking slack out of the trigger, now aimed at Jack's ear since his head was turned to the side.

"Let me help," Allen said, scaring the shit out of Nick and nearly causing him to pull the trigger. "Hang on, I'll call him."

"Okay," Nick said, keeping Jack in the scope.

Jack turned and began walking back toward the doors.

"Hurry, Allen," Nick said.

The sounds of the cell phone seemed loud in the van as Allen dialed as fast as he could.

"It's ringing," Allen said.

Jack was three feet from the door when he stopped, and reached inside his jacket for the phone.

"Tell him to look up at the garage," Nick said. "That you're going to be waving."

"Okay," Allen said. Allen then said hello into the phone. "Hey, Jack, look down the road toward the parking garage."

Jack turned and began to squint, and as he did Nick put

the crosshairs back on Jack's left eyebrow. The rifle seemed to be moving a lot as Nick began to slowly pull back the trigger. The top of the captain's chair and the tight roof made for one of the worst shooting positions he'd ever had to take. Unable to focus perfectly on the eyebrow, Nick dropped his aim to Jack's eye, since it would make a smaller, steadier aiming point.

Nick was trying not to listen to Allen, who was chatting away about something. He didn't notice the pain in his arm, which was making serious gripes about the uncomfortable position he'd been in for more than five minutes. He didn't notice men and women dressed in business attire walking in and out of the doors behind Jack. All he focused on was a clear sight picture, perfect point of aim of the brown eye of Jack, and trying not to jerk the trigger. The shot needed to surprise him, so he wouldn't flinch.

And then the rifle exploded like a cannon, its sound amplified to a deafening boom in the small, dark, enclosed van. As the gun knocked Nick back, his right hand was already working the bolt to reload.

Jack never knew what hit him. Like all long shots, the bullet ripped into his stomach before he ever heard the shot. Jack, now lying on the ground, remembered two sensations. The feeling of being gored by a charging rhino and an even worse feeling. The feeling of having a grappling hook tied to a racecar being jerked through his innards as the bullet passed through him, taking a healthy helping of guts and blood with it. Grabbing his stomach, he screamed. The deep bellowing yell seemed to match the echo of the shot in the corridor. It even overpowered the shrieks of women now darting across streets and into the nearest door.

"AAAHHH!!!" His screams were panicked. Feminine. He couldn't get up, though he was trying. His legs were pushing and kicking and his head was rocking back and forth like he was having a seizure. It was a sickening sight and Nick watched it with the keenest interest. He debated another shot, but enjoyed watching Jack, the beached whale, flopping around helplessly.

Nick wanted him to suffer, but most importantly die. He had seen a lot of men die in his time and he was certain the shot, though low and bad, was a killing shot.

Not because it should have been. No, tougher men would pull it together and probably live, albeit in a wheel chair, but Jack Ward wasn't born or made into that kind of man. He was screaming and speeding up the shock that was overcoming his body. Idiot, Nick thought, knowing Jack Ward had been taught during his early training how to overcome shock. That couldn't be said for Anne.

"Nick, we need to go. You going to shoot again?" Allen asked, sounding more nervous than a Boy Scout on his first camping trip around a fire on a dark night, hearing his first unknown sound following some scary ghost stories.

Nick put the safety on the weapon and pulled it from his shoulder. "No," he said without another thought.

Nick didn't recognize the look Allen had seen.

Allen, starting the van up was horrified. He'd just watched a man die, or at least in his last throes of life. And it wasn't that he had helped Nick kill Jack Ward that scared him. It was the look he had just seen on Nick's face. Pure pleasure. He was now convinced Nick enjoyed the heinous murder. Allen realized now that Anne played a small role in the decision for Jack Ward to die.

Driving down the tight rows of the garage, he remembered Nick had said it was about getting in the enemy's head. Killing enough of them to make them ineffective, regardless of how overwhelming their strength was.

Allen knew Nick had just fired the first shots of his war. He doubted the other side had anyone as eager for this war as Nick was. Damn the man was scary.

CHAPTER 42

The get away went off without a hitch. They had paid their ticket, admitted to the employee they had heard a shot, too, but informed him it had sounded like it was blocks away. It had just echoed back and forth in the parking garage, they told him. He actually seemed to believe it.

"Man, K-town is crazy," the staffer said.

They drove to the mall, where they ditched the van for good and grabbed Nick's green Caprice. From there, they headed for their motel outside Knoxville.

Meanwhile, several hundred miles away, Whitaker learned of the shooting and went into panic mode. He had good sources, but he barely beat the media on hearing the news of the shooting of Jack Ward. Of course it was understandable, really. About thirty people had been on the sidewalks around the building when Nick Woods pulled the trigger from the back of his van.

And with the noise of the rifle, the Knoxville Police Department had received more than one hundred emergency calls to 911 in less than sixty seconds. Initially, the Department believed it was dealing with a terrorist sniper. Calls were made for the SWAT team to assemble. But, people were calling the media, too.

The broadcast channels broke into commercial breaks,

and the cable media soon followed. In just over five minutes, CNN was broadcasting "early reports" of a possible terrorist attack in Knoxville. Just moments before CNN had the story, a source of Whitaker's had called him in D.C. and said there had been a shooting at the building where the FBI was headquartered in Knoxville. The man had said he had just heard it on the scanner and would call back when he heard more.

He didn't need to. Whitaker already knew. It fit the profile. Angry vet still madly in love kills man responsible for killing his wife. And with that, he felt a cold fear start to creep up his stomach. Nick Woods wasn't going to hide out in the mountains, thankful to just be alive. No, he was hunting again.

CHAPTER 43

The press releases prepared by Allen Green were written to catch your attention. And they did. The headline of the single-sheet fax said, "So who shot FBI Agent Jack Ward in Knoxville yesterday and why?"

Allen and Nick had driven to Chattanooga, another city with more than 100,000 people just south of Knoxville, the day after the shooting to send out the release. Allen had a list of fax numbers for newspapers throughout east Tennessee, as well as regional and national newspapers. He knew the only chance the press release had was for whoever picked it up off the fax to recognize it. He figured the east Tennessee papers were his best chance.

Allen had hoped to wake up early and shoot the faxes out about 8 a.m., but he overslept, true to his night-owl character, and didn't make it to a Kinko's copy center until just after 10:30 a.m. Allen had a list of fax numbers for practically every relevant newspaper in East Tennessee, as well as all the major national daily papers and magazines.

There was no line so he walked up to the fax machine and began punching in the various area codes and fax numbers. He soon had the machine shooting out his three-page fax -- four with cover sheet -- across the country. Allen had never understood how a bunch of strange beeps and signals sent across phone lines could produce perfectly reproduced faxes, but it didn't really matter. He just hoped those who were on the receiving end were in the right mode to actually fully read, and hopefully follow up on, the press release he had worked on for hours.

The release immediately announced in the first paragraph that FBI agent Jack Ward had been killed by gun-nut Bobby Ferguson, whose wife had been negligently, and wrongfully, gunned down by FBI Agent Jack Ward in a recent botched raid, that was hastily planned and in itself raised all kinds of questions. The murder was revenge at its core level, but the story was actually much deeper.

Allen had then described the story of how Bobby Ferguson was actually former Marine sniper Nick Woods, who had served covertly in Pakistan against the Soviets. The rest of the press release was quite similar to his story in The New Yorker. It ended by not providing any contact information, as was customary in most press releases, saying instead that each media outlet would receive a call later that day or the following one.

Nick and Allen had bought dozens of disposable cell phones from several stores with some of the money from Allen's pack, and it was with these cell phones that Allen knew he would spend the afternoon and next day making the most important story pitch of his life.

The work proved to be the most frustrating work he'd done in some time. Setting in yet another hotel room, this one in Nashville since Nick thought they should leave Chattanooga after sending out so many faxes that might be traced, Allen worked nearly non-stop from eight to five for the next two days.

And with all that work, he achieved nothing. The reasons why no one would pick up the story were many. Reporters were out of the office. Editors had reviewed and shot down the story -- isn't this the same story you just denied a couple of months ago? Even those who got past his denial and began to probe as to why he had later retracted and denied the story thought it was absurd to believe that some secret agents had apprehended and threatened him and planted evidence on his computer. And burned down a building, too? This was all just some kind of new out-of-this-world conspiracy theory.

Allen diligently kept good notes of each phone call and marked off each news source as it became clear they wouldn't do anything on the story. At his highest point, he thought three organizations might do the story: The New York Times, Time Magazine, and 60 Minutes. The Times came closest before bowing out. The reporter from there finally said her editor thought the story might be plausible except that it didn't make sense that Allen would change his story because of secret agents or threats. No good reporter would cave in and give up the truth, she said in a sanctimonious voice.

Of course, he'd once felt the same way. But being abducted, assaulted, and threatened had a way of changing one's point of view.

CHAPTER 44

Whitaker used his key to open a heavy steel door on the side of a rundown warehouse in Fredericksburg, Virginia. He and Tank entered the huge warehouse and slammed the door behind them.

Inside, men lifted weights off to the left. Whitaker had bought enough weights and machines to make most small gyms jealous. Whitaker believed a team should lift and live together as much as possible. It kept his teams tight and forced them to push themselves harder than if they were lifting alone.

The equipment sat on the concrete floor and lacked even the comfort of rubber matting, but his men didn't care. They'd worked out in far worse conditions.

Whitaker heard heavy metal coming from a boom box sitting in the floor and saw the men dripping sweat as they pushed and pulled weight in impressive amounts. He nodded to the leader of Strike Team Two, who supervised the team of eight men.

Whitaker kept walking and fought the urge to join his men. He knew Tank wanted to, as well. Probably worse. Seeing the men of Strike Team Two lifted Whitaker's spirits. These men were professionals. Killers of the highest order. And he had four more strike teams just like them. Five teams. Eight men each. Forty of the best commandos in America. All waiting for a target.

Whitaker knew he could bring Nick Woods down if he could just determine his location. He walked into his office with Tank, which was one of several rooms built out inside the shitty-looking warehouse. From the outside, it looked like those around it. But from the inside, it had been retrofitted and upgraded to a command post, complete with the latest command and control equipment.

Whitaker had located his command post in Fredericksburg, Virginia, for several reasons.

First, it was near Washington, D.C., where he often had to go to meet with his boss or one of his aides -- Senator Gooden did like keeping his distance.

Second, unlike D.C., Fredericksburg lacked the traffic of commuters or a first-rate police force with experienced, nosy detectives. It had less than 30,000 people and an average police force.

Finally, the city was close to Quantico, where the Marine Corps had plenty of ranges for practicing weapons drills and assaults. It also had miles of woods for the teams to practice in. Strike Team Five, in fact, was in Quantico training today.

Whitaker always felt the location of his command post had been nothing short of brilliant. Actually, the entire set up of his unit by Sen. Gooden was brilliant, and everything could keep going as planned as long as he took down Nick Woods and Allen Green.

Whitaker took a seat at his desk and breathed a heavy sigh. Tank sat across from him in a guest chair.

"What's ailing you, boss?"

Whitaker rolled his neck in a circle and sighed again. Tank said nothing. He knew when to keep his mouth shut. Whitaker took his eyes off the ceiling and looked at Tank.

"We've got one shot to get Nick and Allen," he said.

"Why's that?"

"Because," Whitaker said. "We know they're going to go after Colonel Jernigan. He's their only remaining clue at the moment. But if we miss taking them down during their hit on him, then we'll be stuck on the defensive. We'll have no idea what their next moves are and they'll pick us apart if they choose to."

"Then we need to make sure we take advantage of this opportunity," Tank said.

"Indeed. We've got two teams here on rotation, doing nothing but training. I want to take both of them with us to North Carolina."

"Sixteen men, plus us. That"s a lot of firepower."

"We may need it."

"And do we warn Col. Jernigan that he may be in deep shit?" Tank asked.

"Of course not," Whitaker said. "He brought this on himself, so if he catches a bullet, it just saves us the effort. Plus, I don't want him looking nervous. Nick Woods can smell a trap from a mile away. We can't let him get away this time."

"He has a habit of that. Afghanistan. Just recently."

"Don't remind me. Let's hit the locker room and change into gym clothes. We'll hit the weights hard before we saddle up tonight."

"Roger that, Boss."

CHAPTER 45

Nick Woods watched Col. Russell Jernigan through a pair of binoculars as he stepped from his home and walked to his Jeep Grand Cherokee. Jernigan followed the same habits as he had the three days prior.

Nick scribbled a notation in his sniper logbook and noticed Jernigan was running three minutes ahead of schedule today. Still, the man left his home each morning between 7:45 and 7:48 a.m.

And besides noting Jernigan's habits, Nick also noticed a few men who also had their eyes on Jernigan. Two sat in a car at the end of the street. There were at least four in full camouflage in the woods behind his house. And Nick figured there were probably a couple more somewhere he hadn't seen. But, still, the shot was doable from where he lay more than seven hundred yards away.

He was across the street from Col. Jernigan's home, and more than twelve homes down. It was a cattycorner shot, angling away. Difficult, even for Nick, but he'd pulled off more difficult shots. His best shooting location for the shot was in the other direction, but Nick had seen several men in full camo working their way around it. So, he'd use this second location. Not ideal. But safer. And more unpredictable for his enemy.

Nick had upgraded his rifle. Two weeks earlier he'd

snuck onto the base where the Marine Corps hosted its sniper school training grounds. Quite quickly, he selected a couple of poorly trained snipers in their first week of sniper school, and snuck up on them at night. He'd hit them with a bright flashlight and surprised the shit out of the tired and exhausted trainees.

But through the light, they'd seen his pistol and given that they were unarmed -- no live ammo, just blanks -- they had little recourse. Nick hadn't planned on shooting them, but if it had been necessary, then he would have winged one of them.

In the end, he'd talked them down into voluntarily giving up their weapon. Nick even fired a round into the air so that their story about being robbed by some crazy man had more credibility. And then Nick had booked it out of the area, humping across the woods through an escape route that avoided roads and hit nearly every thicket and swamp he could find. It was only two klicks to the road where Allen was driving up and down waiting to pick him up.

None of that extra precaution on the escape had been necessary as the training staff hadn't been in the field and the two men hadn't been given a radio for their routine training exercise. It took more than six hours before the MPs were even alerted, and by then Nick lay on his bed in a hotel room just twenty miles away in Jacksonville, N.C.

He'd already showered and cleaned up.

Nick had spent the next week getting familiar with the rifle he'd stolen, which felt like an old friend from back when he served. It was the same rifle caliber and scope as he'd used, so it took little time to get familiar with it. He'd fired more than a hundred rounds through it on an abandoned farm thirty minutes away, while Allen Green spent the week working the phone and a laptop to find exactly where Col. Jernigan lived on base in Camp Lejeune.

Allen had worried he'd have to stake out the bar scene again, as he had the first time, but in the end he managed to get through to a couple former friends from the news world. Enough time had lapsed since his child porn charges that several were starting to believe Allen's crazy story of being framed.

He had, after all, had an impeccable reporting record for the past thirty years. And all the insiders had known he'd been working on a major story for months and months. To have been that mistaken about a story and then turn around and admit he'd been wrong was so farfetched for a veteran reporter of Allen's stature that many former friends were kicking themselves for abandoning him so quickly. One of his best friends had paid back an old favor and tracked down Col. Jernigan's home address through a couple of military contacts he had a relationship with.

And now just a little more than three weeks after drilling FBI Agent Jack Ward from a parking garage in Knoxville, Nick Woods lay behind a much better rifle and planned to blow away Col. Jernigan the following day. He'd prepped the battlefield, studied his exit route, and had all kinds of surprises in store for Whitaker's men who were "guarding" Jernigan.

These dumb sons of bitches were about to tangle with one of the best warriors America had ever produced. And they'd been getting sloppy after guarding the same man and following the same routine for three weeks straight. In a word, they were screwed, Nick thought.

CHAPTER 46

Nick Woods lay behind the M40A1 rifle the next morning, watching Col. Russell Jernigan's home as the sun burned off the early morning fog.

The rifle felt familiar, and it should. It was the precise weapon he'd used to hunt down the Russkies in Afghnaistan. He had worried when he stole the rifle in the dark from the two training Marines that he might end up with an M40A3, something the Marine Corps began fielding around 2003. The M40A3 was heavier and used an improved scope, which wouldn't have bothered Nick. What would have bothered him was learning the new rifle with the level of familiarity he had with the older M40A1.

In short, he wouldn't have been able to in just a matter of weeks. Nor, in even a year or two.

He'd spent hundreds of nights and days with an M40A1, some cold, some wet, some hot. Many nights in training and quite a few in war.

And lying behind the M40A1 sniper rifle all these years later, he felt the comfort and familiarity one might find with an ex-girlfriend they've dated for years. With this rifle, he knew her tendencies, and he knew how to make her sing.

Col. Russell Jernigan's door opened, and there he stood in his camouflage uniform looking down at his keys and an attaché case. Just another day at work, or so he thought.

Nick Woods cursed under his breath, feeling real anger that such a despicable man had reached the rank of Colonel. The man couldn't control his mouth and protect Top Secret information, something Lance Corporals and Corporals did on a regular basis -- for about one-tenth the pay.

Seeing his face through the scope, Nick swallowed down his emotions and tried not to think about the fact that this man was responsible for Anne's death.

Nick buried his raw anger and worked to forget the sight of Anne in their yard laying in her nightgown, blood pooled below her. The sight of the scope tracking Jernigan across the yard reminded Nick of dozens of shots from his past.

How many had he killed? He'd once known, but after a while they ran together, and the real professionals stop keeping track.

Colonel Jernigan walked toward his truck, looking calm and unhurried this morning. Jernigan always paused in front of the door to his truck, and since it was an older model 4x4, he had to unlock it manually with a key. Nick planned to take the shot at this moment, when Jernigan wasn't moving.

Jernigan took his final steps to the truck and Nick felt time slow down and his senses sharpen. Some kind of bug climbed his leg just above his boot and he shifted his mind from the sensation to focus on the crosshairs and Jernigan's body. The wind remained constant, blowing just slightly from left to right.

Nick began easing back the trigger, as delicate as you might test the blade of a razor-sharp knife with your finger.

CHAPTER 47

"Cruel Angel, this is Team 4 Leader actual. Do you read, over?"

"Roger, Team 4 Leader," Whitaker said. "This is Cruel Angel actual. Read you loud and clear."

"Be advised, Cruel Angel. We have November Whiskey in our sites."

November Whiskey stood for Nick Woods, and Whitaker could not contain the joy those words brought to him. He nodded to Tank, as they sat in a hotel room off base in Jacksonville. Whitaker knocked his smile off and decided to confirm the news.

"Team 4 Leader, are you absolutely certain you have November Whiskey in your sites?"

"Roger, Cruel Angel. We can see his position and the outline of his body."

Whitaker could barely contain himself.

"Roger that, Team 4 Leader. Follow original plan and do not intercept until after the shot is taken."

Tank laughed and Whitaker looked up from the radio.

"What?" he asked.

"You're an evil son of a bitch," Tank said.

"Might as well close the final loose end. Plus, it ties off nicely with the story that will emerge."

"Still, pretty cold blooded to let Col. Jernigan get

wasted."

"It is," Whitaker said, "but we deal in big schemes, and in the big scheme of things, it's a minor footnote."

Whitaker glanced down at his radio again. He wished he was out there with his troops. The one bad thing about command was how quickly you got pulled away from the front lines. Eventually, you found yourself looking at maps and listening to radios. You found yourself perfecting plans and studying strategy, and Whitaker knew he had a great strategy in place here. He'd overseen countless plans and this was one of his best yet. And like all great plans, it started with first-rate intel.

Whitaker knew Nick Woods would go after Col. Jernigan. And he knew he had a civilian-made .308 hunting rifle, which was not nearly as effective as a military sniper rifle. So, figure 300 yards as a max range for Nick. Really, that was barely outside assault rifle range, so Nick's greatest strengths as a sniper were severely diminished.

From there, Whitaker had drawn a 300-yard circle around Col. Jernigan's home, as well as his office, though both Whitaker and his team snipers felt Nick would shoot Jernigan around the home. The office was too jammed up with people and buildings to be effective.

But playing it safe, Whitaker had set up surveillance at both locations, and then they'd seen Nick around the home. It had been so tempting to take him out early on, but Whitaker's plans relied on Nick taking Col. Jernigan out.

The advantages to this were numerous. First, it closed a final loose end. Second, the shot would be a flat-out murder that would further undermine Nick's outlandish story involving conspiracy and threatened news media. Third, after the shot, Whitaker's men could kill him in a way that would allow Marine Major Hawkins of the MP unit on base to take credit for just happening to be in the right place at the right time.

Hawkins was the Marine who'd helped Whitaker get on

the base to begin with, and even allowed him to borrow a couple Hummer's on his first trip to Camp Lejeune. This would be a huge repayment of that favor. Major Hawkins was about to become a real-life hero, and his career would be set for good.

Whitaker had ordered all members of Team 4 to arm themselves with H&K MP5 submachine guns, since these fired 9 mm rounds. Best of all, the H&K MP5 came with a suppressed model that all of Whitaker's teams used regularly, so they were familiar with them.

And once the men had killed Nick Woods, Major Hawkins would come roaring up in his Hummer and fire the appropriate number of times into the air that Nick had been hit. The Team 4 leader had assured Whitaker they could take Nick down with two good center mass shots, and maybe one in the head.

That would be three shots for Major Hawkins to fire in the air while Team 4 policed up their brass and got the hell out of Dodge. Investigators wouldn't even take the time to run ballistics on the rounds. It'd be a routine shooting and no one would question the integrity of Major Hawkins.

"Shot fired! Shot fired!" screamed Team 4 Leader over the radio.

"Here we go," Whitaker said to Tank.

"I hope they nail the bastard," Tank said, and Whitaker looked up and thought he heard something in Tank's voice. Had Nick Woods gotten in Tank's head?

CHAPTER 48

Nick felt the rifle jerk as the shot surprised him and he worked the bolt in the automatic habit he'd developed through the years. He moved the rifle back on target and prepared for a follow-up shot, but saw Jernigan go down, blood sprayed across the truck door.

Nick knew the shot had felt good and figured he'd hit Jernigan within a few inches of the heart -- certainly through one of his lungs. The man stood no chance, unless an ambulance pulled up in the next thirty seconds, and even that would be a stretch.

Nick began to push himself up from his position. He had a four-mile hard evasion route in front of him and he mentally prepared himself for it. Then he caught movement and ducked back down. A van came roaring down the street toward a fake hide he'd placed right at three hundred yards from Jernigan's home.

Nick had placed it there in case there were any counter-snipers watching for him. And he'd set it up a bit obvious, even placed a cheap scope he'd bought at Wal-Mart among the bushes so that there'd be some reflection there from the morning sun.

Nick pulled the rifle back up as the van slid to a stop just yards from the hide, which sat just inside the treeline. As the men jumped from the truck and aimed silenced

H&K MP5 submachine guns toward the hide, Nick realized these were not MP's or Marines. They wore Marine uniforms, but Marine MP's didn't carry silenced weapons or deploy like an assault team.

It dawned on Nick that these were men of whatever shadowy unit it was that was hunting him and Allen Green. And he also realized he'd been given a golden opportunity. One they had forced him into. After all, his plan didn't include trying to outrun eight men who had vehicle support. He'd expected some pursuit, but by men who were also trying to avoid getting seen by MP's or other base personnel.

The sheer audacity of these men brought up some fear Nick hadn't expected. And then he remembered the fake FBI agent, who's name turned out to be Nancy Dickerson. And just as he finished twisting the range down on his scope and placing the reticule on the first man, he thought of how they'd rounded up Allen Green and destroyed the man's life, to say nothing of how they sold Nick and his partner out in Afghanistan.

By the time Nick pulled the trigger, he'd decided he'd kill every one of them if he could. His first shot blew a man off his feet.

* * *

"Where'd that come from?!" yelled the Team 4 Leader. "Spread out! Eyes outboard! Communicate, God damn it. What do you see?"

His men spread out into a quick 360, each taking a knee and looking for where the shot came from.

* * *

Nick racked the bolt and aimed at the leader standing and shouting. He fired fairly quickly. After all, it was just four hundred yards away now, instead of seven hundred.

The man went down hard, and Nick dropped a third man before they went prone.

* * *

"Where are those shots coming from?" screamed one of the men, real urgency and fear in his voice.

"He's to the west, I think," another said.

"Get online," one man yelled. "He's this direction," he said, pointing with his rifle.

The men not facing toward Nick jumped up and ran to get on line, except now everyone was in the prone.

"Cruel Angel, this is Team 4," yelled the next in charge into the mic in his vest that connected to the radio in his pack. "Team 4 actual is down, as are two other team members. We're taking very effective fire from several hundred yards away. Request support, over."

Tank saw Whitaker look down at his radio with a sick look. They had no support in the area other than a few men even further away, who were at the best sniper position that Nick should have used, but which he'd not scouted around. They may as well have been several miles away, Whitaker knew.

"Team 4, support is on the way, but it'll be a few minutes getting there," Whitaker said. He saw Tank look up at the obvious lie, but continued, "You must try to fire and move toward him. He can't hold you all off, and that's your best chance."

The Team 4 member who was next in command didn't answer Whitaker. He looked up and said, "All right, guys, we're going to fire and move and take this fucker out."

"Come on, Lewis," someone said. "We've got piss-ant pee shooters that barely shoot a hundred yards. We're dead men if we try to run him down."

A shot sounded and the telltale whack sounded. A moist slap that caused all the men to squirm lower to the ground.

"Who was that? Who got hit? You all right?"

"We need to go," another Team 4 member said. "If we make a break for it, some of us can make it out of here."

Lewis was not convinced of the wisdom of making a break for it instead of trying to take Nick down. "Sounds good," he said. "Get ready for some covering fire."

* * *

Nick had a hard time seeing them now, and he knew they'd probably make a break for the van. He pulled his nearly empty magazine from his rifle and threw a fresh one in. He had five rounds and four targets left.

In the distance, he could hear sirens approaching, but that was as much a threat to him as it was to the men lying in the grass before him.

Suddenly, two jumped up and rounds started zipping by him, some low -- striking the dirt -- and others high -- cutting branching and leaves.

Nick took a chance figuring only bad luck would cause one of them to catch him while he lay in the prone. He aimed at the man jumping into the driver's seat and fired, his shot shattering the glass but missing from the deflection it caused. He worked the bolt and sent the second shot into the side of the man's face. Either the man's head or the passing shot -- or the two in a combined motion -- slammed into the driver's side window and busted it out.

Nick aimed at the second man who'd jumped into the back of the van. He lost him behind a seat and then the other two were jumping to their feet and running to the truck. He shot the one heading toward the back of the van and blew him into the van, before his body slid out.

The second of the last two made it to the driver's door and was yanking it open and pulling the screaming man from the driver's seat when Nick put a bullet right into the front of his face. Both men fell and Nick worked the bolt again. He aimed toward the rear of the van, trying to decide where to fire when he had a better idea. He'd let the final man live -- and any others who were tough enough to survive taking a well-placed 7.62 mm bullet. Their stories would intensify the fear among the rest of the opposition's troops.

And with that thought, Nick slid back from his position and exited the area with the stealth that only a sniper can command.

CHAPTER 49

Allen Green grew increasingly worried following the day of Nick's mission. Nick had said it might take a day or two -- maybe even three -- to get off the base depending on how tightly they clamped it down following the shooting of Col. Jernigan.

News channels had shown the complete devastation after a Marine leaked a video clip taken from an iPhone. Bodies lay busted and broken across the landscape. Best of all, the men that Nick had killed had left a treasure trove of intelligence for the Marine Corps investigators, as well as the FBI, to work with.

Now media throughout the country were reporting that the violence hadn't been a terrorist attack as initially reported, or if it were, it had been an internal militia group; possibly from out west.

All the men found dead or wounded were carrying various forms of identification that stated they ranged from private investigators to former police officers to former federal agents, including even one former FBI member. Neither the Marine Corps nor the media could figure out exactly what had gone down yet, but all the bodies had helped the dialogue between Allen and his former press friends.

More and more were starting to buy into a conspiracy

of such scale and width as to be mindboggling.

One, a reporter from The New York Times, had begun to seriously dig and ask questions to DOD and the CIA. His name was Ken Leonard, and he had already been publishing bits and pieces of an upcoming story on his blog. Readers began weighing in on comments and offering suggestions on what they thought was happening.

On the second day following the shooting, Allen Green again dutifully drove down a barely used state road that bordered the Marine base and, more importantly, the training area that Nick planned to exit from.

Nick had told Allen to drive down the road each night and look for a series of signals along the road at a pick-up point the two had agreed would work best -- both for the man in the woods and the man driving the car. And just as he did on the first night, Allen drove down the road more nervous than shit, looking for a branch in the road, followed by a RC Cola can, followed by an old red shirt that would be lying in the gravel alongside the road.

Allen had worried other trash might confuse him, but the two had driven the spot that would be used and confirmed it was relatively litter free prior to Nick leaving for the op. Besides, Nick had asked, how many RC Cola cans have you seen lately? Not to mention the red shirt he'd be packing in with him.

But despite how hard Allen squinted in the darkness of that second night, he saw none of the three signs when he passed the area at midnight as directed. He arrived back at his hotel room dejected and increasingly worried, but that negativity was soon replaced by joy once Allen checked The New York Times website and saw a news story -- third down from the top, in fact -- that had been written by Ken Leonard, the reporter who'd been jumping more and more on Allen's side in regards to the conspiracy.

Ken had asked Allen earlier in the day if everything he had told him in the previous few days could be used on the record. Allen, now a fugitive on the run, figured he had nothing to lose by having his name used in a story with quotes and statements from him.

This agreement to be quoted on the record with his name attached had been the decisive factor in Ken Leonard's editor at The New York Times giving him the green light on his article.

And as The New York Times so often does, they'd placed the article online around midnight, which almost always meant the article would appear in the next day's print edition. Allen clicked the link and waited impatiently while the page loaded.

The headline read, "Colossal conspiracy or frantic felon, full of foolish fancy?"

Well, Allen thought, they sure nailed the alliteration.

He read on full of anticipation. Sure enough, Ken Leonard recounted the story from beginning to end with flawless precision. Of how an award-winning reporter had worked for months on a huge story. Of how the story had claimed that American snipers had engaged Soviet Spetnaz troops in Afghanistan, despite years and years of Americans adamantly claiming no such thing ever occurred. Or even nearly occurred. Of how those same snipers had been sold out to close up any loose ends and determine who a Soviet mole actually was.

And then the article described how Allen admitted it was all false the very next day, and how the police said he set fire to his apartment and had child pornography found on his computer. The article followed these two points with a quote from Allen himself, now hidden allegedly somewhere in the south, according to the article.

"It's absurd that I made that story up and would withdraw it the very next day," Allen Green said in an interview. "I've been writing articles for thirty years and had only two clarifications in that time. Yes, two clarifications and no, read zero, corrections. And child porn? Wouldn't you think that if I looked at child porn, I wouldn't have done so from my work computer, which is monitored by my employer? This is part of a huge government conspiracy. The government couldn't allow this story to stand, so they came after me with some secret group."

Allen smiled after reading his quotes. They read well in print, and he was glad Ken Leonard had quoted him accurately.

The article continued to say how the once respected reporter had skipped town and later begun issuing press releases claiming the sniper mentioned in the story was actually alive and was tracking down the shadowy organization that was plotting against the two men.

The story only had a couple paragraphs about the gunning down of Nick Woods's -- err, Bobby Ferguson's wife -- then a bit about how the two names were the same person, and how Nick Woods had proudly shot down FBI Agent Jack Ward in retaliation for his gunning down of Anne.

And now, Allen Green was willing to go on the record and claim that Nick Woods had gunned down U.S. Marine Col. Russell Jernigan at Camp Lejeune as part of the recent huge news involving a massive shootout at the sprawling base. Green also said Nick Woods had been responsible for the death of the men (called militia, for now) from the shadowy group who were protecting Jernigan.

The article reported that the Marine Corps refused to confirm or deny whether a Col. Russell Jernigan was involved in the shoot out until the investigation was concluded.

Amazingly, much to Allen's delight, Ken Leonard had interviewed a former CIA official (while not naming him) who said that while the claims by Allen might seem outlandish to most readers, the truth was they rang pretty accurate, according to the former agent.

"It can get pretty mixed up while you're in there serving," the former CIA agent had said in the story. "And often as not, you're as likely to be sold out as picked up after you complete a mission."

Allen stared at the screen a few more minutes, looked to confirm the article didn't allow comments, and then leaned back in his chair. He pulled a cigarette out of the pack and lit it. And as he smoked it -- slowly -- a conclusion began to run through his mind.

Son of a bitch, he thought. We're honest to God going to nail these bastards after all. The media -- with its vast powers and resources -- has the story in its sights, and more than likely they would pull no punches tracking down this story. It was too big not to. And as Allen settled on these thoughts, smiling as he smoked the cigarette, he felt more and more certain that he and Nick Woods (with the help of the media) would take down Whitaker and his group. As well as whoever was behind it.

CHAPTER 50

While Allen Green enjoyed the story and tasted the first thoughts of victory, Whitaker and Texas Sen. Ray Gooden made their countermoves.

Whitaker called Sen. Gooden the moment one of his men alerted him to the story, and Gooden didn't even waste time reading the story.

"What's it say in a ten-second nutshell?" he asked.

"It's bad," Whitaker said. "Pretty much tells the whole story. Accurately."

"I've got to chair the Armed Services Committee tomorrow, and still need to review some material. I don't have time for this shit."

"I know, sir. I have a plan for dealing with it."

"You damn well better," Gooden said.

He listened to Whitaker's plan and then made one phone call. It didn't matter that it was nearly midnight. And it didn't matter that his request probably broke about twenty different laws -- all felonies.

Gooden called the Deputy Director of the National Security Agency and when the man answered, groggy from just having fallen asleep, Whitaker said, "Bruce, hate to wake you, know it's after midnight, but I've got a national security emergency. I need you to alert your staff on duty that I've got a man on the way to your front gate, and he needs some quick research done on a crucially important matter. Feel free to wake up the Director if you want, but he's aware of this situation. We'd hoped we wouldn't have to drag you into this, but the situation turned south on us in a hurry."

Bruce, the Deputy Director of the NSA, had said no problem, and picked up the phone to call the night staff at headquarters to make it happen. Since he trusted Sen. Gooden, he never bothered to confirm with his Director whether he was indeed aware of the situation. No need to wake him.

Instead, he intrinsically trusted Sen. Gooden. How could he not? The man had been running things on the Senate Armed Forces Committee for nearly thirty years.

And this was a good thing, since Gooden had just told one of the most dangerous lies he'd told in more than a decade. And as Sen. Gooden ended his call with the Deputy Director, somehow managing to hide his anger at Whitaker and just able to swallow down his fear as he related the lies to Bruce, he decided that if Nick Woods didn't kill Whitaker, he would do so himself.

Whitaker, with all his mistakes, had jeopardized decades and decades of work. But first, he'd use Whitaker to get that damn reporter Allen Green and see if he could stop Nick Woods. And while Whitaker worked to make that happen, Sen. Gooden would be looking for his next commanding officer. Because if something didn't drastically change, he'd be burying one man and bargaining to retain a new one in the very near future.

CHAPTER 51

Whitaker stood behind a goofy looking dude who sat in front of three computer monitors, completely focused. The guy had curly hair, looked like he weighed ninety pounds, and had ear phones that ran down into a mesh of wires scattered on the desk. Whitaker had assumed the ear phones were work related, until he'd followed the cord to their destination, which was an iPod on the far corner of the desk.

Whitaker had never been around some of the top computer geeks employed by the NSA. He usually just received data dumps and intel files electronically, but tonight was an exception. A major one, he thought, wondering how far past midnight it was now.

The computer geek kept working -- oblivious to the man standing behind him -- and Whitaker closed his eyes and rubbed his temples. The past two days had been complete hell, and had reminded him of fierce combat in other war zones he'd encountered across the globe.

Whitaker remembered how confident he'd been just prior to Nick Woods dropping Col. Jernigan. And then how that confidence had been shattered by the brutal ambush of Team 4. The shooting had barely stopped before he was scrambling and making frantic attempts to get his men who'd survived off the base, but he'd had no luck. The MP's had swarmed and there were more generals and officers involved in the situation than he could possibly get around.

Whitaker wasn't even sure how many men from Team 4 were dead and how many were hooked up to machines in the base hospital. And as soon as he'd realized it'd be impossible to get the men off the base, he'd had Tank order his best available sniper in the states to get to Camp Lejeune. And fast. The man had collected his gear -- he'd been training on a sniper range in Quantico -- and jumped on a waiting private jet that Whitaker had arranged to land nearby.

Then Whitaker had spent the next few hours planning the mission with the sniper and getting his Marine Major on the phone so that the sniper could get on base, which currently was under heavy security.

"Where do you think he'll be?" Whitaker had asked, looking at a topographical map of the terrain around Col. Jernigan's house.

The sniper, who'd been studying the map for nearly an hour while Whitaker worked the mission's logistics, said nothing at first. He continued to study the map, looking at the lines that indicated elevation and the colors that portrayed heavy vegetation. He tried to put himself in the shoes of Nick Woods. What would he do? Would he have hauled ass after the shot? Or, buried himself deep in a hide until the pandemonium ended?

The sniper had an "x" placed on the map where the shot and resulting ambush had occurred. And around that "x" he had measured one mile in each direction -- north, south, east, and west. And then he'd drawn a curve connecting all four points until he had a circle on the map exactly one mile out from the shot.

Then, he'd repeated the task for two miles, three miles, four miles, and finally five miles.

The sniper knew Nick Woods was within those circles, since the shot had been just a few hours earlier. And he knew Nick would pick the same evasion route as he would, since they'd been trained the same. So, he studied it a couple more minutes and then saw precisely where Nick would go.

The sniper estimated the pace he would move at if he were Nick, added some extra distance to be safe, and then looked for the nearest insertion point. He wanted to be in position and waiting when Nick came by.

The sniper looked up at Whitaker and pointed to the map. "He'll be here, and I need to get a ride and be dropped off here."

Whitaker nodded and had told him he'd make it happen. After setting up the insertion of the sniper, Whitaker had nearly gone nuts the next two days. He'd tried to focus on his other teams that were deployed and the training of teams not deployed, but he couldn't stop worrying about whether his sniper had nailed Nick Woods. Since the man purposefully carried no radio, Whitaker was in the dark.

And then after two days, the article had broke on the New York Times and he'd talked with Sen. Gooden, who'd set him up -- pulling who knows how many strings -- with the NSA. And while the agreements worked their way down from the top of the NSA to its operations center, Whitaker had been aboard a private jet flying straight to a nearby airport.

Now, still standing behind the geeky NSA operator, he tried to let the worries about his sniper and Nick Woods go. He couldn't control that situation. Right now, he had a single focus, and that was Allen Green.

"How long should this take?" Whitaker asked.

"Depends on how complex and paranoid our friend Ken Leonard is," the NSA guy said.

"What do you mean?"

"Well," the man said, his fingers still typing, "it depends on how complex his password is. Whether he used numbers in addition to letters. Whether he used punctuation and symbols. And whether he used a longer password than most."

"Is there any way you can't break this?" Whitaker asked.

"No. Just a matter of how long it will take."

The geek, who Whitaker found rude, certainly knew his business. He'd broken into The New York Times server in less than ten minutes, though Whitaker thought he'd made it look like it took that long. Whitaker suspected they hacked into The New York Times regularly, but didn't want to give that piece of intel away to some guy they didn't know.

Now, the annoying little dude was trying to crack into Ken Leonard's personal email account. And from there, they hoped to find the e-mail address from Allen Green, and from there they wanted to get his IP address. Once they had that, they would use national security requirements to get the hosting company to give up the specific address -- and not just the city or general location.

Once they had that hotel -- and maybe even the number, but the geek had said that would be a lucky break -- then Allen Green was a dead man.

"One more question," Whitaker said. "Give me a best case and worst case scenario."

"Best case? An hour to break into his e-mail and four hours to work the approvals to get the exact location. Worst case, maybe four hours to break into his e-mail, plus the four that follows it."

"Great," Whitaker said. He stepped away from the computer workstation and pulled out his phone. He ordered his on duty officer at his operations base in Fredericksburg to alert Strike Team Three, which was on light training following a difficult deployment to Afghanistan, to mobilize and get ready to move out.

Whitaker hadn't caught any breaks yet, but taking Allen Green out would end the real threat. Without Allen Green's skills and connections, he'd just be dealing with a barely educated sniper who lacked any outside resources. And with luck, that barely educated sniper was already dead.

CHAPTER 52

Nick Woods moved through the woods. He followed low ground, as much as possible, and stayed in dense, impenetrable cover. And yet even in such impossible thick brush, he moved like a ninja.

He crept along in a crouch, each footstep half as long as a normal stride. With the shorter stride, he was able to keep his balance and place his toes down in a spot free of dry leaves or twigs. He'd add weight to his toes and then bring his boot down along its outer edge, slowly adding weight and pressure. The movement was so slow that sound was minimized and once all his weight was on the front leg, he'd lift his back and repeat the process.

In his pocket, the fired brass cases no longer put out heat. He congratulated himself on remembering to grab them after the unexpected ambush. And now just an hour after the shooting, he'd regained his composure and he slipped -- very s-l-o-w-l-y -- toward his extract point with the kind of confidence and potency you might find in a jaguar sneaking through the jungle.

Nick smiled to himself as he crept through the woods. Wonder what Whitaker is thinking now, Nick thought. He's probably not feeling so cocky, Nick thought, having missed his best chance to nab me. He knew I was coming and he still missed.

Nick smiled at this thought though in truth he'd never seen the van coming. And in truth, had he not stolen the sniper rifle prior to the op, they'd have buried him back there having perfectly guessed where his location would have been.

That thought did trouble him a bit. This guy Whitaker had guessed where he'd fire from with his hunting rifle, hid his men for nearly two weeks, and executed a flawless counter attack. Just in the wrong spot.

This thought brought Nick up short. Never underestimate your enemy, sport, he reminded himself. After all, Whitaker had been cautious enough to send the FBI to round him and Anne up following Allen Green breaking the story. And he'd done this with the near certainty that Col. Jernigan had leaked the info, not Nick. But, still, he'd had the FBI go on short notice nonetheless.

And he'd also flawlessly nabbed Allen Green from his very office, in a very public building, in a very public city. And he'd even had the tenacity and discipline to go after Nick and his spotter after the Afghanistan ops. And he'd done that just to be safe. Just so he could tie up a couple loose ends. Loose ends involving two of the best-trained Marines America had. There would have been no chance that Nick or his spotter would have leaked that info.

But this guy Whitaker, if that was his actual name, he didn't take chances. And he didn't lose very often.

Nick continued to move at his incredible slow pace.

So, what would you do, he asked himself. If you were Whitaker and you were trying to nab a crazy, well-trained sniper at the one opportunity you'll have. The last possible opportunity you have. You have this great organization facing a serious internal threat and you have one chance to save your organization. What would you do?

Nick knew he had a knack for figuring out what the enemy would do. It's what had saved him from the Soviets and what had protected him in countless other situations.

Think, Nick, he commanded himself. What would you

do?

He admitted the idea for a strike team rushing in by van was good. And then Nick stopped in midstep and a cold fear hit him. He felt sweat break out on his forehead and his heart start to race.

Because at that moment, Nick knew damn well what he'd do if he were Whitaker. He'd send in a sniper to back up the assault team. One not in the op area, since that wouldn't be necessary, but one staged in a trap to cover Nick's evac route in case the assault team missed him.

And with that thought, Nick got the eerie feeling that he was being watched. He'd come to the most open and dangerous part of his route -- the perfect place for a sniper to cover -- and as he instantly dove to the ground, fearing the shot he knew was headed his way, he thought of Allen Green and knew that if he were truly Whitaker, he'd do more than send in a sniper as back-up to take out Nick.

He'd also find a way to track down Allen Green and take him out at the same time. Because Allen Green, with his contacts and research capabilities, presented every bit as large a threat as Nick did.

CHAPTER 53

Whitaker's Strike Team Three had assembled at their warehouse compound in Fredericksburg, Virginia. They had their camouflage packed and stood around waiting in various forms of civilian attire. A couple looked like red necks in jeans. Others wore sharper, preppy clothes. Each carried concealed firearms.

The main goal was for them to not look the same. Their camouflage and heavy weapons were packed in containers in two work vans that would be driven by support members. They'd be riding in three SUVs, each driving with about two minutes distance between each other, with the two work vans in the middle of a widely spread-out convoy.

They'd be following speed limits, and each carried legal permits for their handguns, but in the event one of the two vans got pulled over and searched, they knew they might have to take down a state trooper before back up could be called.

That had never happened though, in all the history of the teams.

The team members didn't know anything about Nick Woods or Allen Green or the grand conspiracy story. Whitaker followed "need to know" protocol, and in his mind, none of these men needed to know.

All they knew was the following "situation:" a middle-aged man in his fifties, located near Jacksonville, N.C., needed to be nabbed. Their mission outline stated the man had been selling military secrets to the Chinese from the nearby Marine base at Camp Lejeune.

Some knew it was bullshit, most didn't. None cared.

They did believe they were acting as a part of the country's vital national security defense, and that was rewarding in its own right. And their over-the-top pay and constant excitement settled any other questions they may have.

They stood by their SUVs, each different in color and brand to help camouflage their unit. They waited impatiently for their commander. The support guys waited by themselves near their vans. They knew they didn't fit in with the actual trigger pullers on the Strike Team and had given up trying to long ago.

Strike Team members lounged about with the ease of hardened veterans who'd learned to master the hell of hurry up and wait years ago. The men joked, laughed, and bitched, but thought little of the mission. Nabbing one man, with no support element, no training, and likely unarmed? That had the word "cakewalk" written all over it.

Just moments after the NSA guy cracked the precise location of Allen Green, Whitaker called his Team Leader. A few questions were asked and then the Strike Team Three Commander walked out of an office, looked down at his notes one more time, and then said, "All right, guys. Let's load up and get on the road."

And with that, the men broke from their groups and climbed into their heavy vehicles, which were souped-up and modified in the front so they could ram obstacles without fear.

CHAPTER 54

A freakish silence hung over the woods. Nick Woods had hit the ground hard, after stalking in complete silence. But, he hadn't worried about the noise because if he'd been in some sniper's scope, then silence didn't matter.

Nick had landed hard and the sound of his body smashing leaves and sticks had sent birds scattering and squirrels up trees.

Now, he lay still, panting. His heavy breathing came not from exertion but from fear. He had no idea how close he'd just come to dying, but his gut told him it was within milliseconds.

After all, the woods in front of him allowed roughly two hundred yards visibility -- behind him was thick brush and cover. For a sniper, two hundred yards was spitting distance. Hell, even a good rifleman without a scope could drop a man at this distance, even using a worn-out, standard-issue assault rifle.

But for a sniper, with a scope and finely tuned rifle, you were talking about being able to hit something just a bit bigger than a half dollar. A good one would hit within two inches at two hundred yards.

So, assuming a sniper waited out there watching for Nick, he'd probably have wanted to drop him immediately as he exited the thick cover. And that's exactly what Nick had done when he got the feeling of being watched. Which meant the opposing sniper had probably already let half his breath out and had been taking slack out of the trigger waiting for it to surprise him. Which meant Nick had been milliseconds from death.

A perfect shot. An instant death.

Nick knew he was in a terrible situation. The sniper would be perfectly hidden in a ghillie suit that provided excellent visibility. He'd be behind some light brush or leaves, hidden in depth behind the moving foliage.

Nick lay between a couple big trees, and while he knew his rear was secure, he also knew he couldn't move forward. Had the sniper been able to see even a bit of Nick, the man would have shot already. After all, his surprise had been blown by Nick, even though he hadn't done a thing wrong.

Nick glanced behind him to confirm he had at least ten yards before he could make it back into the thick cover of the swampy thicket. While Nick didn't know where the sniper was located, he felt certain that there'd be no way he could go ten yards without exposing part of him, which the man would immediately blast. It's exactly what Nick would do -- in fact had done in some of the sniper duels he'd survived in Afghanistan.

Once surprise was gone, you wanted to wound the other man and frustrate him. Make him have to try to patch himself up so you could either move into a position with a better view or hit him again while he attempted to stop the bleeding.

So, Nick couldn't go backward. That was for sure. And he couldn't go forward or move to either side. To do so would be to risk exposing himself and getting winged by a man who would be driving nails at this distance with a grin on his face.

A risky move would be to jump up and try to dart back to the thicket. That had a small chance, especially if he rolled one way or the other, but at this distance, the sniper wouldn't need to hold his breath or work hard to make a great shot. So, the roll would alert his opponent and increase the risk, and just trying to get up would be equally deadly.

Nick figured the man was aimed in on the spot where he'd hit the deck. Waiting to see some movement he could blast. If Nick rose up, it'd just be a quick trigger pull and that'd be it.

Great job, Nick, he said to himself. You're about to get bagged by some sniper who's probably embarrassed at how easy this is going to be. Hell, there were fat, out-of-shape police snipers who shot twice a year who could handle this situation with ease.

Since he couldn't move, Nick had one thing left to do. And he'd soon find out who the tougher, more patient hombre was.

CHAPTER 55

Nick lay on the ground, listening. He had no idea how much time had passed, but he'd guess it'd been at least two hours. The birds and squirrels had calmed back down just minutes after he dove to the ground, and he'd kept his head down for the first twenty or thirty minutes.

He knew from long experience that keeping your head up while in the prone would quickly lead to neck cramps. And he knew his opponent wouldn't move in the first few minutes, until he was certain Nick had gone to ground.

So Nick had kept his head down, but strained for all his might to keep his hearing super alert.

After waiting roughly twenty or thirty minutes -- he refused to look down at his watch -- he lifted his head as slowly as one might raise the flag at a particularly moving memorial ceremony.

Nick wished he had his old ghillie suit. Not only would it hide him far better than his camouflage uniform and boonie hat, it also had a reinforced, padded front to it. This made laying in the prone more comfortable. And as Nick shivered in the cool fall air, he remembered it also helped keep you warm.

But Nick needed to focus. He pushed the thought of a more comfortable ghillie suit out of his head and pulled his rifle toward him, adjusting the knob on the top of the scope to two hundred yards.

He lifted his head and scanned the area to his front. He worked his head from left to right, moving it slowly and looking closely at the underbrush and deep shadows. It took him ten minutes of close study to confirm he could see nothing that looked out of place.

But he hadn't planned to see anything out of place. If this guy was any good, and if he had a ghillie suit on, then he couldn't be seen.

But Nick knew there was also the chance -- and it was really good -- that the sniper wasn't in a place where Nick could see him. If he were, after all, then the man would be able to see, and thus shoot, Nick. But, he wasn't most likely and now Nick needed to memorize exactly what the area to his front looked like. He felt sure the sniper would soon be crawling toward him, and it'd be difficult to pick up his slow movement.

Nick's best chance was to see a difference in the way things looked, and the moment he did, he planned to put a bullet right into the space.

But, no sounds reached him and no shadows changed. Minute after minute passed and Nick felt impatience and doubt creep up on him.

Maybe he hadn't felt someone looking at him? And maybe laying here, with his back to the thicket was a guaranteed way to die? Couldn't more men be on his trail, maybe even with silent trialing dogs? And one of their handlers would step out of the thicket and see their target lying there, facing the wrong direction. A double-tap to the back and that'd be it.

But the feeling had been so real of being watched. Could he have imagined it? So many times he'd trusted his gut, and it'd almost always been right. And it was only when he'd ignored his gut that he'd lost. Like allowing Anne to wear down his awareness, or paranoia as she called it.

The minutes turned to hours and Nick felt his body

begin to cramp. Two hours is a long time to do nothing, and Nick was far older than he'd once been. And he was also severely out of practice of the painful hell required of snipers.

Just trying to stay semi-alert and focused was difficult, and he felt his mind drift to Anne as the tactical situations left his mind -- hell, there were no tactical scenarios, just wait till the other man moves; first man to move, loses.

He hadn't thought of her much the past few days. Really, since he'd read about Allen Green in the newspaper and hauled ass up to New York to try to save his life. Nick wondered if Anne would approve of his shooting of the FBI Agent and the Marine Colonel, both of whom had caused her death.

Nick wondered if his opponent was thinking of a girl. And again, if a sniper even lay out there? He also wondered if Allen Green would freak out later tonight when Nick wasn't at the pick-up point.

Well, one thing at a time, he thought. First, he needed to try to survive this conundrum. And even pulling this off would take all the discipline and tenacity he could find.

Nick could hear nothing, but he wondered if he'd be able to hear a good sniper crawling two hundred yards away. The leaves were fairly dry, but a good man would move so slowly that the crushing of them would emit almost no sound.

Nick wanted to look down at his watch. About as much as he wanted to get off the cold ground. He figured if he looked at his watch, he'd give himself another fifteen minutes.

But looking down would not only take his eyes off the area, it would also create movement. And it'd also demoralize Nick since he felt confident less time had passed than he'd imagined. And if he did look at his watch, he really would set a time to get up and get moving. And such an idea, while tempting, also probably had death written on it. And so he pushed the thought from his mind and tried to concentrate on the job at hand.

The sniper across from him was no doubt dealing with the same thoughts and Nick just needed to be more disciplined than him.

More minutes passed and turned to hours. Nick needed to piss. He needed to scratch several mosquito bites, especially one on the back of his neck. But he fought these distractions and cursed his weakness. The urge to piss became so painful that he could no longer hold it, and so he pissed where he lay. Without undoing his pants. Without moving. The warm mess felt bad enough, but as it crept along the ground and up his stomach, the urge to get up nearly overpowered him.

Could any man other than himself lay this long? He didn't know the answer, but if the person was in a hide with food and water accessible, and piss and shit bags, then the answer was certainly "yes." But if the man wasn't in a hide, had just been sent on a quick reaction-type mission, then there wouldn't be a good hide or piss and shit bags or candy bars. That man would be beyond the breaking point by now. And with any luck, that man hadn't seen as much shit as Nick had, and would thus be weaker.

Nick considered that thought. Had any snipers in Afghanistan these days, or in Iraq, been in as tough a situation as he and his sniper partner had been in against the Soviets?

Nick figured the answer was "no." No way had any of them operated against a highly trained group of Spetsnaz, who had air support and infantry companies supporting them. And mobile units including tanks and armored jeeps. And even perfect intel provided by the U.S. government itself who had sold him and his partner out.

No. No way had this man been through what Nick had been through.

Suck it the fuck up, Nick. Suck it up for your sniper spotter. Suck it up for Anne. Suck it up for Allen Green. Suck it up so you can take out whoever's behind it all.

And suck it up Nick did. He didn't move. He fought off the urge to sleep. He drove away the temptation to scratch. To stand. To scream that he gave up and he couldn't take it anymore.

And hours after he went to ground, and hours after pissing himself, he noticed a spot two hundred yards away look a bit different. Darker than it once was.

Nick brought his rifle up moving as slow as he could and got his eye behind the scope. It took him more than twenty seconds to find the same location in the scope and as he scanned it in the detail of 10X magnification, he began to doubt he'd seen any change.

But as he lay there staring at the dark blob behind loads of leaves, he saw it move.

He smiled, thanked his old drill instructors for being such assholes, and fired. The shot rocked the quiet day and the target jerked and yelled, before immediately cutting it off. Nick worked the bolt, ejected the round, and rammed a new shell home. He moved the reticule back on target and fired again. Again the greenish shadow moved and screamed louder, unable to bite down the pain anymore.

Nick worked the bolt again and leaped to his feet. He ran, stumbling at first from legs that were stiff, toward the man. He arrived winded and approached carefully, looking about for a spotter that may be with the sniper.

But just as his gut told him someone was watching him, so, too, it told him that the man operated alone. Partly, he figured it was because whatever snipers were available would be split up to cover various evac routes. And partly it was because Nick figured whatever unit was out there, they couldn't have that many snipers available.

After all, none had been in New York when he went to pick up Allen Green. And only one, if any, (he'd seen none) had been back at Col. Jernigan's home.

Nick slowed his pace to a walk, aimed at the man, and covered the final distance. Blood spread in a pool below him, and covered leaves as high as waist high.

It's nasty getting hit by a high-powered rifle, Nick thought.

The sniper looked dead. He'd rolled on his back and no longer looked camouflaged.

Nick jogged the final few steps and kicked him in the jaw with the toe of his boot as hard as he could. The head yanked to the side and Nick heard the sound of teeth rattling, but no sound emerged. He's dead, Nick thought, and checked the area again to make sure the man didn't have any friends.

Nick then searched the man, grabbed his wallet, and stole his Beretta 9 mm pistol, along with both magazines. He'd gone fifty yards before he stopped and jogged back to the body. He then smiled and stole the man's ghillie suit, placing it in the crook of his arm.

Nick knew from prior experience that the blood would turn dark and not hurt the effectiveness of the suit.

CHAPTER 56

Two men from Strike Team Three sat outside the Holiday Inn in Jacksonville, N.C.

They watched Allen Green's room, though they didn't know the full story as to why Allen Green needed to go down. All they knew is that some guy named Allen Green was selling secrets to the Chinese that he was somehow getting from a few Marines inside Camp Lejeune.

Strike Team Three intended to hit Allen Green's room at 3 a.m. There was no better time for a night strike. Too late for the night owls to be up and too early for the early birds to have risen.

The team would stack quietly and hit the door with a battering ram -- no warning, no knock-ee, knock-ee.

Two support members would trail the eight-man strike team and wait in the hall. They'd be wearing khaki's and polo shirts and wearing Glock pistols on their hip. Anyone who opened their door to investigate the noise would be approached by an angry "cop" flashing a quite-real looking badge and told to stay in doors for their own safety and to not bother calling the cops. The situation was under control.

Inside the room, Allen Green would be either taken alive -- bound and gagged -- or riddled with bullets from silenced MP5s. His choice. Neither Whitaker nor the team members cared.

The time was just after 10:15 p.m. and the two Strike Team Three members watching Allen's room had been bored for nearly two hours now.

The team member in the driver's seat said, "Did I ever tell you about the best blowjob I ever got?"

"Yeah, you did. When we were doing that surveillance up in Buffalo, New York. Her name was Sarah, and you were on a plane. Stepped into the lavatory together."

"Actually, it was Sandy, but yeah, that was it."

The team member in the passenger seat heard the disappointment, but what the hell. He didn't want to hear the story again. He did hate the tension he now felt in the car. Maybe he should have pretended he'd never heard the story. Then, he saw the curtain in Allen Green's room move.

"Hey, hey, hey. What do we have here?" he asked.

"What is it?" the team member in the dirver's seat asked.

"The curtain moved in his room --"

But before he could say more, the light turned off and the door opened. Allen Green checked the lock and stood in the walkway up on the second floor.

"Call it in," he said.

And while the call worked its way up to the team leader, they saw Allen walk down the walkway and down the steps.

CHAPTER 57

Allen Green drove the entire way to the pick-up point full of mixed feelings. On the one hand, Ken Leonard from The New York Times had written a great article the night before. Doubt continued to grow among the public and the authorities.

On the other hand, Nick Woods should have been at the rally point waiting just in the trees on night number two. Now, it was night three and Allen couldn't shake the feeling that something bad had occurred. And it was so frustrating because they were so close to busting the conspiracy wide open and getting their lives back -- even though Nick said they'd never truly have their lives back. Allen disagreed with that, but regardless, that was beside the point.

They were so close to their safety and freedom again, and yet it seemed something had happened to Nick. Allen lit his second cigarette of the past ten minutes and tried to push his fear out of his mind. Maybe he should just keep driving if the signals weren't in the roadside tonight. He had nothing in the hotel room that mattered. Maybe they were after him now. He felt a cold chill work its way down his neck. Nonsense. He'd been around Nick too long and was growing too paranoid.

He drove on, turning the radio on and pushing the

thought from his mind.

Behind him, Strike Team Three scrambled to gear up. The two men who'd been watching his room followed from a safe distance, while the rest of the team grabbed weapons and loaded into vehicles from a nearby hotel.

They had been waiting in a hotel room while their team leader sent a call in to Whitaker, telling him their target was on the move. Whitaker digested the news and told the Strike Team Leader to follow the man and take him down at the first chance they got.

Whitaker debated briefly in his head as to whether he should mention to the Strike Team Leader that their target might be meeting up with a dangerous sniper and former veteran, who'd bagged a bunch of people in his day and was still on the hunt. But in the end, Whitaker passed.

He knew the Strike Team Leader was in an open room with the rest of the men, so everything he said would be heard by all. And it certainly doesn't inspire confidence among the men when they learn they've been flat-out lied to. (Okay for them to partly suspect, but not to out-right hear.)

And there wasn't time to tell the Team Leader to step outside and call him, so he could brief him. Thus, Whitaker made the decision to not mention it.

"Listen," Whitaker said. "Follow him and the first chance you get where there aren't any witnesses, just take him out. I don't care if it's open road or a dark, deserted parking lot. Just make it happen and get out of there."

"Roger that," the Team Leader said. Then, to his men, he yelled, "Let's go. We don't have time to screw around. He's getting further and further away and we can't go speeding after him if we're armed for bear. Everyone, just grab pistols and ignore your vests or sub-machineguns. This should be easy. Now, let's go. Move. Move. Move."

The six remaining Strike Team Three members and their Team Leader piled into their two SUVs and headed in the direction that their target -- or Allen Green --

traveled.

CHAPTER 58

Nick Woods watched the road in front of him. He waited in the kneeling position, leaning against a tree. He had the sniper rifle slung across his back and the bloody ghillie suit that he'd taken off the sniper balled up in front of him.

He had his .45 pistol out and in his right hand, nice and ready. Extractions usually proved dangerous, and Nick didn't plan to take any chances. Besides his .45, he also had the 9 mm Beretta that he'd taken off the sniper stuck in his waist, just below his belly button.

Right on time, he saw headlights headed his way.

* * *

Allen Green drove down the road, his eyes searching the ground in front of his eye beams. And then he saw a branch where it was supposed to be.

"Come on," he thought. "Please, RC can, where you at?"

And then his headlights picked up the glint of a blue RC Cola can. And just beyond that, the old red shirt laying in the gravel of the road's shoulder.

Allen felt huge relief, the fear and stress suddenly gone. There was just something about the confident, hard Southern man that Allen had trouble putting into words.

Allen cut his lights and slowed. But, as he pulled to the side, he noticed a vehicle behind him hit its high beams and roar toward him. And behind it came two more.

* * *

Nick heard the convoy before Allen saw them. Nick's senses had been on full alert in the darkness, and his ears picked up the traffic coming his way.

Nick immediately left the ghillie suit and started running through the treeline toward the coming vehicles. As Allen had approached he had kept his eyes shielded from the headlights in order to maintain his night vision. And then the other vehicles hit their lights on bright after Allen had slowed and cut his off and Nick still worked to look away from the glare hoping his adjusted eyesight might play some advantage if things got rough.

Nick raced through the woods, limbs smacking his face and his boots slipping and sliding. He made it roughly fifty yards and then darted out of the woods and into the grass alongside the road once he'd run beyond the vehicles.

The three vehicles -- two SUVs and a business car of some kind -- lined up behind each other and men burst out of the cars, guns drawn and shouts as they raced forward.

Nick ran, too. Toward them. He kept his eyes squinted, wanting to protect his night vision. Thankfully, he just had the red brake lights to contend with, not the bright lights from the front of each vehicle.

The men all raced to the right of each vehicle. It made sense from a tactical perspective. If they approached from both sides, then they'd be in each other's line of fire. Like this, they'd be on line and could fire safely.

Nick had closed to within ten yards and they still hadn't heard him in their own noise. Then he saw Allen's brake lights go brighter as he pushed the brake. It was obvious he planned to throw the car in gear and drive off -- he'd frozen for what must have been five or ten seconds, but that's what civilians do, Nick knew.

"Shoot him before he drives off," someone yelled, and Nick saw pistols get raised their final necessary inches. He stopped running and started shooting.

He couldn't see his sights, but he didn't need to. They were just six feet ahead. He pointed the pistol as if he were pointing his finger. It was just like he'd been trained, and he trusted his body to intuitively aim correctly.

His shots rocked the night as only a .45 can, and as his rounds tore into the rear man -- and on through him -- the team hesitated. They'd been told there'd be only one man, and Nick took advantage of their hesitation.

He fired eight shots from the .45 in three seconds and dropped the pistol, yanking the Beretta out and firing off the entire magazine from the kneeling position.

The men in front of him tried to turn, to maneuver around their screaming and bleeding buddies, but every time one got close to getting some return fire out, they caught rounds themselves. The entire line of men were perfectly illuminated and blinded by the bright lights of the three vehicles. They could barely see a shadow or silhouette, and some pistol flashes, but their views were one-one hundredth of what Nick Woods saw.

And Nick Woods fired until the pistol locked to the rear, out of ammo. Nick reached down, grabbed his .45 from the ground, and reloaded it with a second mag. And as men groaned, cried, or reached for pistols or other weapons, he walked among them and fired final rounds into each of their heads.

CHAPTER 59

After the echoes of the gunfire ceased, Allen Green wanted to haul balls out of there, but Nick told him to hold up.

Nick ran to the woods and grabbed the ghillie suit he'd taken from the sniper.

"I might need this," he said, throwing it into the car.

"I thought you said you didn't have one," Allen said.

"I didn't, but somebody decided to let me borrow it."

Allen looked back over the seat and saw what looked to be dried blood on it.

"I'll bet," he said.

"Oh, before we leave, let's get all the money we can from these chumps," Nick said. "May need it."

"We'll be leaving our fingerprints, though."

"Won't matter," Nick said. "You'll be writing this up as one of your press releases, right?"

"True."

The two quickly searched each of the men and wiped the inevitable blood they couldn't avoid off on the dry pieces of clothing they could find. Despite the sticky hands, it proved worth it. They found more than $860 in cash on the men, and an MP5 and six magazines fully loaded in the back of one of the vehicles.

"Not a bad night's work," Nick said as they drove off.

"Easy for you to say," Allen said. "You didn't have eight dudes aiming guns at you about to blow your head off."

"The hell I didn't," Nick said. "Who do you think they were aiming at after I started firing. Not to mention a damn perfectly hidden sniper nearly took my head off."

"How'd you get by him?"

"I'll tell you later. We need to get the hell out of here, grab our stuff from our room, and get out of Indian country."

"And then what?"

"First, a shower for me. Then you can update the media on what happened. With as many bodies being piled up, they're going to catch on soon that something pretty serious is going on."

"Actually, on that note, I have some good news. A New York Times reporter named Ken Leonard has been writing up the story. Believe me, the press is coming around to seeing things our way, and I've been getting more e-mails from reporters I once knew."

"That's great news, Allen. It really is, and it's an important part of what we need to get done. But just remember, in the end, this war will be won by bullets, not barrels of ink."

"Don't be so sure," Allen said, pulling out a cigarette.

CHAPTER 60

Whitaker lost a lot of sleep that night. After losing radio contact with Strike Team Three, he'd tried to stay calm. Surely, a tactical situation made it necessary that they stay off the air. Surely, not all nine of his strike team members were dead. All nine? Could that even be possible?

These were some bad motherfuckers. Delta Force. Navy Seals. Army Rangers. Marine Recon.

One Marine and a soft liberal from New York taking them out?

Impossible.

So, Whitaker had shook the thought and done everything in his power to not look like the panicked commander in the rear with the gear.

But, three hours with no communication and Whitaker could take no more. It was after 2 a.m. and his team commander had broken every Standard Operating Procedure in the book. It seemed impossible that between cell phones, pay phones, and three vehicles, that the team leader hadn't found a way to contact him.

Whitaker finally relented and called up his support guys, ordering them to head out to the unit's last known location and report what they saw.

They called twenty minutes later, reporting a huge

crime scene up ahead. Dozens of police cars, ambulances, and night lights. Whitaker told them to turn around and avoid trying to get closer or drive down the road.

"For Christ's sake," he said. "It's after 2 a.m. and you're a bunch of guys driving down a dark road, all of you carrying weapons. The last thing I need is for you all to be arrested and add to my problems. Get the hell out of there while you can."

And then Whitaker had sat heavily in his office in Fredericksburg, Virginia. He poured himself a shot of Tequila and just thought.

Certainly, he was in deep shit. What would he do if he were Sen. Ray Gooden? Was there any way he'd keep the same man in charge?

And that brought up an interesting dilemma. After all, Gooden would probably do far more than fire Whitaker. How did you fire someone who knew so much? Who'd done shit-tons of illegal stuff, and probably had files and files of hidden documents that could bury you.

Whitaker glanced at his office door, ensuring it was locked.

Tank was in his office and Whitaker wondered whether Tank would kill him. Considered whether at this very moment he was getting a text from Gooden telling him to take Whitaker out.

Whitaker pulled out his .40 caliber Glock from its hip holster and laid it on his desk. Much easier to go for it while it lay there than trying to draw it out while sitting. But, would he open the door with it in his hand, should Tank knock?

What if Tank merely had a simple question or message to relay? How weak would Whitaker look then? How long before his troops would start to talk, saying the old man had lost his nerve. This old war horse -- a paranoid loner who was good with a rifle -- had finally got the best of the ole' veteran commander. The man who'd hunted the VietCong like a mad man, and led troops on nearly every continent.

One loner and a journalist, for God's sake, had finally bested him. Whitaker shook the thought from his head.

He stood, holstered his pistol, and unlocked his door. One way or the other, he wouldn't go out a coward.

CHAPTER 61

Allen Green and Nick Woods returned to their hotel room, Nick grabbed a quick shower then they retrieved their hidden cash and gear, and drove out of Jacksonville, N.C.

Nick was beyond exhausted, nodding off before they'd driven five minutes.

"Why don't you catch some sleep?" Allen said.

"I may just do that, partner. I'm flat beat."

"Any particular direction you want me heading?"

"Just head south. We'll find somewhere far away from civilization and recoup a bit."

"I need to stay near Internet access. This story is blowing up, and more and more reporters are e-mailing me."

"That's fine. Just head south, and we'll get another hotel room."

* * *

A lot happened the next few days. While Nick rested up, and eventually got back to his running, calisthenics, and countless pistol and hand-to-hand drills, Allen worked his magic.

Based on the advice of a colleague from the Washington Post, he set up a website that detailed and catalogued everything he knew (and suspected) about the conspiracy. The tone of the website was one of a questioning doubter. Allen used it more as a, "If there's no conspiracy, then how do you explain this? Or that?"

By then, news media had descended again into the Jacksonville/Camp Lejeune area. Nine more men killed -- one, an obvious sniper, the others piled up by the side of the road. Again, no real clues.

Allen wrote on the website his version of what happened. He claimed Nick Woods had acted in self defense to defend him from a carjacking or abduction. Granted, he came across as crazy, but how to explain all those bodies. Who, by the way, were armed and not found to be licensed law enforcement of either the state or federal government.

The web hits started growing from day one, and Allen's site became both a media resource and a destination source for an increasingly fascinated public. By this point, even Nick could see the value of the information war Allen was waging.

He begrudgingly began to accept that Allen's methods were gaining them loads of allies, which translated to plenty of brains helping with their strategy and even volunteers willing to hide them out or support them in any way they could.

Nick appreciated the support, but worried about some of them.

"Someone in that list of e-mails you have is a plant," he said. "He'll show up and blow our asses away."

"Precisely why I've told no one where we are."

Things improved even more the next day.

First, Allen received a message on his website claiming to be from the FBI stating they'd found some irregularities in their investigation into the shootings and believed some of what he was stating had merit. The FBI requested the two men come in for questioning and protection.

Nick was dead set against this idea, and Allen was only marginally more for it. It seemed fraught with danger, and this group that hunted them seemed to have plenty of sources and connections.

But, an even better idea emerged when the New York Times offered to have an artist sketch out the face of the man who'd gone by the name of "Whitaker." Allen wanted to jump on this idea, but Nick still worried that the artist could be followed, assuming he wasn't a plant to begin with.

Nick and Allen reached a compromise when the New York Times offered to host a secure video-conference with the artist. Nick agreed to let Allen do that, but he insisted they start moving hotels twice a day instead of every day.

"This is really burning through our money," Allen argued.

"Beats having some of the guys from this group come busting down our door. We don't know what abilities they have to track us electronically."

But, those abilities had vastly deteriorated. The NSA was done letting Whitaker use their resources. Allen's website about a Marine hero and a reporter just looking for the truth had completely swayed public opinion. The story was so big that an opinion poll had been done and now only 18 percent of the public believed Allen Green had ever looked at child porn or made up his original story. And as the public perception turned, the media piled on in Allen and Nick's favor.

And as for Nick Woods, the public wanted him exonerated from the shootings he'd been involved in and granted military honors for his sacrifice in Afghanistan.

Nick showed no concern for these realties. He remained convinced more blood would flow soon. But, Allen pressed on and soon had the sketch drawn up with the artist. Once it was completed, Allen promptly uploaded it to the website.

And that's when things really started to go Nick and Allen's way.

CHAPTER 62

Whitaker stood before Sen. Ray Gooden's desk. Again, Sen. Gooden was ignoring him while he scanned through a half-inch report.

Sen. Gooden finally paused, pulled down his reading glasses, and said, "Why are we here today?"

Whitaker thought of a half-dozen smart-ass responses, but figured humility should win the day.

"We're here," Whitaker said, "because I've failed to either bring in or take down Nick Woods and Allen Green."

"Well, that's certainly clear. A bit obvious, if you ask me."

"Yes, sir."

"But, it's more than that," Sen. Gooden said. "Exactly how many men have you lost?"

"Too many, plus Nancy Dickerson," Whitaker said. Unfortunately for him, he knew the number exactly. Knew most of their names. Their dreams and aspirations. With units like his, men didn't come and go. These men had been there for years and Whitaker knew them all.

Sen. Gooden said nothing, letting these facts further sink in for Whitaker. Oh, he's good, Whitaker thought. He's good.

"So, nearly two dozen men?" Sen. Gooden asked.

"Yes, sir."

"And one cop?"

Whitaker swallowed. He'd forgotten about the California police officer. "Yes, sir."

"And one FBI agent?"

Whitaker looked harder at Sen. Gooden. Surely he wasn't laying the death of FBI Agent Jack Ward on Whitaker's hands. "But, sir," Whitaker said.

"Don't 'but' me. That man only died because of a failed op that you asked the FBI to conduct. But the bigger problem here is you're taking part in what is increasingly looking like a full-blown war inside our very own country."

Whitaker tried to show nothing, but his heart raced and sweat beaded up on his forehead.

"Do you know," Sen. Gooden asked, "that the few people who know of our program -- and believe me they are few -- are wondering why this wonderful operation has gotten so sidetracked that its more focused on a former, honorable veteran and reporter, who frankly, is a loyal citizen, as well."

Sen. Gooden stopped, looked to the side, and picked up a cigar. While he cut off the end and slowly lit it, Whitaker said nothing. He knew better than to interrupt the man when he was making his point. And Sen. Gooden liked to take his time making his points. A showman, through and through, with a Texas drawl and a murderous look.

Sen. Gooden blew some smoke into the air and looked down at the cigar.

"Fine cigar," he said, as if he wasn't in the middle of chewing Whitaker's ass out.

"And so," Sen. Gooden said, "one of the few people who know of our program asked me recently, 'Senator, why is this beautiful operation, which has worked so well for so long, why has it gotten so sidetracked that its more focused on a hero and well-regarded reporter."

Sen. Gooden looked down at the cigar and took

another puff.

"Do you know how I answered that question?" Gooden said.

"No, sir."

"I didn't. And I didn't because I don't know the answer. But, I told them I'd soon have an answer for them. And so I called you up here--" he took his time and blew a line of smoke straight toward Whitaker "because I figure you have the answer to this question. Because otherwise, we've got a problem that's quite a bit bigger than you, I assure you."

Whitaker took a deep breath and said, "Sir, we didn't get sidetracked. Following an operational security breach, in which some early secrets of our organizational history were leaked in a national publication by, as you said, a well-respected reporter, I took action to do some serious damage control. Such damage control helped prevent months and months of news speculation and likely Congressional Hearings.

"This in itself, was a major success. However, a unit not under my control, along with terrible luck, led to Nick Woods, or the former Bobby Ferguson, not being in his home. And the superbly trained, decorated hero soon joined forces with Allen Green. And let me remind you, sir, that these two men represent the most formidable of threats to our organization. That, sir, is why I got sidetracked."

Sen. Gooden said nothing. He sat, leaning back in his chair, and watched Whitaker with a sick smile on his face. He smoked two full inhales and exhales on his cigar, his eyes locked on Whitaker.

At least thirty seconds passed and Whitaker didn't dare break eye contact.

"Strike Team Two?" Sen. Gooden asked. "Why haven't you sent me any reports on them the past few days? Weren't they closing in on America's second, most-wanted terrorist?"

Whitaker nearly gasped. "Sir, I apologize. My second in command has been working liaison with them, and I'm sure he can answer any questions you have regarding that operation. I apologize, again, for not keeping you in the loop. I've been distracted and in over-drive since the shooting at Camp Lejeune?"

"Which one?" Sen. Gooden asked. "There's been about three separate incidents in the past three days."

Whitaker nodded. "Point taken, sir."

Sen. Gooden's smile grew wider. He took a sip of his Jack and Coke and said, "I want you to take your time answering this next question. Your life, quite possibly, hangs on how you answer it."

"Yes, sir."

"Are you scared of Nick Woods and Allen Green?"

"No, sir," Whitaker said, a little too angrily.

"So, you're not? You've deployed entire teams of men to kill him and he's slaughtered them like sheep and you're not concerned?"

"No, sir."

"Ah, good," Whitaker said. He took another puff of his cigar and smiled sickly. He pushed a button under his desk and four men in suits entered.

Whitaker had been disarmed before entering -- no one got near the Chairman of the Armed Services Committee carrying a pistol, it didn't matter who you were -- but these weren't Secret Service agents who normally guarded Sen. Gooden.

The men formed a cauldron around Whitaker. Two by the desk, between Whitaker and Sen. Gooden. Two behind him. All four had their arms crossed, ready for action. And not the kind where you draw a pistol, but the kind where you beat someone's ass.

"Whitaker, I've asked a few men to witness the ending of our meeting because I don't want you to over-react and do anything stupid. Now, I've taken a couple main points from our meeting.

"One, it's quite clear you've botched about every aspect of this damage control mission since the beginning. You've lost more than a dozen people, destroyed two Strike Teams, and severely damaged our ability to operate inside the country. We've got half of the country's media looking under rocks for our group, which is where we started when Allen Green broke his story. At this point, it would have been better to have done nothing in the beginning, because we're back to the start except we didn't pass go and we for damn sure didn't collect two hundred dollars.

"For failing so miserably in this operation, I now relieve you of command. I've already alerted a man in your command, who I won't name, that he's in charge. Your passwords have been changed, your team leaders, your entire organization already knows you're no longer in charge. That your words, threats, and pleas carry the weight of an overpaid janitor, who's no longer on the good side of the principal.

"That's the first point."

Sen. Gooden paused to take another sip of his Jack and Coke, and Whitaker tried to control his face. To say he was stunned to have lost his command was beyond obvious. He could see being killed, but stripping a man like him of his command, that was actually far worse. The two men in front of him looked eager for Whitaker to do something stupid.

Sen. Gooden laid his drink down and looked back up.

"Now, you've said you don't fear Nick Woods and Allen Green. I figured that much. And though you've been relieved of command, I want you to know that I've never doubted your courage. You mean a lot to me and Martha, and I'll always welcome you at our table. But don't go planning to come by anytime soon. Because effective immediately, you and Tank, who's also been relieved of his duties, have one single mission. You are to hunt down and kill Nick Woods and Allen Green. No more, and no less. And you'll be issued a credit card with a balance of

$250,000. That's all the support you get. No weapons from the warehouse in Fredericksburg, where your code no longer works. No intel. No nothing. Because officially, you no longer exist to this organization. Of course we'll monitor you. You go to the press or even hint at leaking national security information, --"

"Sir, I would never --"

Gooden raised his hand to stop Whitaker. "I know you wouldn't, but I've got to say this. If you even hint at leaking national security information, you'll find yourself at Guantanamo Bay. No American prison. No open trial. Nothing like that. Files have already been prepared and delivered to the NSA and FBI describing every hair on your ass, all your friends, your current bank balances, along with their numbers, you name it. If anything changes, even so much as a single dollar starts to move, then you'll be apprehended.

"And how will we apprehend you? Oh, that's even grander. You'll be fitted with an ankle bracelet after you leave my office. If that thing ever comes off or leaves the country, then you're either a dead man or headed to Guantanamo. You know these men are good. You trained them. Now, get out of here, go get Tank, and get after Nick and Allen. Bring me their heads on a plate and we'll talk about finding you another fit in a good line of work. Don't expect to get your command back. You've caused too much damage for that, but I can offer you my good graces again and a steady income with exciting work. That's the best I can do. Maybe you'll earn a command again someday.

"Now, get the hell out of my office and make it happen."

Whitaker finally smiled and said, "Consider it done, sir."

"For your sake, you better hope so."

CHAPTER 63

Allen Green hit the jackpot the day after Whitaker lost his command.

Allen had posted The New York Times artist's sketch online. The media and public already knew the story of Whitaker, and how he'd interrogated Allen in a hidden room after the story broke.

And within two days of posting it, reports started to come in from California that the sketch of Whitaker looked exactly like a man that was wanted in a police shooting. Allen looked that incident up and knew the minute he saw the video footage from the police department that he was looking at the man that had destroyed his life. Whitaker, until he learned the man's real name.

And then the hunt sped up as it hit its next stages. Reporters from dozens of newspapers and TV stations were combing through photos of graduating classes at West Point and the Naval Academy, hoping to find out who this guy named Whitaker really was.

Worse, even former graduates and officers from all four branches were trying to figure out who he was. This man had gunned down a cop and abducted a reporter in some kind of unbelievable CIA-like conspiracy. You didn't do that, even in the post-9/11 world.

The public smelled blood and desired payback, and the media fanned the flames as only the media could.

CHAPTER 64

"What's our plan?" Tank asked.

He and Whitaker sat in a corner booth of Waffle House. It was after midnight, and Whitaker needed some coffee and time to think, and Tank could always use more protein for his ever-starving muscles.

"The bottom line is we need to kill Nick and Allen," Whitaker said. "If we do that, then their website goes inactive and eventually the public will move on. We'll keep a low profile during that time and hope for the best."

"How do we pull this off now that there's a sketch out of you? That sketch is a good one, at that, and they may have your actual name before long. They'll find you from your West Point annual. There just aren't that many West Point grads of your height and who would have graduated in the time period that you did."

"All true," Whitaker said, reminding himself yet again that Tank was no dummy. The man had more than just bulging muscles. "And, of course, we really have no intel or any way to figure out how to find them."

"Which means, what?" Tank asked as he forked down a load of eggs.

"It means we need to e-mail them through the website and arrange a meeting somehow. And at such meeting, we kill them."

"Why would they risk that? They'll know what we aim to do?"

"That's a fact," Whitaker said. "So, we'll need some bait to help bring them in."

CHAPTER 65

Sen. Ray Gooden sat behind his desk. It had been hours since he talked with Whitaker and it was now after midnight.

Gooden had cancelled attending an important fundraiser with some Texas constituents who had flown in by private plane, sending his No. 1 aide instead and explaining a national security situation had held up the Senator.

Now he rested at his desk. Half drunk. His tie loosened and his shirt a wrinkled mess. He knew the situation was spiraling out of control right before his eyes. And it was moving at a speed he found difficult to comprehend. Things were moving at the speed of political campaigns, except in this case it involved national security and too many felonies to count.

With every passing day, the chances for a Congressional inquiry grew. And once those began, then the risks increased still further. There'd be tough questions asked out loud and broadcast throughout the country. There'd be asshole former military officers, maybe even a few current ones, who -- too straight-laced and honorable for their own good -- would leak info or even testify about what they'd heard rumors of. These men had no idea about real national security, Gooden thought. You couldn't protect all of America while following the law to the letter. You had to blend it a bit, adding in some terrorism of your own. You had to exist in that shade of gray, in an ugly world where nothing was black or white.

But, the speed and danger of this situation had Gooden more scared than he'd been in a long time. Probably since he'd trailed Democratic candidate Bob Kile. Yeah, this situation felt as dangerous as that had felt -- much worse than those investigations by the Senate Ethics Committee.

Gooden smiled as he remembered that firebrand, Bob Kile. He grinned harder and thought, "Well, Bob, I'm betting that twelve-point lead and endorsement by four different newspapers didn't matter much as your plane raced toward the ground."

Bob Kile had been two days away from burying him in an election and he'd still found a way out. Now, he just needed to find a similar way to end this crisis.

Certainly in just a day or two, the media would figure out who Whitaker actually was. And from there, those bastards would start pulling that small thread and following it to its source. And with so many recent deaths from among his troops, and so many of their family members and friends who may have seen or known Whitaker, the risks were skyrocketing.

Gooden felt his stomach rumble and wiped his sleeve across his forehead.

Oh, they hated him, and he'd pissed off and attacked so many people that what allies he had might turn on him this time. That was the problem with power. You had to exercise it, and yet with each time you used it, you gained more opposition and animosity.

Gooden gulped down the rest of his Jack and Coke, and slammed the glass on his desk. He immediately refilled his glass, mixing it about with about 60 percent Jack Daniels and 40 percent Coke.

He took another large swallow. He couldn't shake the thought that he needed this to end fast. At this point, it didn't matter whether Whitaker and Tank lived or died. He just need them to either take Nick and Allen down or die trying. If they succeeded, then Allen's website would cease being updated and the story would soon die. And if they failed, then there'd be the body of Whitaker and Nick and Allen could claim victory.

With luck, Nick would head back to the woods of Tennessee and a life of construction, and Allen would probably win some kind of award and be offered some senior reporting slot again.

There'd be danger immediately after the death of Whitaker and Tank, but the CIA would deny any knowledge of the men's group, which was of course the truth, and the public would again suspect the CIA knew very well about the group and its operations. There might be some increased oversight from Congress and some articles written, but it'd all die down soon. Too many terrorists out there to hammer the CIA too hard.

Gooden chugged the rest of the glass and wiped his mouth with his sleeve, further soiling his shirt.

Damn, he needed this to go down soon. Like in the next day or two. Regardless of who came out the winner. He needed it over.

He refilled the glass again. What was this? The fifth? Or eighth? Or was it even higher than that?

Gooden didn't care. He had an aide and driver who could get him home, and in the depths of the back of his mind, he could feel a possible solution coming on. He stood and started pacing the room.

He walked in a line, back and forth, thinking hard and sipping his drink. Yes, he liked this idea. He could arrange the showdown. Make it happen fast. And then whoever won, won.

The idea came further together. He'd contact Whitaker and Tank and claim he'd changed his mind. That due to the urgency of the situation, he needed it resolved quickly. Therefore, he'd decided to use all the political leverage he had to have the NSA get involved one more time. And that they had the rough location of Nick and Allen, so Whitaker and Tank should stage themselves at one of their CIA cabins not currently in use deep in the woods.

Whitaker knew just the right location to put them at. It wasn't near anything. The two sides could have their war and the public would be none the wiser.

And while Whitaker and Tank waited, Gooden would be leaking their location to Nick and Allen. He felt certain Nick would overpower Allen and insist on going to get them, even if it *was* a trap.

Nick wouldn't allow Allen to bring in the cops. And Allen was still wanted by the police, and Nick probably wasn't in the clear either. Lots of bodies had been felled, including one FBI agent who was operating officially in his legal duties.

Yeah, Gooden thought. This could work.

He pushed the "page" button on his phone, and when his aide picked up, Gooden said, "Vaughn, get me a clean laptop. Brand new. And have our tech people set up a clean email account with no history. And I don't want that laptop logged onto the Internet or anything else that might leave an IP address or any other kind of internet history. You understand?"

"Yes, sir. I'll start making it happen immediately."

Gooden turned his speaker phone off and leaned back in his chair. He looked at the drink that remained on his desk, but it no longer called him.

He felt his confidence returning and started worrying about an upcoming hearing he needed to chair in two days.

CHAPTER 66

"You've got to see this," Allen said.

Nick looked up from his ninety-third pistol drill of the day. He only had seven more reps of this exercise.

"What is it?" he asked.

"Could be the jackpot," Allen said. "Got an e-mail from someone who says they're in Whitaker's group. Says they want to give away his location so we can take him."

Nick grunted. "Sounds convenient. How stupid do they think we are?"

Allen shook his head. "I don't know. The e-mail is pretty long and detailed. It talks about all the offenses Whitaker has committed and says he's giving up Whitaker and his bodyguard -- some guy named Tank -- because they're out of control."

Nick smiled and said, "Sure they are."

"I agree at first glance it seems like a trap, but I don't know. He talks in here about how he didn't know Whitaker had shot a cop, or started to torture me."

"Keep dreaming," Nick said, completing repetition number ninety-eight.

"He says this organization is pivotal to the war on terror, but that it's gotten off track under Whitaker's leadership. He doesn't want to sell out his buddies. Just Whitaker, who he calls a maniac."

Nick finished his pistol drill and reloaded the weapon. He slid it behind his back and walked over to read the e-mail. The e-mail seemed legit, but that meant nothing.

"Tell him we need proof he's telling the truth," Nick said. "Ask him to send three different photos of Whitaker, as well as a good one of this guy named Tank. If he's as close to them as he says he is, he should be able to get them or already have them. Units are usually tight. I had photos of all my buddies."

"Great idea," Allen said. "I'll e-mail him now."

CHAPTER 67

Whitaker's phone rang, and he recognized the number as a Washington, D.C., area code.

He flipped it open and said, "Go ahead," having learned a long time ago you never said your name when you didn't know who was calling. And sometimes even when you did.

"Whitaker, this is Gooden. Change in plans here."

"Go ahead."

"This whole thing is spiraling out of control and it needs to end fast. So, I've called in every favor I've got left with every friend I know in the NSA."

"And?" Whitaker asked.

"They're going to do it. In fact, they're already doing it. They've got Nick and Allen's location pinned down somewhere in the mountains of East Tennessee. They're having more trouble this time though. Allen has some tech guys from various news organizations, as well as some really talented hackers, working with him. You know how the hackers love conspiracies like this."

"Can they get it?"

"They say they can, but when they do, I want you and Tank nearby. Ready to strike. Otherwise, their hackers may pick up that we've pinged them and we'll have blown our only chance. You know if they split, we'll have no way to find them again."

"Where do you want us?"

"The CIA has an unused cabin way up in the mountains in East Tennessee. It's miles from anywhere. Go there and wait. I'll text you the location. This might even take a couple of days they say, but you two stay rested up. I want you ready to move within minutes whenever we get their location."

"Sounds like a plan."

"Where you all headed right now?"

"New York. We had every intention of nabbing Jennifer."

"Jennifer? Who the hell is Jennifer?"

Whitaker laughed. "Alan's sweetheart. We'd planned to use her as bait."

Now Gooden was laughing, too. "You sick bastard."

"I learned from the best."

"Indeed you did."

CHAPTER 68

"We got photos," Allen said.

"You're shitting me," Nick said.

"Nope, plenty of them. And there's even coordinates and a map of where the two are."

"Get out of here," Nick said, standing up from the prone. He'd been "snapping in" with his rifle -- at least that's what he'd told Allen he was doing -- but in truth he'd been just pulling the trigger and re-cocking it, completely lost in thought. He'd been missing Anne more and more, and he wondered what he'd do if he survived this mess. Even scarier, he wondered if he even wanted to survive it.

Allen read Nick's face as he climbed to his feet. No doubt about it, the days of waiting had begun to take a toll on Nick. He seemed grumpier and angrier than he normally did. And while he wouldn't say it, Allen knew he was missing his wife. And he knew more than anything else that Nick needed to see a counselor. The man had so many demons running through his head, and that was before Anne had been gunned down.

Nicked stopped halfway to him. "What the hell you looking at like that?"

"Nothing," Allen said. He reached for a cigarette and lit it. "Check out these photos. These are definitely photos of the guy named, 'Whitaker,' who interrogated me. And this is definitely the NFL linebacker-sized dude who was with him. It says in the email that this guy's name is Tank. And here's the cabin's location. It's near your old stomping grounds."

The two spent a half hour looking over the photos. Zooming in and looking for any sign of manipulation. And then they began scoping out the cabin. The cabin lay outside Gatlinburg, Tenn., backed up to the Great Smoky Mountains National Park. Whoever had built it had buried it by itself literally ten miles from the nearest other dwelling.

Allen spent ten minutes using satellite shots from Google Maps and Bing to study the cabin and the woods all around it. There was only one road to it, and it turned into a dirt road more than two miles from the cabin.

"Awfully isolated," Allen said.

"It is."

CHAPTER 69

Whitaker and Tank arrived at the cabin exhausted. The planning of the abduction of Jennifer and all the driving toward (and back from) New York left them spent. And worrying about the likely end of their careers, if not their lives, had emotionally drained them.

On top of all this, their senses had been working overtime, as well, because both knew deep down that their lives could be taken at any moment. They faced as great a danger from Sen. Gooden (maybe greater) than they did from Nick and Allen.

They sat in the car, watching the cabin with slight unease.

"Gooden said there'd be no one here, right?" Tank asked.

"Right," Whitaker said.

"Then, let's enter weapons drawn just in case," Tank said.

Whitaker nodded. They exited the vehicle, yanked out pistols, and glided toward the front door. Whitaker stood to the side of the door -- in case someone shot through it -- and used the code he'd been sent to unlock the key-panel lock.

As soon as the door unlocked, the two burst through the door. Whitaker went right, and Tank cut left. They cleared the two corners of the room first and then turned away from the wall toward the inside of the room, which they both immediately recognized as a living room. They scanned the ceiling and moved on to the next room, the kitchen.

Room by room, the two cleared the cabin silently. They checked the closets, the crawl spaces, and underneath the beds. The cabin had no attic, so they immediately without a word began checking for sensors, listening devices, cameras. Forty minutes later, they felt safe talking.

"Nothing seems out of the ordinary," Tank said.

"I know, and that worries me more," Whitaker said. "Hasn't been that long ago that we were both relieved of our duties, thrown to the side, and assigned tracking bracelets."

"Good point."

"Let's check the woods for a sniper. We move fast and zig and zag so they can't get a clean shot on us. If one of us gets hit, the other runs for it if he's not close enough to take the sniper out. And don't go for the car. They'll be waiting for us to do that. Whoever survives the shot takes off at full speed into the national park. Emerges days later as far away as possible. Maybe even a week. With a pistol, the survivor ought to be able to kill something to eat and extend the time he can hide out."

"Sounds like a game plan. I'm ready when you are."

Whitaker nodded and walked to the back door. Tank stacked against him and he ripped open the door and sprinted away from the cabins and into the woods. They rushed from tree to tree, zig zagging and darting about like two mad men in the sights of someone's scope.

Thirty minutes later, they ended their search of the woods around the cabin. No sniper or sniper teams stalked them from afar. Nor had they seen any sign of men crawling or lying anywhere in the days prior.

"What now?" Tank asked.

"We see if the fridge is stocked with something stiff

worth drinking."

"I'm down with that," Tank said.

CHAPTER 70

Nick Woods worked his way forward. He wore the ghillie suit he'd picked up off the dead sniper inside Camp Lejeune. As he'd known, the blood had dried and left some darker spots, and it still blended perfectly. And it was a great ghillie suit. Its owner must have spent weeks and weeks on it.

In the movies, sniper work is sleek and sexy. But the reality couldn't be further from the truth. It's slow, methodical, and painful.

Nick moved slower than a snail, and his senses tried to pick up even the slightest thing that might be off. Both he and Allen had worried this could be a trap, but both also had a gut feeling that it wasn't. That this was what they'd been searching for so hard, and it'd been handed to them in quite the surprising twist.

As a precaution, in case it was a trap and Nick was taken alive, Allen agreed to pack and leave the hotel room he'd been staying in. That way, worst case, Nick couldn't give up his location even if tortured. Nick honest to goodness didn't know where Allen was heading.

But, Nick couldn't think of that right now. His entire focus was on sensing anything that might be wrong. Sometimes it was a sound. Sometimes a shape. Sometimes a feeling.

Yet nothing felt wrong at all. Nick felt more nervous in his hotel room than he did out here. But, he wanted to be thorough, so he crawled, slid, and scooted around the woods he'd approached from.

Convinced it was clear, he started to work in a 360 around the cabin. A single truck -- a gray Toyota -- sat in front of the cabin, which was connected to civilization by a dirt road that was covered in leaves. Nick knew if it had been used much, it would have been muddy or hardened dirt. But, it lay flat with the forest ground, lacking ruts and covered by leaves, a barely used trail to a barely used cabin.

Nick also noticed the cabin had no power. Just a rough outpost powered by generator and without a satellite antenna in sight. That probably meant the place had no communication, but Nick couldn't be sure. These days there was cell phone service just about everywhere, but this was deep in the mountains and miles from a single-lane road, which itself was about fifteen miles from other homes. So, there was a chance it had no way to communicate outside.

Nick completed his reconnaissance and left the area. He needed to re-coordinate with Alan and find out where their new hotel room was for the night.

Then, it'd be planning an assault and hopefully the end of Whitaker and Tank, assuming those were their true names.

CHAPTER 71

Whitaker and Tank left the cabin again. They drove down the nearly invisible road with weapons in their laps and senses at caveman-like intensity.

"What if we don't hear from Gooden today?" Tank asked.

"We give him one more day if we don't," Whitaker said. "And we consider the idea that if we don't hear anything tomorrow, that we probably ought to make a break for it. Cut off the ankle bracelets and run for our lives."

"Agreed," Tank said. He gripped the stock of his MP5 and said, "And heaven help the assholes who try to stop us."

Two hours later, they returned to the cabin. Gooden himself had called them today -- not just an aide -- and he'd told them they'd nearly nailed down Nick and Allen's location. Had it down to within three blocks, and that they were still in Gatlinburg -- a small city just twenty minutes from their location.

So, they'd stopped for a pizza and rented a hotel to get real showers in before heading back with additional grocery supplies. They knew how to hurry up and wait, and if they needed to camp out another night, they could make do with canned goods and cards for entertainment.

It was the life of soldiers around the world.

CHAPTER 72

Meanwhile, just a short distance from Whitaker and Tank, Nick and Allen finished making their plans.

"You can do this, right?" Nick asked.

"Yes," Allen said. He had an MP5 in his hands, and was holding it about like a recruit would. Nick had shown him how to use it before, and had just showed him again. Making sure he knew how to release the magazine, yank the bolt back, and know the various selector switch settings -- semi, three-shot burst, and fully automatic.

"Let's go through your drills again," Nick said.

Allen did, feeling more comfortable with his abilities, Nick helped him load up his six 30-round magazines. Then he and Allen packed up everything else and loaded it into their car. (They carried the rifle to the car by putting it in an old seabag, with clothes stuffed around it.)

They left the small town they'd holed up in wearing their civilian clothes. Two miles away from the nearest building, they pulled onto a dirt road and drove back a hundred yards out of view. They changed into camouflage -- Allen, some basic hunting stuff they'd bought at Wal-mart -- and Nick into his Marine ghillie suit.

Nick backed the car up the dirt road and pulled back out. They were mission "go" now. They knew if a cop got behind them they were screwed, but it was a chance they had to take.

They drove the remaining distance to the dirt road that led up to the isolated cabin. Nick eased his car up the dirt road and when he could no longer see the road behind him, he let the car coast to a stop between two stout trees. He didn't touch the brakes so they wouldn't squeal. With thick woods on both sides of the drive way, they'd effectively trapped Whitaker and Tank inside the woods. Even if the two men got away from the cabin, they wouldn't be driving away. They'd have to hoof it out on foot, and Nick felt certain they wouldn't get away from him in a one-on-one fight in the woods. Especially since he had the great ghillie suit he'd taken off the dead sniper.

Nick and Allen exited their vehicle and grabbed their weapons. They pushed the doors closed so the interior light wouldn't run down their car battery, but did so as quietly as they could. Then Nick crossed in front of the car and entered the woods, Allen following.

Nick walked point silent and smooth. He crept through the woods, his heart beating through his chest, and sweat dripping down his face. This was finally it. Was it a trap? Could there be sensors that might detect them? A satellite looking down from space with thermal cameras? Three helicopters loaded with heavily armed commandos waiting to swoop in? Or, maybe in the air already on the way. He paused and looked up, listening as hard as he could.

He swallowed hard and remembered that at this point it lay in fate's hands. If this was a trap, then they were dead. If it wasn't, they had a chance.

He glanced back at Allen and saw the man looked focused, though nervous. Nick had told him going in that his only job was watching his step and being quiet, and true to form Allen had his eyes peeled at the ground; on the prowl for branches or sticks that would snap and sound louder than an alarm.

A little more than an hour later, Nick had placed Allen in position facing the back of the house. Allen lay behind a thick pine tree, his MP5 aimed at the rear door.

Nick snapped his fingers lightly and Allen looked up. Nick pointed at the MP5's magazine, and then Allen nodded. He laid out the five remaining magazines in front of him.

Nick gave him a thumbs up and a smile, and Allen smiled back. The mission was about to go down, and since Whitaker and Tank's truck sat outside, then this would likely end the cat and mouse game the four had been playing for weeks now.

Nick glided away from Allen, moving deeper into the woods before circling back around to the front. Getting seen now would be about the stupidest thing he could do, and since the cabin had plenty of windows, it was a distinct possibility.

CHAPTER 73

Nick Woods watched the front of the cabin through his scoped sniper rifle -- the very one he'd taken off the Marine prior to gunning down Colonel Russ Jernigan.

Nick wasn't perpendicular to the door. He did not want to see into it when it opened. Instead, he lay along the axis of the door so that if it opened, he would see no one; but if someone exited it, he could hit them with enfilade fire.

Nick knew they'd either run down the wall away from him or up the wall toward him. Thus, he was positioned so that his shots would be straight on, not lateral in nature as they would have been had he been perpendicular and facing the front door.

These were two of the most important shots he'd taken in years. These two men were fierce killers. Well trained and battle tested, and Nick had to face them with just the help of an anti-gun liberal from New York who barely knew how best to hold the MP-5 he'd been practicing with.

Nick eased into his position better. He made sure his rifle rested on his forearm -- bone support they called it in the Corps -- and that no muscular tension was manipulating the rifle. It had to be naturally aligned, and Nick had shifted his body an inch here or an inch there several times to get it right.

Each time he'd aim in on the cabin and then shut his eyes for twenty seconds. If it wasn't where he'd been aiming, he'd shift again.

But he had the position as he wanted now, and he worked to control his breathing. Allen would start firing any moment and Nick lay beneath his ghillie suit -- plenty of light vegetation and cover in front of him -- the epitome of the perfect human predator. Two rabbits would soon dart from cover and he would strike them both like a snake, unseen but just a mere hundred yards away.

Nick Woods settled into his comfort zone behind the rifle. He felt familiarity creep in. He'd spent thousands of hours of his life lying behind a rifle in the prone. He'd used a scope and low profile to conduct reconnaissance. He'd used it to avoid detection, ducking death by the slimmest odds. He'd used it to bag men, both near and afar.

And if all went according to plan, he'd soon use it again. To avenge Anne and avenge his spotter in Afghanistan. To right who knew how many wrongs.

"Whitaker, you've sent a lot of men to hell in your day," he thought. "Some probably needed it. But the country has laws for a reason. And you chose to play cowboy outside the law. Probably made good money doing it, too. Today, it catches up with you."

On the other side of the cabin, Allen Green prepared to execute his part of the mission. He clicked the MP5 off safe and into semi auto. He checked his watch, confirmed it was time, and choked down his remaining anti-violence feelings.

Two months ago, he wouldn't kill a fly. Today, he'd be firing a military-style submachine gun at two humans, in what he was pretty sure would fall into the felony category of premeditated murder.

Allen breathed as best he could and swallowed down his anxiety and fear. He aimed at the side of the cabin and pulled the trigger. The MP5 fired, roaring loud in the quiet afternoon, but Allen appreciated the lack of kick the small 9 mm round created. He paused just a second, then returned to the sights and fired again.

Round after round through an entire mag, he peppered the side of the cabin. And when the MP5 clicked empty, he reloaded and began anew.

* * *

Inside the cabin, Whitaker read the latest edition of The Economist, while Tank flipped through a dog-eared copy of Hustler. Both scrambled for cover when Allen's first shot shattered the afternoon silence. They knew the sound, and knew it wasn't a car backfiring or a balloon popping or a firework exploding. They also picked up the caliber from the sound, as well as the thud of the round hitting the wall of the cabin.

And as they rolled behind cover and retrieved weapons, they also calculated the gap between the sound of the shot and the impact of the bullet. This happened instinctively, without conscious thought or effort. Years of range time and combat provided them with more data than two dozen inexperienced civilians would have picked up in twice the time.

"He's at the rear of the cabin," Tank said.

"Probably fifty yards away," Whitaker replied.

"Agreed. Let's hit the front door before they rush us or burn us out."

Whitaker nodded, scrambled to his feet, and darted to the door, as more rounds smacked the cabin and one shattered a window and buried into an interior wall. Tank raced after him, his body leaning forward and low.

The two men burst through the front door opposite the direction of the incoming fire. Whitaker and Tank scanned their sectors in the front yard, and felt relief to see no stacked troops preparing to assault the cabin. They paused only a second before stacking up and moving along the wall toward its edge.

* * *

Meanwhile, hidden from them, Nick Woods watched the two men through his scope. He smiled, wondering how his plan had worked so well. Nick's scope rested on the second man to exit, the one in the rear of the formation and the only one he could see. He assumed it was Tank. The man stood at least 6'5" or 6'6". The two moved toward the end of the wall and Nick forced down the pressure of how little time he had to make his shots.

Time slowed, he squeezed, the rifle fired.

It roared in the woods, easily twice as loud as Allen Green's MP5. It fired a round twice the size of Allen's submachine gun (which shot merely a pistol bullet) and the heavy round ripped through Tank. It clipped his spine, exploded his heart, and tore a three-inch hole out of his chest. The wobbling bullet hit Whitaker, too, going nearly an inch deep in his back.

Whitaker felt like he'd been hit by a red-hot, fire poker, which had been swung by some power-hitting Major League Baseball player. But as the pain burned and the sound of the shot reached him, he acted. He spun and elbowed the stumbling Tank out of the way.

Instinct told him Tank was dead. The man's legs looked like sponges and snipers didn't miss at this range.

Whitaker raced for the door while Nick rushed to reload and get back on target. Both just made it.

Whitaker darted through the door as Nick yanked the trigger. Whitaker made it inside. Nick scored a brutal shot to Whitaker's side. Blood exploded against the side of the cabin and both Nick and Whitaker knew he would die without immediate medical attention.

And without question, both knew it'd never come.

Nick reloaded, eased from cover, and exited the woods. Allen ceased firing after hearing the two loud shots.

"Did you get them both?" Allen yelled.

"Sort of. Stay in the woods out of sight and work your way to me."

Inside the cabin, Whitaker looked at his bloody side. He felt the burning in his back, the blood flowing there, as well, and he knew shock was his worst enemy right now. He threw his M4 on the couch and limped to the bedroom. He kept his right arm pinned to his side, desperate to slow down the bleeding from there.

Whitaker ripped the comforter off the bed and grabbed the sheet underneath it. He yanked it off the bed and cut a one-foot long strip of it with his knife down its entire length. He wrapped the sheet around his side -- across his full body -- four times and then stuffed it inside itself, as you wrap a towel around your waist. His back bled, but that didn't matter. He thought for a second, realized he had no one to call for support or reinforcements, and accepted his fate.

Whitaker moved back to the living room and retrieved his M4. He positioned himself in the corner and waited in a kneeling position, his rifle across his knee. The door to the cabin remained open, but he didn't want to chance walking through the opening to close it. The sniper may have relocated himself to cover the door's opening and more importantly the space that was visible inside. Besides, locking the door achieved nothing. They'd either breach the door or burn him out.

Whitaker flexed his fingers on the weapon and tightened his arm against his side. He'd been in tough positions before. He wouldn't go down easy.

CHAPTER 74

Allen Green knelt next to Nick Woods. Nick watched the open front door of the cabin from a kneeling position behind a tree, his rifle slung and his .45 resting easy in his hand aimed in the general direction of the door. Now, just thirty yards away, he'd prefer the semi-auto pistol over the bolt-action rifle with its over-magnified scope.

"How do we know he won't hit the back door while we're both up front?" Allen whispered.

"We don't," Nick said. "But if he does, he won't get far and we'll be able to track him. I hit him good. Look at the wall there. And if I were him, I'd stay inside, hidden. Ready to whack whoever comes in."

"What do we do?"

"We burn him out," Nick said. "Finally, all your smoking is going to pay off."

The two stayed on the side of the cabin, keeping an eye on two curtained windows as they quietly stacked limbs and logs against the side of the cabin. They moved silently and since the curtains never moved, Nick assumed Whitaker continued to wait inside. Unless he'd run out the back, but Nick doubted that. The man was probably building up a position, Nick guessed, unless he'd been hit harder than Nick thought, in which case he was playing field surgeon on himself.

Nick and Allen built a leaning fire shelter in just a few minutes, and, with a pile of leaves at the bottom, it lit and spread quickly. The dry branches and limbs caught fire and ignited thicker limbs. The side of the cabin smoked and both knew the cabin would catch soon.

"Let's stay together," Nick said. "He's still dangerous and armed to the teeth."

They moved to the front of the building, both covering the door -- Allen with his MP5 and Nick with his .45 pistol. The fire spread and they soon heard coughing from inside. Minutes passed and still he remained inside.

"Come on out," Nick yelled. "Tell us who your boss is and we'll let you live."

Whitaker fought tears and tried to filter the air through another piece of sheet he'd cut. He lay on the floor trying to stay below the smoke, but it barely helped.

He considered his options again, for about the hundredth time in the past ten minutes. He could run out the back, but he wouldn't make it far. His side still gushed blood and fatigue wrapped its arms around him like an evil mistress out for your soul. Whitaker wanted to succumb to her. To rest his head on the floor and surrender to peace and rest.

The room blurred and became unfocused and Whitaker smashed his M4 against the top of his head. The pain drove off the evil bitch trying to seduce him and brought him back to reality. To pain. To the impossible situation before him.

He shook his head and tried to think clearly. He remembered he couldn't run. He coughed on the smoke and realized it was now or never. It would either be a warrior's death or the kind of movie-like ending you only dreamed of: a main character emerging from certain death an unstoppable hero.

Whitaker climbed to his feet. His legs wobbled and doubt assailed his mind. This wouldn't work, he thought, but then he fought down the pessimism. Come on motherfucker, he said to himself. He whacked his rifle against his forehead and roared as he stumbled through the door.

"Ran-gers!" he yelled as he exited the cabin, angry hatred on his mind.

* * *

Nick Woods heard the yell and saw the tall, blood-soaked man burst through the smoke like some kamikaze-charging, doped-up samurai. He admired the man's courage and determination and thought in another time on another day, he'd have been honored to serve under this man. But then he remembered his spotter in Afghanistan, blown to bits. He imagined dozens of broken laws. Saw Anne's body in the grass.

And Nick's heart turned from admiration to righteous vengeance. Whitaker's M4 angled toward Nick and began firing on automatic. Nick saw the fire and flash from the barrel and felt the air turbulence of bullets as they zipped by, snapping in his ear like a bullwhip.

Nick fired a pointing shot in Whitaker's direction with his .45 that missed, even at the short distance of six feet. But Nick's body never paused and moved to the kneeling position where he two-handed the pistol and fired some more. Yet Whitaker's weapon still tracked toward him, spewing out molten death, and Nick rolled to the side.

* * *

Whitaker saw Nick and moved his weapon toward him, his finger yanked back on the trigger. Live or die, he'd take Nick with him. The M4 moved to Nick's head and

Whitaker smiled as he imagined seeing Nick's head explode.

But just as the weapon got on target, Nick's head moved. Whitaker lost Nick for a second between the smoke in his eyes and the speed of Nick's movement. Then he felt the first slam in his chest. Like a horse kicking him. He felt it again and realized Nick had ducked to the kneeling position.

Another jolt pounded his stomach, and he knew death was no longer an "if" but a "when." But he wanted to take Nick with him worse than anything in the world.

This hero bastard who always did right and believed in honor and black and white. And as Whitaker's weapon tracked to Nick's path and his subsequent roll to the side, he knew he had him. They'd leave this world together and Whitaker would have the pleasure of knowing his organization could survive in the wake of Nick's death. America needed men like Whitaker. Men who weren't afraid to break the law to protect its people.

* * *

Behind Nick, Allen watched the whole thing in sick fascination. Whitaker firing, Nick dodging by kneeling and rolling. Each time just a split second ahead of Whitaker. But Nick fired a pistol, while Whitaker wielded an automatic assault rifle with a stuffed-full magazine and a body doped up on death's adrenaline.

Allen realized Whitaker would get Nick at the end of his roll to the side. He knew from Nick's drills that he had not practiced a move that would help him avoid this situation, and only those hours of practice and their resulting speed had spared him thus far. And then Allen remembered the MP-5 in his hands. He pushed the weapon to full auto and began firing from the hip as he brought it up. Twenty 9 mm rounds poured through it into Whitaker's body and still Whitaker tracked Nick's movement.

Then Allen thought of the brain and knew only a head shot would end this sick death dance. He pointed at Whitaker's head and noticed the sights automatically lined up -- German ingenuity knowing no bounds. Allen fired ten more rounds, each sickeningly on target, wrecking teeth, bone, and brain matter.

* * *

From the ground, Nick knew the bullets hammering into Whitaker's face had saved his life. He reflected on how close death had come to him again as he held an empty pistol and watch Whitaker's riddled body fall to the ground.

"That man took a lot of killing," Allen said.

Nick lay looking at his pistol, its slide locked to the rear on an empty magazine and started shaking. It looked absurd, he felt certain, but he couldn't stop himself. He often got the shakes after intense combat.

"You okay?" Allen asked.

"I just need a minute. I owe you," Nick said, looking up at Allen.

Allen saw respect in the look and felt a pride in his killing of Whitaker that would have made sick the Allen of just six months ago. He smiled.

"Told you that you'd enjoy it," Nick said. "Remember?"

Allen thought back to the car and the bully and pawn speech.

"Give me a cigarette," Nick said, reaching up, his hand still shaking.

"You don't smoke," Allen said.

"Special occassion. Now give me a damn cigarette

before I kill your suddenly cocky ass."

Allen laughed and dug out a cigarette. He lit it for Nick and the two smoked while the cabin burned and Whitaker bled out, brain dead and paralyzed. Allen took a seat next to Nick, who hadn't stood and still lay on the ground. The two sat like that for several minutes, listening to the cabin crack and pop as it burned stronger and stronger.

"What's next?" Allen asked.

Nick blew out smoke. "We go after his boss, whoever that is."

"Got to be the head of the CIA or someone in Congress. Maybe the President."

"Doesn't matter," Nick said, serious.

"You must be joking."

"Nope."

Allen watched Nick take another drag and realized he wasn't joking. Then Allen started laughing. "You're serious?"

Nick said nothing.

"You realize," Allen said, "that even with all my sources and reporting friends, I could spend years and never find out if it was the head of the CIA, someone in Congress, or the President? And then once you find out, you've got to somehow kill them. You're certainly not going to get them indicted or incarcerated in jail."

Nick sat thinking. Allen shook his head in disbelief.

"You're nuts."

"What else do I have. They took Anne."

Allen lacked a response to that. His cell phone rang. Both men jumped, and before Allen could recover, Nick was loading a mag into his .45 and looking around.

"I thought there wasn't cell phone service here?" Nick asked.

"There's not."

"Who has your number?"

"No one. Never called any one on it. It's one of our cheap pre-paid cell phones that we bought."

Nick looked up at the sky and imagined a satellite looking down on them. "Answer it," he said gruffly.

"Hello?" Allen said.

"Put the phone on speaker," Texas Sen. Ray Gooden said. But Nick and Allen had no way of recognizing the man's famous voice. A computer program altered and digitized it into a deep sounding bass.

Allen pulled the phone down and fiddled with it until he figured out how to put the unfamiliar, cheap phone on speaker. The moment he did, Sen. Gooden continued.

"Well done, men. I've watched the whole thing go down and I must say you performed well."

Nick grabbed the phone from Allen and said, "We're coming for you, you no good, son of a bitch."

Sen. Gooden laughed into the phone and it sounded especially evil in its altered state.

"Let me give you a quick reality check," the voice continued. "Right now, three drones are circling you both. They carry among them half a dozen Hellfire missiles. Their operators are veterans of Afghanistan. Quite good shots, really. Have killed dozens of al Qaida sympathizers and terrorists in Northern Pakistan."

Nick and Allen searched the sky.

Gooden laughed again. "You can't see or hear them, you idiots. How else would they work so effectively if you could? But, if you managed to outrun them, I have two hundred men from Delta and Seal Team 6 staged twenty miles away in helos."

Allen, bold reporter again, yanked the phone from Nick. "You wouldn't fire a Hellfire missile in the States. Even you're not that stupid."

"Indeed," Gooden said. "But military aircraft have been known to crash during routine training ops. I'm sure that's all that happened. Pilot parachuted safely, of course. But that's assuming it's even noticed. You've forgotten that you're miles from anywhere. I doubt it'd even be noticed before our teams serviced the area and removed any identifying missile pieces."

Allen lowered the phone, while Nick searched the sky.

"Now," Gooden continued, "you've heard Option 1. Either a fiery death or a fun traipse through the woods pursued by heavily armed commandos and helicopters loaded with all kinds of sensors, like infra red, as well as machine guns and rockets. So, Option 1 is death. Guaranteed. Certain. Swift. Would be over in less than an hour, assuming you dodge the missiles, and frankly I'm okay with this plan. Even prefer it actually. It's safer for me, since there'd never be any leaks or chance for the truth to emerge. Option 1 is far safer for me. And America."

Nick dropped his eyes from the sky and met Allen's. Neither said anything.

"Good. I see I've got your attention and you're finally listening."

Nick shook his head in defeat, searching for an angle out of the dilemma. Behind them, the cabin burned fiercer, popping and crackling.

"Option 2 is more pleasant. Our drones fly home, their pilots bored and frustrated. Our Delta and Seal operators return to base, pissed about another false alarm. And you two live.

"Allen, you'll be famous. The two of you successfully took down an out-of-control Homeland Security/CIA leader and his right-hand man. Since Nick will avoid the spotlight, Allen, I imagine you'll become a sensational hero. Best of all, you fired the final shots that took down Whitaker. All charges against you for kiddy porn will be dropped and proven fraudulent, you'll get your job back, and sell several million copies of a book retelling all of this. Minus this small part we're discussing right now of course. More than likely, your girlfriend Jennifer will enthusiastically take you back. Women do have a thing for rich, courageous heroes. Trust me, I know.

"Moving along, Nick, you get a new identity. You can make up your own back story or we'll provide you one.

Even better, we're giving you two million dollars since you won't be publishing some colossus best seller. Move where you want. Do what you want. We don't care."

Nick looked at the woods just fifty yards away. He had his rifle across his back and pistol loaded and ready to go. He wondered if he could make it. What was the flight time of a Hellfire missile?

"Don't even think about it," the deep, altered voice said. "I can see you looking at the woods, thinking about running. Trust me, I will obliterate you in a heartbeat. Gladly."

Nick looked to the sky again. Allen wiped sweat from his brow and tried to stop his hands from shaking.

"I'm letting you two live," the voice resumed, "because you've done our nation a great service. Nick, you've done so twice, and yet you were betrayed terribly after your service in Afghanistan. But, I will put this nation's security over your two lives. In a heartbeat. Our nation needs the program you nearly unraveled, and I have shown my virtuosity by relieving Whitaker and his assistant of their command, and leaking their positions to you two. I can do no more without weakening our nation beyond a level I'm comfortable at. And that's why I directed my two men to such a secluded area. Had you two failed and they survived, I'd have placed them back in charge and they would have never forgotten either their reprimand or how it felt to lose control of their men. Leaders fear irrelevance. But you two aced them, so the ball's now in your court. I am prepared to give a single order and engulf you both in fiery explosions and the sights of two hundred trigger-happy men. Make your decisions. Quickly."

Allen, too quickly, said, "Nick, you know what I want to do."

Nick nodded.

He knew he couldn't give up. Couldn't surrender and let this man go free. To continue his reign of abuses.

Nick looked at the distance to the woods and judged

his course and where he'd hit the deck. Could he find some cover and either low ground or a dead fall to protect him from the shrapnel? He looked at Allen who read his mind and shook his head "no" in utter disbelief.

"Don't do it, Nick," Allen said.

Nick didn't care what Allen wanted. Days and days together or not, in the grand scheme of things, he was still just a piss-ant liberal from New York. Nick looked up again and at the tree line. He doubted he could avoid the three drones with their Hellfire missiles and two hundred men following in their wake, but he had survived a battalion of Soviets who'd been given his location by his sell-out commander, and then, he'd been behind enemy lines in a country where he didn't speak the language.

Nick prepared to make his move. He judged the distance to the woods, checked the sling holding his rifle around his back, and then confirmed his pistol was loaded. But seeing the pistol, he paused and thought back to another pistol. This one taped under a sink and discovered by Anne. He smiled at the memory, recalling the anger and sadness from her that followed.

Looking at this pistol, which had been hidden as well from her in a cave, he realized that the one thing Anne had wanted above all else was for him to be "normal." To not be paranoid or worried all the time.

Nick considered this a moment.

With the death of Whitaker, he'd avenged Anne's death and that of his spotter in Afghanistan. Not to mention likely many other heroes who Whitaker may have betrayed and abandoned in a foreign land.

Nick, with Allen's help, had tracked down and killed Whitaker and his right-hand man. Nick could race for the woods and pursue an even more difficult search for the man behind this all -- certainly a Congressman or senior CIA official (and possibly the President) -- but that's not what Anne would want. Not even close.

Nick holstered his pistol in his belt in the small of his

back and looked at Allen, whose face had gone from horror to relief as he'd read Nick's thoughts.

"We'll take your deal," Nick said toward the speakerphone.

"Wise move," the voice said, and before the sentence ended they heard the sound of helicopters rapidly approaching.

"This was a trap," Allen said with incredulity.

"Seems it was," Nick said, swallowing down relief. That was nearly the second time he'd died within the past fifteen minutes.

And as a black, unmarked Blackhawk descended into the clearing, the two men watched as more than a dozen other Blackhawk's circled above it, covering it like a swarm of hornets.

"Glad you took the deal," Allen yelled over the helicopter's roar.

Nick nodded and looked up to the clouds. He thanked Anne for saving his life, yet again; both after she found him when he was in the deep abyss of anger and paranoia more than ten years ago, and just now.

Nick couldn't believe how wrong he'd been on this one. On how he'd missed the trap devised by whoever was above these guys, and on how the helicopters were far closer than he'd ever expected. He'd have certainly been dead within five minutes.

Allen turned and walked toward the landing helicopter, and Nick followed. "I hope you can see me now, my love," he thought, tears streaming down his face. "But for you, and I'd be a dead man right now. It took me years and years, but I finally listened. I'm burying the hatchet. I'm picking peace over paranoia."

EPILOGUE

Texas Senator Ray Gooden's predictions came true.

Allen Green turned into an instant hero, famous and rich. The charges against him for child porn were dropped and proved to be part of a grand conspiracy. The New Yorker hired him back. And after an awkward start, things went back to better-than-ever with his girlfriend Jennifer, who eventually forgave him for not calling her early on.

Nick Woods received the two million dollars he'd been promised. He promptly withdrew it from the bank, transferred it a half-dozen times, and eventually withdrew it all in a series of cash withdrawals. He disappeared from the radar screen and mastered the art of safely caching his cash in dozens of spots he marked in his journal in code. Anne would be a little frustrated by his behavior, but not much, as he soon dropped most of his paranoia and lived a life of hunting, fishing, and reading. So far, he's still failed to settle down and marry.

Texas Sen. Ray Gooden found new leadership for his covert organization. It rebuilt both its bank accounts (through drug running) and its ranks, through hungry young men anxious to further serve their country.

Gooden continues to rule both the covert organization and the Senate Armed Forces Committee through fear and intimidation. Neither the CIA, nor America's newest President, has found the nerve to take him on.

The End

ABOUT THE AUTHOR: Stan R. Mitchell lives in Oak Ridge, Tenn, and he and his wife own a small weekly newspaper, The Oak Ridge Observer.

When he's not working, which he does too much of, he's writing fiction, practicing martial arts, or exercising.

Prior to his current life, he served in the Marine Corps. During his active duty service ('95-'99), he and his platoon members received Combat Action Ribbons for their work in Operation Silver Wake, the evacuation of U.S. citizens from Tirana, Albania. Stan spent all four years in the Marine Corps as an infantryman in Alpha Company, 1st Battalion, Eighth Marines.

Learn more about Stan R. Mitchell and his other works at www.stanrmitchell.com.

Also by Stan R. Mitchell…

Little Man, and the Dixon County War.

Made in the USA
Lexington, KY
07 January 2015